Triple Crossed

R.C. Hartson

BLACK ROSE writing

© 2016 by R.C. Hartson
All rights reserved. No part of this book may be reproduced, stored in a retrieval system or transmitted in any form or by any means without the prior written permission of the publishers, except by a reviewer who may quote brief passages in a review to be printed in a newspaper, magazine or journal.

The final approval for this literary material is granted by the author.

First printing

This is a work of fiction. Names, characters, businesses, places, events and incidents are either the products of the author's imagination or used in a fictitious manner. Any resemblance to actual persons, living or dead, or actual events is purely coincidental.

ISBN: 978-1-61296-706-6
PUBLISHED BY BLACK ROSE WRITING
www.blackrosewriting.com

Printed in the United States of America
Suggested retail price $16.95

Triple Crossed is printed in Garamond Premier Pro

For my wonderful wife, Lynie. Without her encouragement, understanding and love, this book would not be possible.

Triple Crossed

R.C. Hartson

Chapter One

The two men rode in silence. At three in the morning the highway was a desert of concrete and the only sound inside the car was the droning hum of the Buick's engine. The night sky was cloudless, with just a sliver of moon providing light. Even the trucks were scarce and the headlights from traffic on the other side of the median were few and far between.

Forty miles had passed since Walker attempted to turn on the radio, but his partner, who was driving, shoved his hand away from the dials. A large man with a face like a bulldog and a personality to match, he was driving eight miles over the posted speed limit of sixty-five. He had large, watery eyes and wore a slumped look of exhaustion like a beaten boxer forced to go one too many rounds.

He scowled at Walker. "We don't really need any bullshit music right now, Ace."

Walker didn't argue. He continued to stare off to the side and watched the car's headlights wash over the pines along the side the highway. He sighed and grunted as he slid a pack of Marlboro Reds out of his pocket.

"Okay, but I sure could use a cup of coffee, couldn't you, Toad?"

The silence that followed stretched into a moment, then two, before his partner responded.

"Yeah, I could use some java, I suppose."

The dash lights illuminated the big man's unhappy expression.

"Crank your fuckin' window down while you smoke that thing," he growled. His chin sunk into the folds of fat around his neck and he clutched the wheel with hands the size of catcher's mitts.

"Why you so pissed off, anyway?" Walker asked, his cigarette dangling from his lip. "You worried about this job or somethin'?"

Toad didn't answer.

Walker lit up, rolled his window down an inch or so and then expelled a huge plume of smoke. He quickly took another drag. The cloud drifted back into his eyes, making him squint.

Triple Crossed

"Well, as far as I'm concerned, this gig is no different than any other job we've had," he said.

Toad said nothing.

Walker scooted his seat back and huffed a quick sigh.

"Well? Okay. Spill it. What the fuck is eatin' you this time?"

"Nothing."

Walker felt Toad's eyes on him.

"Dammit, I need to think and I can't with that radio on. Or with your mouth running." He spoke slowly and paused between his words when no pauses were required so Walker never quite knew when he was through talking.

Walker stared at the floor as he listened. His face was a blank. His eyes always seemed to be seeing everything and nothing at the same time. After a moment, he looked at Toad and grinned.

"Hey, what the fuck? I'm just trying to make conversation here. Help keep you awake is all."

The silence swelled and Walker took a last deep drag, crushed the cigarette out in the ashtray and blew the smoke out his nostrils with a sigh of disgust. After a while he took the initiative once again.

"Yeah, okay. I get it. You think this deal is something real special for some reason. You're not bullshitting me. Well, I say relax. That package in the trunk isn't going anywhere."

"That's for sure," said Toad. His voice was phlegmy.

Walker gazed out his window, remembering the scenery from hours earlier. They were in the country for sure. Subtract a few houses, eliminate a few McDonalds or other food and fuel stops, and the Pennsylvania landscape was mostly hills and woods. He squirmed around a bit and tilted his seat back. He was a thin man with thick, dark hair brushed straight back. It was too long and it curled over his ears. He had a dark mustache and a tuft of black hair that showed at the vee of his silk shirt. He wore stone washed designer jeans and tan snakeskin cowboy boots.

"So, what is it then, partner? You and me been working together since snow was cold, and I can tell you've had a hard-on about something ever since we left the Ohio line. I'd probably get more conversation outta that mark in the trunk and he's so far gone, he'd let us yank out his liver if we wanted."

"Yeah. I'm just wondering if we shouldn't be getting more for this whole deal. Fifty large is okay, but you know as well as I do that Cosgrove has something huge up his sleeve to have us kidnap this guy. You can bet there's a ton at stake for him and that grease ball, Tony Cicotto." Toad paused for one of his strange beats. "Kidnapping is federal. You know that, right?"

"Yeah, no shit. So what? We knew that going in. But our passenger has to ID us, and that ain't gonna happen. He never saw either of our faces, Toad. For Christ's sake, I don't give a shit what Cosgrove's up to. I sure as hell can use my share. It's a lot of green from where I sit right now."

"Yeah, I'm fine with it too, but I'm just saying we probably should be getting a lot more for this. It's one hell of a risk we're taking. You don't have to be a weatherman to know which way the wind is blowing, but there's a lot we don't know, and maybe we oughta know, seeing as how we're doing the heavy lifting here. See what I mean?"

"Aw, bullshit. Since when do we care what's underneath the paint? Don't sweat it. It's not our business. Cosgrove knows it all, done it all. He's no dummy. So we should trust him to be smart, right? You and me, we just grab our green and leave the rest in his lap, I say."

Toad cleared his throat, rolled down his window to spit, and then cranked it back up.

"Well, I'll admit the boss has done pretty fuckin' good for himself," he said, "Probably busted a lot of heads to get to the top. Some say he was a big hero in Nam. Had Staff Sergeant stripes and killed a shit load of gooks all by himself. Got wounded a couple of times, too. That's why he walks with that limp...got to respect that."

"Bullshit!" said Walker. "I don't believe any of it. I don't think he was even in the Army. Cosgrove wouldn't know Ho Chi Minh from sweet-and-sour shrimp. And, as far as that goes, Cicotto is an asshole. I think he's a loser, so blind to shit he couldn't find his dick if it glowed in the dark. He's all mouth, too."

Toad cleared his throat. "I don't know about that. He's one vicious son-of-a-bitch. In fact, Cicotto's the meanest prick I ever met." He paused briefly. "If he lost his hands, he'd bite you to death. You can't trust him, that's for sure."

"Fuck Cicotto," said Walker. He opened his mouth and then his eyes clicked away, as if he were thinking over what he'd been about to spit out. There was silence for a beat.

"Listen, we just have to do this shit and we're home free, the way I see it," Walker continued. "Cosgrove wanted the guy snatched. We got him. Now all we gotta do is deliver him to Jersey. Big deal." He leaned over and checked the fuel gauge. "I need that coffee and you should be stopping for gas pretty quick. I gotta piss, too, so the sooner the better."

Triple Crossed

"Yeah, I need to stretch my legs," said Toad. "Keep an eye peeled for a sign for gas and burgers. We'll stop. Hope we can find somethin' open at this hour way out here in the boonies." He glanced at his watch in the light of the dash. "We're making good time. We should be hitting the Jersey border before dawn."

Ten minutes later Walker lit another cigarette. "I still haven't seen any signs for eats, Toad. Maybe we should pull off in a rest stop first anyway. Check our friend back there. It wouldn't be too swift opening the trunk at a truck stop with a bunch of eyes around."

Toad agreed. "I saw a sign back there. One should be coming up pretty quick. About three miles, I think."

Toad pulled the car into the rest stop and parked on an angle close to the cement block building. He turned off the car, scanned the area and looked over at Walker.

"I think this is as good a spot as any. What do you think?"

"Yeah, but hold on." Walker rolled down his window and craned his neck to see a dimly lit jogging path that appeared to circle the building. It snaked through the patches of trees on his right. To the left was an open field with swing sets and wooden Flintstone structures for kids, barely visible in the light from a few well-placed streetlights. The only person in sight was a gray-haired woman who was walking a poodle to her car.

"She's leaving. I'll go take a leak while you pop the trunk and check our guy," said Toad. He reached inside his jacket. "I'm sure he's still out, but in case he's awake, give him another shot of this."

He handed Walker a small baggie containing a hypodermic needle.

"Yeah, okay, then I'll go in when you get back. Hurry up, though, my hind teeth are floatin'." He pulled his iPhone out, checked the screen a moment and put it back in his pocket. "Nothing, no messages. That's good, no?"

"Yeah." Toad pulled his right trouser leg up over his sock, exposing the hideaway .25, Velcro-strapped to his ankle. "All set. I'll be right back."

Walker lit a cigarette, reached down and popped the trunk. He got out and did a half squat to get the kinks out of his legs before moving to the rear of the car. He lifted the trunk lid slowly.

The man they abducted still lay in a fetal position. He was about forty years old, medium height, light weight and dressed in a dark-colored Hugo Boss suit that was more than a little rumpled. Duct tape was wrapped around his ankles and wrists. A blindfold covered his eyes, and his short black hair, with silvering temples, was badly ruffled. His mouth was covered with the tape, too, and he wasn't moving.

Walker bent down and slid the blindfold up to the man's forehead. Seeing the man's eyes were still closed, he lowered the bandana and slammed the trunk closed. Hiking up his pants, he casually surveyed the area and stood. His eyes searched up and down the walkway as though he heard voices in the wind. He interlaced his fingers out in front of himself and cracked his knuckles. Deciding he couldn't wait for Toad, he ducked behind a bush, pissed, and zipped up.

Toad was coming out of the building just as a new Dodge Caravan pulled in and parked about thirty feet away from him. A middle-aged man and a woman got out and headed for the restrooms. Walker sucked the Marlboro down to the filter, the ash glowing red as he tossed the butt, and got back in the car. Toad got in and said, "Well?"

"Well what? I already pissed in the bushes."

"Well, what in the hell do you think I mean...the guy in the trunk? Is everything okay?"

Walker tilted his seat and slumped back. "Yeah, he's fine. I didn't even have to juice him up again. He's out."

Triple Crossed

Chapter Two

I sat at my desk with my feet up, reading the Chicago Sun Times, when the woman flounced into my office. Things had been slow and I was daydreaming. The windows were open and the hum of the evening rush-hour traffic drifted in along with the smell of tar and gasoline. Even though it was late September, it smelled like July.

Deckle, the homeless guy I had sort of adopted, was sitting on a hard-backed chair in the corner, snoring.

"Excuse me for not getting up. I didn't hear you knock," I said.

I focused on Deckle: "Deckle! Hey, Deckle! Deckle!"

"Huh? Wha...?"

"Time to scoot, partner. I've got company." I nodded towards my new arrival.

"Oh, yeah, yeah, gotcha, Cleve." Deckle was only half awake but got up, wobbled a bit and tipped his grubby-looking Chicago Cubs cap to the visitor before he hustled out the door.

I figured her to be in her thirties. She was beautiful, but wore too much makeup, I thought, and the strong perfume told me that she felt it vital to impress the male population with the essence of herself. Either that or she had a nose problem, perhaps an ignored sinus infection. It wasn't a pleasing fragrance. She was built like the proverbial brick shithouse and wore a gray skirt that stopped just above the knees with a matching soft gray v-necked blouse. Her lipstick was candy apple red, her skin had a caramel tan and her highlighted blonde hair was thick and freshly brushed.

"Good afternoon, Ma'am." I extended my hand. "Cleve Hawkins. Can I help you?"

She frowned, glanced back at the door and said, "Yes, I suppose so." She looked me over like she was bidding on a used car. "Are you the private investigator?"

"I'd better be, ma'am, or we have to report a B&E immediately."

She stared for a moment as if she wasn't sure she heard me right. "My name is

Bethany Hubbard, and it's Mrs. Please don't call me ma'am," she said. "I don't like it. It sounds too old, too ma'am-ish." She raised a diamond-clad ring finger as if I needed proof of her marital status. "You may call me Beth, and I do apologize." She glanced sideways and sat down in one of my two client chairs. "I didn't mean to interrupt the meeting with your rather tawdry friend."

I was caught off guard by her frankness. "Oh...the guy who just left?" I grinned. "He's sort of a fixture around here. Runs errands and so on. His name's Deckle and you might say I've adopted him on a part-time basis."

"Thank you." She postured herself firmly upright, elbows on the chair arms, hands folded in her lap. Crossing her legs was a production as she glanced slowly around the room and looked at me as if she was expecting something more in the way of furnishings.

We were quiet. The late summer air moved gently through the window and fluttered some papers on my desk. I said nothing while Mrs. Hubbard stared out the window behind me. My theory is that when you do the silence bit long enough, you can get a sense that the other person is at the start of an explanation of sorts. So the best thing is to give that person the space and wait for them to fill it.

During the pregnant pause, I fiddled with a paper clip. I dropped it on my desk blotter and figured I'd best take the initiative and move along since it was getting late and I was thirsty. "Well, how can I help you, Beth?"

She readjusted the gold watch on her inner wrist and said, "My husband is having an affair." Her voice was dry and hoarse, like wind whispering over sandpaper. Her words were deliberate, her diction precise.

"I'm sorry. A lot of that going around," I said.

"Yes, well, I need to prove he's screwing around before he blows all of our money on some tramp and writes me out of his will." She had a pout on her lower lip that she seemed to be aware of and she moistened her lips often with her tongue.

"So, you want me to tail him and report my findings, is that it?"

"Exactly."

I pulled a yellow pad out of my center drawer and began to take notes.

"Okay...what's your husband's name?"

"Thad. Thad Hubbard. Well, Thadeous, actually. But everyone calls him Thad. She re-crossed her legs and sat back in the chair, somewhat relaxed. "How much do you charge?"

"That depends. Let's see what's involved and go from there, how's that?"

Triple Crossed

She appeared dismayed so I continued. "I get a thousand up front and work off of that. If I bust your husband and satisfy your curiosity as to his unfaithful behavior rather quickly, there'll be no refund. And my expenses are not included in that thousand, by the way. They are to be paid separately."

Her eyes widened, but she didn't flinch, so I marched on. "Are you two currently cohabiting or separated?"

"Co habit...whatever. That means together, right? Yes, we are living in the same house." The blood had risen in her face, and her eyes were shiny with embarrassment.

I had a fairly good opinion of her intellect at that point. "...and your address?"

"It's in Oak Park. 5150 Cherry Hill Road. But you won't be coming by the house, will you? If you do, Thad will know I hired you, and that won't work, of course."

"Of course. Well, I don't see any reason to come near your home at this point, Mrs. Hubbard. Unless of course you want me to be on hand when he does get home. Then I could hide in the bushes, jump out and yell 'Boo!'"

After I said that, she became pensive and bit into her bottom lip. I could see the heat intensify in her face. She stared and said, "I see. You think you're humorous, don't you, Mister Hawkins? This is serious business and I want you to handle it accordingly. Is that clear?"

I shrugged and smiled. "Just trying to keep things light, Mrs. Hubbard. It makes everything, including my day, slide by much easier. Tell me, where is your husband right now?"

Her frown told me she didn't buy what I'd just said. She fidgeted a bit before she said, "Thad is at his office, as far as I know. Two days ago he told me he'd be working late. Nothing new of course, but I didn't believe him."

"You think he has a girlfriend instead, then."

"Exactly...out with one of the whores he works with, no doubt." She began to fumble around in her purse and pulled out a pack of Virginia Slim cigarettes. "May I smoke?"

I nodded. "I don't have the habit, but I can understand the addiction." I reached into the bottom drawer of my desk and handed her an ashtray. "Go ahead."

"Thank you," she said as she lit up. She closed her eyes, massaged the lids slowly and at length while blowing a thick plume of smoke toward the ceiling. "This entire situation has me so stressed. That chiseling bastard thinks he's going to drop me like one of his slutty playthings. He's got another thing coming."

"How long have you two been married?"

She sighed and answered as if I were taking up too much of her time. "About a year and a half."

"Newlyweds."

"Ha! Not really."

"Any kids?"

"Not by him. I have a daughter and a son. They're both living in California, though."

"You've got a pre-nup?"

She shook her head. "No, and I'm damned glad we don't."

"That's one way of looking at it, I suppose. What does your husband do for a living, Mrs. Hubbard?"

"Call me Beth, please, and I'm not sure, exactly. He works for a rather large firm in the Loop. Carrington Engineering Enterprises. You've heard of them?"

"Sorry, no." I leaned back in my chair and braided my fingers behind my head. "What does he do there?"

"What's his job entail, you mean?" She shrugged and shook her head. "I just know he's in the Research and Development section. He's a chemist by trade. I have no idea what they research though. He doesn't tell me anything about his job...never has. He's a very secretive man, know what I mean?"

I nodded. "I think so."

"I have been up to his office a few times, but the receptionist always had to call him on the phone and announce me. Each time it took forever before he finally came out through a special door. Isn't that odd? Like, what's the big deal? I'll bet his boss doesn't have to get permission to bring his wife back there, you know what I mean?" She took a deep drag on the cigarette and snubbed it out in the ashtray before continuing.

"They've got two of those security guard guys standing at the door, too. Look like apes. And the secretary is just there, doing nothing but polishing her nails. There's not even a typewriter on her desk."

"No computer?"

"Oh, I don't know. I never noticed." Beth adjusted the gold watch on her inner wrist again as she awaited my next question. I tapped my pen on the pad for a moment and tried to keep a straight face.

"It sounds like they're very security oriented over there," I said with all the enthusiasm I could muster.

"I'll say. It's so ridiculous."

Triple Crossed

The silence swelled and I put down the pen and leaned forward. "Tell me, exactly what makes you think Thad is cheating?"

"Ha! That's easy. For one thing, he had been working late at the office three nights a week for the past four months. Now, recently it's become four and sometimes five nights. And he's never home before midnight. I can smell perfume on his shirts, too."

I already knew she had no clue about the scent of perfume, but I continued to roll with her thought process.

"Now last night he didn't even come home at all. No call or anything."

"This working late…is that the reason he always gives you for being late?"

"It's always the same. The project they're working on is behind schedule and the push is on, whatever that's supposed to mean. He doesn't even come to bed when he gets home…sleeps in the guest room most of the time."

"I see. Do you ever question him about that part, the not coming to bed, I mean?"

"Yes, of course, and I always get the same answer: 'I didn't want to wake you.'"

I paused a moment. "So, what happens on his days off?"

"Saturday and Sunday? Ha! Usually he plays golf with his buddies from work…or he says he does. He does grace me with his presence on Sunday night. Big deal. If you were me, what would you think?"

"I'd probably think about hiring a private eye to snoop and see what Thad's up to."

She looked at me and made a little sound that might have been a laugh, smothered, and then she frowned. "This is serious business, Mister Hawkins, and I don't appreciate your sarcasm." She had lit another cigarette and blew a huge cloud of smoke my way. "I've heard about you."

"Sorry, I didn't mean to sound sarcastic. Really. Just curious, though, what have you heard about me?"

She hesitated for a moment and let her dangling foot rotate in small circles. "Well, you used to be a homicide detective with the city and you quit to become a private eye. I've also heard that you're a good detective, but quite frankly…well…a smart ass."

I gave her my best surprised look. "No…really? Well, you shouldn't listen to everything you hear, Mrs. Hubbard. Pardon, I mean Beth. The excellent detective part is correct, however. Now then, does your husband have any friends he hangs out with on a regular basis, in his spare time, I mean? Who does he play golf with, for instance?"

"Well, none of our neighbors associate with him, if that's what you mean. He does hang around with Glenn whats-his-name. Plays golf with him and Jerry Berg, as far as I know."

I grabbed my pen again. "Okay, what's his name?"

She smiled. "Sorry. Jeff Dahms. He's one of the guys Thad works with. They hang out, play golf, handball at the gym, go to the bars, whatever. Why?"

I stopped writing and looked at her. "I'm just attempting to get as much information as I can before I can get started, Beth. I'll need a recent picture of your husband, too."

"Certainly." She began to paw things around inside her purse and retrieved a beige wallet. She handed me a picture of her husband, Thad, who looked geeky and reminded me of Mister Peepers from the old TV show. It wasn't a head shot. He was wearing an ill-fitting blue blazer over a collarless black shirt and gray slacks. For a man of his apparent position, his clothes had the worn and rumpled look of a thrift store sale. He had a small round face, very little hair on his head and he wore wire framed glasses which did nothing for his appearance except make him look even more Mister Peeper-ish.

"This is the only one you have? I mean, you don't happen to have a portrait-type picture with you, I suppose?"

"Sorry, no." She opened her wallet. "No, I only have these pictures of my girlfriends. I do have some better ones of Thad at home."

"Okay, maybe you can find a better one before we meet again. I would appreciate it. Now, on another front...do you have any idea which bars he frequents? Does he have any favorite restaurants, that sort of thing?"

She shrugged. "No, how should I know? I told you, Thad tells me very little, if anything. We talk on the phone more than we do at home. That's another thing that makes me suspicious, by the way." She leaned in and squinted as she said, "Hang ups. I get phone calls and when I answer, nobody is there. Ha! Who does he think he's kidding?"

"Hang ups, you say?"

"Yes. Probably three or four in the past couple of months alone. Not on my cell, but we still have the landline and when I answer, nobody's there. And this always happens when Thad is supposedly at the office, working late."

"Hmmmm. Boggles the mind." I sat forward and scratched my head. "What kind of car is Thad driving these days?"

"A Chevrolet Monte Carlo, two-thousand and two, I think. It's black, if that helps. I don't know his license plate number."

Triple Crossed

"That's okay. I shouldn't have any problem getting that."

Beth puffed on her cigarette and the room was quiet for a moment while I jotted down a few more notes. She sighed with impatience. "Well?"

"Well, what?"

"Well, are you going to help me catch him or not?"

I stood and circled the desk. Sitting on the front edge, I said, "Cleve. Call me Cleve, Beth, and of course, I'll take the case. You can make the check out to cash."

She pulled a checkbook from her purse and I stood up as she leaned over my desk to write. With that done, she handed the check to me and said, "I am depending on you. Please don't let me down."

She offered her hand and I shook it. With that I watched her hips sway as she walked out on high heels in a gait that reminded me of a gazelle's. She was a woman in a hurry, haloed by a cloud of smoke.

I imagined what a life Thad must have with her. I sensed she probably went about her life with the abrasiveness of a carpenter building coffins with a nail gun.

I strolled over and closed the door, went back and dropped into my swivel chair and peered out the window. Deckle was sitting on the curb watching Beth as she hurried down the block to where her car was parked.

This should be easy money, I thought.

R.C. Hartson

Chapter Three

Thad Hubbard stirred and tried to remember what had happened.

It didn't take long to realize he was trapped in the trunk of a moving vehicle. He wasn't sure how, but his head felt as though somebody had jabbed it with a knife. He tried to extend his legs, but he was consumed by pain and his body seemed to absorb each bump in the road as if he'd been thrown down an endless flight of stairs.

His eyes fluttered open, but he felt the snugness of a blindfold wrapped around his head. Barely conscious, he sensed the vague odor of exhaust and burning oil. He was breathing through his nose and realized that his mouth was covered with tape and his hands and ankles were also bound in some way. His straining against them accomplished nothing.

Thad tried to remember anything that would help, but he felt himself slipping back into a dreamlike limbo and he stayed that way until much later when he sensed the vehicle slowing down. His eyes blinked open again when it jerked to a stop.

The evening sky was ribbed with purple and red clouds when Toad and Walker eased their Buick around a corner and disappeared down a tree-lined side street that looked like an illustration clipped from a 1939 issue of *The Saturday Evening Post*. The taillights flickered just before they pulled into a long, winding cement driveway in the affluent community of Alpine, New Jersey.

"Did Cosgrove say he wanted us to park and go in or what?" asked Walker.

"When I called to check in, he said people would be watching for us. He said we should just pull inside the garage and we'd be told from there," Toad said. As he approached the garage he added, "Ha! Look at this. A fucking four-car garage. We should have plenty of room to park in there."

"Yeah. What about the flake in the trunk?"

"Take the shit outta your ears, will you, Ace? I just said somebody's gonna tell us what to do. There...see, the doors are opening now. Talk about timing." He glanced over at his partner. "Put that fuckin' cigarette out, will you?"

Triple Crossed

He eased the car into an open bay in the garage. The two adjacent stalls were filled. A sleek Mercedes-Benz CL was parked in the one next to them and a huge cabin-cruiser, covered with a tarp, occupied another bay by the outside wall.

A petite woman with blonde hair and no chin opened a side door leading from the garage into the house. She wore a white and pink apron and smiled as she held the door open and stepped out of their way.

"Come in gentlemen. Right this way. Mister Zagaretti is expecting you."

The two men followed her through to a foyer where a chandelier the size of a beach umbrella hung and then they entered a pine paneled living room furnished with English antiques. French doors led to a study where the shelves were filled with encyclopedias, science and history books, fiction novels and plastic-bound collections of classics. The couch and the chairs were red leather and a glass-covered mahogany desk fit for a CEO sat in front of wide bowed windows.

The room was softly lit and on one shelf, squarely in the center of an ego wall, was a collection of stars and planets. The mantle above the fireplace displayed miniature oil derricks of various sizes.

A woman suddenly edged in behind them. "Gentlemen." She glanced at the woman in the apron. "I'll take it from here, Chiela. Thank you."

"Yes, Ma'am," Chiela answered, feigned a curtsey and left the room.

The woman extended her hand. "You may call me Trebecka."

Toad shook her hand. "I'm Keith, but everybody calls me Toad."

Walker took her hand. "Walker's mine. Glad to meet you."

Trebecka was a middle-aged woman, slightly overweight, with carefully coiffed hair that changed color weekly. She wore dark slacks, gray pumps, and a white silk blouse that hung over her waist. A real pearl necklace graced her neck. Her face was fresh and cheerful, and the light and dark streaks of blond in her thick hair gave her an elegance seldom seen in maturing women. She stood facing them with her fingers hooked in front of her stomach like an opera singer.

"Nick will be with you momentarily. Meanwhile, help yourself at the bar over there," she said with a saccharine smile. "Jamie will take care of you." She nodded at the man behind the bar.

He was in his early thirties and had massive arms and spiked hair that looked as if he'd just put his finger in a light socket. Taking out a pack of spearmint gum, he selected a stick and after unwrapping it, folded a piece into his mouth. His eyes were on the wide-screen television that sat across the room showing re-runs of *Law and Order SVU*. He quickly muted the sound as the visitors approached.

When Toad saw the man's hair, he mumbled to Walker, "Jesus Christ."

Jamie overheard him and said, "I don't think so. No beard. No sandals."

The man put together a fairly good smile, sort of an Elvis number, part sneer and part grin as he stuck out his hand. "Hey, gents. I'm Jamie."

They all shook hands and Jamie shoved two ashtrays in front of them. "Feel free. Smoking lamp's lit."

Walker quickly fumbled around in his jacket, found his pack of Marlboros and lit up. Both men sat down on the leather-covered barstools.

Toad regarded Jamie with the thinnest hint of a frown touching his wide, lipless mouth. "Got any munchies…chips or somethin' maybe?"

"Gotcha covered," said Jamie. He reached under the bar and tossed Toad bags of mini potato chips and Fritos. Then, snapping his gum, he said, "What'll you guys have to drink? I got it all. Beer, wine…you name it."

Toad ripped open a bag of Fritos and started cramming them into his mouth while he and Walker checked the inventory behind the bar. The long row of bottles arranged like soldiers in front of the mirror glistened in a shimmer of colors along the dimly lit area.

"Cutty Sark on the rocks," said Toad.

"You got it," said Jamie as he grabbed a tumbler and made the drink.

"How's that Rheingold beer I see back there on tap?" Walker asked.

Jamie plunked some ice into the tumbler and shrugged. "Ah, it's a pretty decent brew. New York favorite, you know. Where you guys from?"

Toad glanced at Walker and rolled his eyes. "Out of town."

Jamie gave Toad his drink and drew up a tall glass of draught for Walker.

Walker looked around. "I hope we don't have to pay rent here tonight." He brushed some cigarette ashes off his slacks by flipping his nails against the cloth.

Toad finished his chips, wadded up the sack and popped it with the flat of his hand before he tossed it on the bar. He pressed his palms together and twisted them back and forth, his calluses scraping audibly. He opened another bag as Jamie threw the empty in a small garbage can.

Toad drank until his glass was half empty and then rested his hands on the bar. He studied Jamie's hair and shrugged. Rubbing his huge hands over his face, he licked his lips and caught the latent taste of the Cutty Sark.

Walker stuck a toothpick in his mouth, furrowing and un-furrowing his brow as though hundreds of thoughts were flying through his mind. He inhaled his cigarette and blew smoke at an upward angle into the air. Out of the corner of his eye he saw Jamie's eyes wander to a spot just beyond Toad's right shoulder. "Here's Mister Zee now," said Jamie.

Triple Crossed

Toad and Walker swiveled around on their stools.

Nick Zagaretti was a thick dark man with a Vandyke goatee and small eyes kept barely apart by the bridge of his flat nose. He was a strange looking individual. His head was long and narrow and his ears were tiny and were pressed tightly against his head as though part of them had been surgically removed. His hair grew in gray and black curls that were tapered on the back of his neck like the rim of a helmet, and his smile exposed teeth that were as perfectly shaped as Chicklets gum.

He was dressed in a dignified gray-on-gray that complemented the short salt and pepper goatee he wore, perhaps to hide the ancient craters of rampant teenage acne. Puffing on a cigar, he squinted through the smoke and kept his eyes focused on Toad as he extended his hand.

"I'm Nick." He nodded his head sideways at the bartender. "You can leave us now, Jamie."

Toad and Walker took turns shaking Nick's hand and introducing themselves. The Patek Phillippe on Zagaretti's wrist spoke of pampered wealth.

"Good to be here," said Walker. "It's quite a haul from Chicago, ya know?"

Zagaretti didn't answer right away, but tried to grin good-naturedly even though his eyes seemed to peel the skin off Walker's face.

"I appreciate you guys having my package intact," he said. "I trust there were no unforeseen difficulties involved."

"Nope. All good," said Toad. "Cosgrove set things up good and tight." He took another swig of his scotch.

"We tried to handle the guy with kid gloves, too, just like we were told," said Walker. "You want us to unload and bring him in now?"

"No, thanks. That's all been handled. A couple friends of mine took care of him a few moments ago." He chuckled. "You might say 'Houston, the Eagle has landed'." He laid a hand on Walker's shoulder and squeezed ever so slightly. "I believe Cosgrove is taking care of your fee. Is that correct?"

"Right," said Walker.

Zagaretti stuck his cigar in the corner of his mouth. He reached inside his coat pocket and pulled out a banded stack of cash. He ran his thumb over the end of the bundle and fanned it a few times. Staring into Walker's eyes, he spanked the palm of his hand with the cash and handed it to Walker. His dark eyes scanned both men.

"Good job, gentlemen. This is a little token of my personal appreciation. I trust you are going straight back home. I'd hate to think of you losing any of this at our rather selfish casinos in Atlantic City.

"Thanks," said Toad as he took the bundle from Walker's hands. "We appreciate the tips...both of them. Don't we, Walker?"

"What? Oh yeah...yeah. Thanks."

Zagaretti smiled. "Good. I may be able to use you men again some time. Enjoy your drinks. When you're done, Jamie will show you out."

He turned and began to walk away then stopped and turned to face them. "Oh, I strongly suggest you invest in another vehicle by the way. A model that's sparkling clean both inside and out, especially the trunk." He winked.

. . .

Thad Hubbard lay on a bed in the dark. At least it felt like a bed. His eyes fluttered to stay open and he could hear his own breathing in the silence. The stabbing pain had returned to his head. He realized the blindfold was missing and the tape had been removed from his mouth, wrists and ankles, but an intense throbbing racked his entire body.

HIs attempt to sit up failed, and he fell back onto the bed feeling groggy and sick to his stomach. He no longer felt the swaying motion inflicted upon him in the trunk of a car. He tried to keep himself awake by blinking his eyes.

Where am I, he puzzled as he lay there.

He wasn't sure how long it was before he heard the sound of jangling keys and the unlocking of a door.

He heard approaching footsteps and then sensed some light. He rolled his head to the side and saw that the light came from a lamp in a corner that appeared to be far away. Every sound was an explosion that reverberated through his temples. The footsteps became louder as they moved closer to the bed. Thad squinted, but could barely discern the shadow of a person.

"Hello, Mister Hubbard."

The man turned a straight-backed chair around backward and straddled it. "Good to finally meet you, sir," he said.

Thad thought the voice sounded as though it was being piped through an underground tunnel, distant and dream-like.

"Sorry you were transported in such an uncomfortable manner, Mister Hubbard, but as you will witness, sometimes the path to success makes rather difficult turns."

He paused, and Thad saw the flash of a cigarette lighter. The acrid smell of cigar smoke soon reached his nostrils.

Triple Crossed

"Seems like you're coming around a bit. Good. I want you to be comfortable, Mister Hubbard. I'm sure you are hungry, as well as thirsty. You will find that these quarters are very comfortable, and I will arrange to have dinner and your favorite beverage brought to you. Then you can get a good night's rest. We will talk in the morning."

Thad struggled to sit up and talk. His voice came out in a hoarse whisper.

"Where am I?"

Chapter Four

After Bethany Hubbard had left my office, I went back to the business of staring out the window with my feet up on the desk. From time to time I glanced at the yellow pad on my lap and the notes I had taken during our meeting.

I decided to start snooping in the morning.

I knew if Thad Hubbard was screwing around on his wife, he must have been brain dead for staying out all night. Perhaps there was some other reason he hadn't made it home. Then again, maybe the couple saw fit to clear the air, kiss and make up. It wouldn't be the first time that scenario played out in my business.

All of it confounded the mind, but I was ready to go home.

I thought about the bottle of Dewar's scotch stashed in the bottom drawer of my desk. For years I had flirted with liquor, especially scotch. The romance began when I was in the Marines doing a tour in Nam. A couple of times I actually fell in love with booze. Now, years later, after I had accidentally shot that civilian while working homicide and quit the force, I decided I was really in love with it and for about six months there, it was as if scotch and I had been married.

I tried to stay clear of drinking now. I told myself that the bottle in my drawer was for guests, but I knew better. I still had a beer occasionally, but drinking alone was the worst, and I refrained as much as possible. At least, when I stopped in one of my favorite watering holes, like Butch McGuires on Division, I had company and, like a sneaky drunk, didn't feel as guilty. My formula was two beers equaled one scotch and soda. Two scotches equaled one and a half martinis and so on. Of course it was all bullshit. Alcohol is alcohol.

I had my future with Maureen to consider. Much of our relationship was spent in a constant push/pull. One step forward, two steps back, living together, living apart, dating each other, dating others. We had spent tons of time and energy in a long and drawn out dance that nearly ended in smoldered embers.

Now I was committed to a positive relationship with Mo, particularly since the Branoff fiasco in which she basically saved my ass. I didn't want to lose her. For the most part, booze and I were no longer seeing each other. We were damn near divorced and I was proud of it.

I rubbed my face. My whiskers felt rough against my palm. I felt grubby. I couldn't help but wonder how I must have looked to the Hubbard woman. Deckle was nowhere in sight and I decided to lock up and head out.

At the apartment, I shaved and took a long hot shower. My stomach was growling and a Pizza Hut was just up the street on Clark. I had just put on my Cubs windbreaker when somebody buzzed my door.

I hadn't seen my old friend, Jeebers, in nearly two years. I was caught off guard, but nonetheless pleasantly surprised when I saw his rugged mug in the peephole. I opened the door.

"Well, Jesus Christ!" I said.

"Nah, just me," said Jeebers. "Christ is above my pay grade." We shared a hearty handshake.

"How's it hangin' Hawk? Still playing cops n' robbers, I hear."

"Get in here. Yeah. I have to have a badge or I go nuts. Not with the department, though. I'm licensed private now. I take it you stopped by headquarters. That how you knew where I was?"

"Yeah, a lieutenant named Andrews filled me in. He explained that you left the department. And why. That's fucked up. You shouldn't have quit, partner. The looy brought me up to speed on the Branoff deal, too. Said you were there when it all went down. Bad shit. What the hell, I always thought Kris was a good man. Too bad."

I didn't feel justified telling Tyler all the particulars as to Kris Branoff's demise, so I simply agreed. "Yeah, we lost a real trooper there."

Jeebers had been my first partner when we were rookies cruising the South Side in a blue and white. That was before I was promoted to Detective Grade One and partnered up with Kris Branoff. Jeebers hadn't moved up with me at the time, but he made detective about a year later.

His real name was Tyler Mulvaney, and although he wouldn't explain where he got tagged with the name, Jeebers, nobody seemed to care. He was one hell of a good man and I'd trust him to cover my back any day of the week. He was one tough son-of-a-bitch, and a straight arrow if there ever was one. Strong inside and out, an enigma who kept his life scars pretty much hidden.

In his forties with a bumpy complexion and sandy hair, a little thin on top, he had the physique of a linebacker. He was six-two, two-twenty, with a chest like a drum and arms like cable. His hands and fingers were thick, as were his lips. His nose was broad. I saw the shoulder holster and snub-nosed .38 under his sport coat when he shook my hand.

"Wow! Fuckin' A. It's good to see you, hotshot," I said. "I haven't heard from you since you left Chicago. I figured you were in Singapore or some other God-forsaken place. Take off that hat and cop a squat, buddy."

"Thanks, Cleve. Yeah, I left a lot of baggage behind when I went out west. I know I should have stayed in touch, but, well, you know how it is." He tossed his hat on the dinette table and looked around as he followed me into the living room. "Pretty nice digs you've got here."

He reached for his inside pocket and pulled out a red pack of Pall Malls and a Zippo lighter. His eyes met mine as he held them up. "Okay if I light up?"

"Sure, what the hell. Go ahead." I saw his Zippo and I chuckled. "Hey, isn't that the same lighter you had when we worked together back in the day?"

After he lit the cigarette, he flicked the lighter again. "Yeah, same old same old. You forgot I got it at the PX when I was stationed at Pendleton." He grinned. "Never fails to work as long as I keep it juiced up."

I straddled a dinette chair and sat on the other side of the coffee table in front of him. Jeebers had never been accused of being modest. He sat in the center of the couch and said, "Got a cold beer around?"

"Is the Pope a Catholic?" I quipped. I went to the fridge, knowing there were two bottles of Heineken left. I grabbed them both, twisted the tops off and handed one to him. "Let me get you an ashtray, too. My girlfriend, Maureen, smokes when she's here. She works in the office on Michigan Avenue. I don't think she was there before you left. She worked for Branoff for a while."

"Nope. Must've been after I left," he said. "But I'll bet she's a beauty, knowing your taste."

He took a long swallow of the beer. I sipped mine after my first swallow.

"Yeah, she's gorgeous. I don't think I deserve her. To tell the truth, we're pretty serious, though. So, tell me…what in the hell brings you to town, Jeebs? Last I heard you were happy working out west in the land of fruits n' nuts."

Jeebers blew a big cloud of smoke and tapped his cigarette on the ashtray. "Yeah. Southern California…actually Hollyweird. It's so insane out there. I had to come back home. The only time I like Crazy is when Patsy Cline is singing it on the jukebox. I was living near Beverly Hills, but I'm back here in Chicago, this time for good, I think."

"That's great, Jeebs. Maybe we can hang out, just like the old days."

It didn't take long before he upended his bottle and said, "I was thirsty. Got another one of these?"

Triple Crossed

I was a bit embarrassed when I said, "No, as a matter of fact, I don't, but I was just going to get something to eat. What say we go over to The Billy Goat?"

"Ah, I'm not really hungry, but I'll have another beer with you. Come on." Jeebers stood and grabbed his hat. "I haven't been in that joint in four years, at least that long. I know it was way before I left Chicago."

"Well, it hasn't changed. Still a tourist peekaboo."

It was within walking distance, but we grabbed a cab and headed for The Billy Goat Tavern on Michigan Avenue. A nice little bar and a world famous tourist trap for die-hard Cubs fans the world over. Besides, it wasn't that far from my place on Surf Street.

It wasn't crowded with the after work shift and it was a travel day for the Cubs. Only a few home games remained and damned few fans would bother to show for those since the team was thirty-five games out of first place. Jeebers and I slid into a back booth.

The waitress was a red-headed, tired-looking woman who wore oceanic amounts of perfume. We ordered two of the Billy Goat Cheezeborgers and a couple more Heinies. Jeebers sat back a little and stared. We swapped phone numbers.

"I've got to start all over here, Cleve. I found a place over on Chestnut. Not the best, but good enough for now. I'm looking for work, maybe undercover or security, you know what I mean? Bodyguard work, maybe."

His face was flushed. His voice sounded thick.

"Yeah, I can understand that. It's a bitch starting all over again. You know, maybe I could use you myself, from time to time, Jeebs. I've got a couple of irons in the fire right now, and I stay pretty busy since I got serious about this PI stuff."

The waitress came with our beers and Jeebers pulled out his cigarettes.

"Shit!" he whispered. "You can't smoke in these joints anymore, can you?"

I chuckled. "No. Those days are over, pal."

He shoved the pack back in his pocket and I could see gears moving and lights flashing behind his eyes.

"Hmmm. That offer of yours sounds good, Hawk. I'd like that. It would be something at least til I get back in the groove. I don't want to sit on my ass. I'd rather become a bouncer in a retirement home. I don't want no handouts either, though, you know what I mean?"

"Yeah, I understand."

We sat silently for a while.

"There's a lot of big outfits in the loop and plenty of them have need for security," I finally said. "Why not give that a shot? Check out the ads in the *Sunday Trib* and *Sun Times*. I would start there, if you're interested. Nightclub bouncing is bullshit. You know that, Jeebs. There's too many ways to get your tit in the legal wringer with that shit. Like I said, I can use you from time to time, but you can't really count on that, you know?"

He nodded. "Yeah, I'd like that, but you're right, I need something steady. I know how to detect, and you can bet your private eye ass, I'll do a decent job. I used to think I was too good for scut work. I figured I'd wait for a real job to pop up. I couldn't see myself doing Dick Tracy, rattling door knobs and shit like that, but times change...so do minds." He winked, took a long swallow of the beer and held the empty in the air. "Where's that waitress?"

He squinted and thought about what I'd said. "You must be in it for the long haul, huh?"

"Yeah, I can't go back on the force and I wouldn't if I could, to tell the truth. I was with the department for fourteen years and I lost count of the lowlifes I helped send to the crowbar hotel. Is Chicago better for it? You know the answer to that one. The real scumbags were the ones we never got to touch. I'm set for good, the way I see it. I'm my own boss, the money's okay. I get by. I won't give it up, not until I'm pushing the clouds around anyway." I paused and took a long swig of my beer. "You wouldn't back away if I had something for you, though, is that right?"

"No, never," He made a wide arm gesture like an umpire calling a runner safe at the plate. "You know I wouldn't bullshit you, Hawk."

"I didn't think so, partner. I had been thinking about drafting Joe Ortega part time. You remember him. He works in vice, and he's not too happy with the new regime over on Michigan Avenue, either. Internal affairs has been hassling him about one thing or another."

Jeebers shook his head from side to side. "Nah, if it's the same Ortega I knew, you really don't want him though. As I remember, he couldn't find his asshole if you gave him a mirror on a stick."

"Is that right? Hmmm, here I thought he might be a good fit here and there when I'm in a pinch."

"Up to you, but I know you can do better, my friend."

"Speaking of doing better, Jeebs, what's going on in your personal file now? Last I remember, you were pretty hot with that red-headed secretary who worked in the White Sox sales office. What was her name?"

He grinned. "Oh, you mean Shari?"

"Yeah, that's the one. What happened there?"

Triple Crossed

"Simple enough. I wanted to move to L A, she didn't. I don't know where she went after I left here. I haven't had time to check it out. I've been seeing a few hot females, that's for sure. I never let my meat loaf." He threw his big head back and laughed out loud. "Listen to this. I was dating this Chinese waitress from Pomona and one night we're making out hot and heavy and I said to her, 'I'd love sixty-nine' and she says, 'Oh, you want beef and broccoli now?'"

I laughed. "Same old Jeebs. You're full of more shit than a broken pay toilet."

He crossed his heart and grinned. "It's damned good to see you again, Hawk."

"Yeah," I said, "This is more damn fun than string cheese night at Lambeau Field, isn't it?"

The waitress came by and brought us two more beers.

He started peeling the label off his bottle and said, "So what kind of cases you got perking right now, anyway?" He snickered. "I know they're not homicide."

"I've got a client came in today, a woman, a rich looking one...high-strung. You know the type. Right out of *The Great Gatsby*. Her husband evidently has a wandering dick. She wants me to tail him, whatever, and get proof. I had a gut feeling that she was more interested in his money than him, but mine is not to judge. I'll just nail the guy if he's guilty. But see, either way, I get my fee and make money on the deal. I do a lot of that now. You know, errant husbands, cheating wives, scammers, missing persons, cuckolding wives, stolen property. Shit like that."

Jeebers was silent for a moment. He tugged at an earlobe and took out a pack of spearmint gum. He selected a stick, unwrapped it and folded a piece into his mouth.

"Sounds like it's right up my alley. You can count on me, if you need help."

I grinned as I shot him with my thumb and forefinger. "Good deal, Jeebs. I don't think I'll need help on this one though." I looked at my watch. "Hey, I hate to bust this up, but I've got to scoot. First thing in the morning, I have to work out and then get started on this new case."

"Yeah, that's okay. I understand," he replied.

I stood and tossed two twenties on the table. "I've got this, Jeebs."

"Nah, I'll get it." He reached for his pocket and I waved him off.

"No, Jeebs. You can get it next time. You've got my number now. Give me a call and let me know how you're making out."

"It's a deal. Thanks." He stood and we shook hands. "Take it slow and easy,

Hawk."

    I left my old friend, even though I would have liked to spend some more time with him. Nothing in my life had the power to be as distracting as the mistakes of the past and the only cure I had for that was to try to control the present. That meant pouring myself into this new case I had as soon as possible. I grabbed a cab and headed for home.

Chapter Five

I got up early and was at the gym by seven.

Having a new case, no matter how large or small, always got my blood racing, just as if I was back in the homicide division at the department. I knew I was over the top in my mental evaluation of the job, but old habits are hard to break. I often thought back on my years in the Marines, when reveille sounded at five in the morning and the day's choice of events was not necessarily mine to be made.

I checked in with the always sexy-looking Jessica at the gym where I hit the light bag and the heavy bag, sweated out some crunches on the Nautilus and ran three miles around the indoor track before taking a shower. A late breakfast was in order after my workout, so I stopped at Ann Sathers on Belmont and had its Southern Decadence three egg omelet.

Back at the apartment, I dressed in a blue button-down, tan slacks and cordovan loafers for comfort. I strapped on my holstered .38 behind my right hip and donned my leather bomber jacket and Bears cap. I had a blackjack I carried in my car just in case, but I didn't like using it unless it was absolutely necessary. Since I had left the homicide division at the PD, I rarely found a need.

The morning seemed divided between darkness and shadow, the clouds overhead roiling and black and crackling with electricity against an otherwise blue and tranquil sky. I drove my dark blue Ford Explorer. It has decent legroom for guys my size.

Before I left, I called Bethany Hubbard. I needed to know if her husband had come home. Her self-assured attitude had changed since her visit to my office.

"No, Mister Hawkins, he didn't come home last night either," she said with a voice that was one of concern. "That's two days and nights without a word. I hesitated to call his office, but I finally did yesterday afternoon and the receptionist told me he hadn't been there in a couple of days." Mrs. Hubbard was silent for several long moments before saying, " I...I have to be honest here...I'm starting to worry that something may have happened to Thad."

"Well, let's not break the glass for the fire alarm just yet, Mrs. Hubbard. I can appreciate your concern, but we will get to the bottom of it and find him. As a matter of fact, I'm on my way to his office right now."

"My husband's office? Why?"

"I need to check the information you are getting before we start a search or report him as missing. Maybe they are stonewalling you for some reason. I'll see. You understand?"

"Yes, I guess so. I am depending on you, so I guess I'll trust whatever you think."

"Right. I will get back to you later today after I do some checking, okay?"

"Yes. I can't believe this is happening. It's just not like him to stay away like this."

"I'll call later. Meanwhile, you try to stay calm. Goodbye, ma'am."

"It's easy for you to say. Well, Goodbye."

I called Maureen, although I knew she wouldn't be there since she started work at eight in the department. Still, I wanted to check in and confirm our plan to have dinner at Harry Carey's place on Kinzie that night. I left her a message and hauled ass.

I took Lakeshore Drive and watched the wind cut across the lake, kicking up whitecaps and chasing dead leaves across the road. Everybody was in a hurry, as usual for that time of day. All the nine A.M. bees buzzing to their favorite flowers.

I turned west, and once I was in the Loop, pulled into the parking garage at 317 West Adams, tipped the attendant, and walked to the elevator. It automatically stopped on the first floor. The security guard was a short, fat man with a pale, jiggly face who should have gone to Hollywood for acting roles as a corrupt southern politician. He was perched on a stool behind a marble-topped counter. I flashed my badge just long enough to allow him a good look. He quickly attempted to stretch his girth across the counter to scrutinize the ID.

"You a cop?" he said in a hushed tone. His gaze skated off to somewhere to my left.

"Close enough," I said. "The name's Cleve Hawkins. I'm here to see Mister Hubbard at Carrington Enterprises."

The wannabe cop rubbed his nose with the heel of his hand and then flipped through the papers on his clipboard. "Do you have an appointment, Mister Hawkins?"

"No, as a matter of fact, I don't."

"Well, I'll have to call and announce you first…company policy, you know."

"Yes, I understand. Go right ahead. I don't want you to deviate from policy."

Triple Crossed

I opened the door that said Carrington Engineering and saw two mature female clerks situated in cubicles off to the left. They glanced up in unison, reminding me of late night partiers in a bar who stare at the front door each time it opens, as though the person coming in has an answer for the hopelessness that dominates their lives.

Another wannabe cop stood just inside the door. I remembered Beth Hubbard mentioning the Neanderthal-looking guard she saw on her visits to the office. He was slouching against the wall, but straightened his jacket and moved his shoulders like a boxer who'd just gone four rounds.

The receptionist's desk was adjacent to an oversized mahogany door. Standing when I came in, she eased around her desk to greet me. A slender brunette, she wore lots of clothes. Her beige skirt reached her ankles and nearly covered her black-laced high heeled boots. Over the skirt she wore a long ivory tunic and a black leather belt with huge buckle. The aqua bow in her hair was striking.

Her face took on a look of trepidation. "Can I help you, sir?"

I flipped out my badge and said, "I would hope so. I'm Cleve Hawkins. I'm here to see Mister Carrington."

She stared at my hands as I folded my wallet and put it in my pocket.

"I'm sorry. May I see that again, please?" Her voice was calm and measured and soothing, like an FM disc jockey playing easy listening music after midnight.

"Sure." I pulled my ID back out and held it closer to her face.

"Oh, I imagined you were the police, but I see you are only a private detective, is that right?"

"Correct. Sorry to disappoint you, but congratulations, you are very observant, Ms...?"

"Chalmers. Edith Chalmers, and I'm sorry, Mister Hawkins, but if you don't have an appointment, you'll have to call and make one. Mr. Carrington has a very busy schedule."

"Well, this is important and I need to see him now, unless you'd rather I call some friends of mine at the Chicago Police Department to join us in his office." I saw the guard ease forward, but he stopped when Edith spoke again and put her hand up to him like a crossing guard.

"No. If that's what you want," she said. "It certainly won't be necessary to call the police." She folded her arms across her chest, gripping her elbows as if she were cold. "I'll see if Mister Carrington will see you now. Wait here, please."

Carrington came out to greet me. After shaking hands he led the way into his spacious office and closed the door. The room was dominated by a huge mahogany desk occupied with computer equipment. Paperwork and manila folders were stacked in neat little piles. The blotter was clean and clear except for a pen, pencil and legal-sized yellow tablet and one open folder.

"Have a seat, Mister Hawkins." He swept his hand over the choices of three plush armchairs sitting in front of his desk. I picked the one closest to his desk. As in the outer office, the furnishings were oak with smooth modern lines. A framed print of Mallard ducks hung on one wall. The ego wall displayed certificates and awards for whatever. The office was neat and tidy, compulsively so.

Carrington appeared to be straight out of central casting. A tall, gaunt individual, his skin was the color of modeling clay and age had pulled the flesh of his face down, leaving deep crevices in his cheeks and forehead. He was clean-shaven, his pin-striped white shirt neatly pressed, the crease in his gray slacks sharp. A tasteful gold bracelet clung to the left wrist just below the diamond Rolex. There were gold cuff links on his French cuffs and English wing-tipped black shoes. He dropped his files on his desk and sat down heavily in his swivel chair. His gaze went all over me, as though I were an object he was seeing for the first time.

"I understand you said this was of an urgent nature, Mister Hawkins."

"Yes. I'd characterize it as such."

"Very well, we'll get right to it, but may I have Edith bring you something to drink? Coffee, perhaps?"

I watched his body language as he spoke. He appeared to be a man with too much stress in his life and no way out except by heart attack. He was looking at the floor as he talked. His fingernails, I noticed, were bitten down to the quick, and he seemed constantly to be on the verge of trembling. His face was a blank. His eyes seemed to see everything and nothing at the same time. After a moment, he looked at me and grinned.

"No, thanks. I'm good," I said.

"Well?"

I said, "Have you or any of your employees seen Thad Hubbard in the last couple of days?"

"Thad? Why no, as a matter of fact, I was beginning to wonder why he hadn't come in. He's one of the most reliable people on our staff. He hasn't even called." Carrington meshed his fingers, as though making a tent, then pointed the tips at me. "Are you here to enlighten me as to his whereabouts? I can't imagine why a private investigator would be looking for Mister Hubbard, anyway?"

"His wife has hired me. She has some concerns of a personal nature, not the least of which is her husband's location."

Triple Crossed

"What? You mean he hasn't been home either?"

I nodded. "That's correct. No phone calls from him either."

Carrington kept running his tongue behind his teeth while I talked.

"Did you happen to notice any changes in Mister Hubbard's work ethic lately, any mood swings, anything out of the ordinary?"

"Well, of course, I don't see Thad every minute of the day. I'm not as close to him as some other people who work in his section."

"Oh. What section is that?"

"Our laboratory. Thad is our chief chemist."

His answer gave me pause and I had to ask. "May I ask, sir, what exactly does Carrington Engineering do? What does your outfit produce?"

He raised his hand, signaling me to stop, and he stood up. "I'm sorry, Mister Hawkins. I cannot discuss our business with anyone outside of our organization. As a matter of fact we work for the government and our business is top secret. Now, if you have nothing else, I really have to be in a meeting in ten minutes or so."

He shoved his hand out across the desk.

"If you hear anything regarding Thad's whereabouts," he said, "we'd appreciate a call. We may have to report it to the police as a missing person if we don't hear from him soon. Have a good day, sir."

"I wouldn't jump the gun on that. We will find him, I assure you, Mister Carrington."

On the way out, I saw Edith was preparing to leave. She stared at me, straightened her shoulders, slung her purse on her shoulder and walked out the door.

I left and on the way out I thought about my visit with Mister Hugh Carrington. Questioning a guy about a third party was a lot like trying to have sex with someone in the next room.

I checked my watch. The day was running double time and I didn't have a damned thing to show for it. I'd head out to Oak Park to see Mrs. Beth Hubbard.

R.C. Hartson

Chapter Six

Nick Zagaretti stared at his captive for a long moment, assessing him and thinking about where to go next. He edged around in front of Thad, hooked a knuckle under his chin and lifted his face.

Thad's skin looked too pale and was accented by harsh shadows and lines of strain. The man could barely move and after a few moments, Nick decided to let him have more time to get himself together. There was no rush, after all.

Three other men stood behind Zagaretti. They wore plastic theatre masks. Each of them was dressed in a suit, tie and shiny shoes, except for the man on the far right who was wearing cowboy boots and a Roy Rogers hat. One man, named Paul, was obese, bald and built short and stubby like a fire hydrant.

"Let's get this fuckin' show on the road, Nick," said Hank.

Nick's brow knitted and his wide-set, dark eyes were busy with thought. "It appears that Mr. Hubbard needs more time to recoup, gentlemen." He turned to face them. "We'll get nothing of value today, I assure you. Leave him to me and my assistants."

He turned to the obese gentleman named Hank. "I'll call you in a couple of days, Hank. You can relay the information I get to Paul and Dixie. I'll let you know at that time when you all can come back."

"Sounds good," said Hank.

"Goddamned waste of time is what this was," said Paul.

"Come on, Paul." Hank looped his arm around his friend's shoulders. "Hell, there's no rush. We're practically in the driver's seat now." He patted his friend's shoulder and winked at Nick "We'll see our way out, Nick. You stay with our friend from Chicago. Maybe you'll get something sooner, if he comes around."

"I think ya'll are right," said Dixie, a tall, thin man with a distinct Texas accent. He looked over at Thad and said, "That ole boy looks soft, sorta sheltered. The kind of guy you smack and he shatters like cheap porcelain. Easy prey." He laughed aloud. "Everybody likes easy prey. That little fucker's no good to us right now. He's still out of it."

Triple Crossed

Thad found it hard to keep his eyes open, but he heard the footfalls of the men leaving. On the way out Hank said, "Never fear. Underdog is here." He turned around before he left. "Remember that, Nick? I just happened to get it...this weenie looks just like that little television schoolteacher, Mister Peepers, the guy who did Underdog's voice. Ha. Ha."

. . .

As the hours ticked by, Thad's thought process cleared and he gradually became more focused. His throat was sore. After two days -- or was it three, or maybe four -- of screaming for help, he'd lost track of time after he being jabbed with a needle and waking in the trunk of a car.

It was impossible to figure a sense of time in the windowless room that now defined his realm of living. He was lying on a king-sized bed in a family room somewhere. But where, he wondered. Fear and memory loss had poisoned his mind much earlier and it was almost impossible to understand or rationalize anything. There had been long hours with nobody coming in or out, nobody to talk to.

"Oh, my God, who are these people? What do they want with me? Have they taken Beth, too?" he croaked.

He kept himself on the bed and spent most of the time in a half-conscious, half-asleep state that only hangovers and certain drugs can induce. Finally, rolling his head from side to side, he sat up and panic set in once more when he realized he was not in control. This just wasn't possible. He had always been in charge of his life.

His face felt hot and swollen, as though it had been stung by bees. The few words he uttered sounded foreign and disconnected, outside of himself. His hands were sweaty and his pulse banged in his eardrums.

I need to take a piss, he thought, and tried to stand up. His legs felt weak, but he managed to put one foot in front of the other and slowly moved from the bed.

It was not dark by any means. Across the carpeted room, a gas fireplace glowed. There was illumination from a small lamp sitting on the nightstand, as well as from a recessed overhead light and three floor lamps.

He wandered into a spacious bathroom just off to the right of the bed and he found a commode, a set of his and her marble sinks, a framed mirror and a marble rain shower. He sat on the commode. His eyes closed as he continued trying to make sense of it all. He didn't know how long he had been sitting with his pants puddled around his ankles, but when he opened his eyes, he realized he had fallen asleep.

He flushed and eased himself over to the mirror. Taking off his glasses, he studied his brown eyes, bloodshot and underlined with dark circles. His chubby cheeks were shadowed with stubble. The knot in his tie had been jerked loose, and the clothes he had worn on the day of his capture were now rumpled and sweaty.

. . .

Hours later, Nick Zagaretti came back into Thad's room smoking a cigar and he exhaled a cloud of smoke as the door closed behind him with a snick. He was by himself this time. Grabbing the same chair he'd used earlier, he straddled it, smiled at Thad and puffed on the cigar.

"I see you're eyeing my cigar, Mr. Hubbard." He reached inside his jacket pocket and pulled out another. "Want one, Thad? I can call you Thad, can't I?" He suddenly yanked back the hand holding the cigar. "Ahhh, come to think of it, maybe you shouldn't smoke. Unless of course you're feeling better. Are you feeling better?" He paused. "No? Well, let me just say I think you're looking much better than you did yesterday or this morning."

Thad sat on the edge of the bed facing the man he now felt was in charge and who had probably arranged his kidnapping. He didn't respond at first, assessing things, and he finally put his hands up as if to ward off an attack.

"Hey, I'm not rich," he said, "if that's what you want, and nobody is going to pay a fucking ransom for me, either. Whatever it is you want, you've got the wrong guy." He noticed that his voice was tight. Adrenaline was flowing into his bloodstream.

"What? Whoa! Wow! The mouse roars," Zagaretti laughed. "Listen to you. Indeed, you are feeling much better, aren't you, Thad?"

"What is it? What do you want?" His face looked puzzled. "I'm nobody important. Let me go."

"I didn't say you were important, did I?" Zagaretti paused, stood up, and began to pace back and forth in front of his captive. "But you must realize, not important to some may mean a great deal to others. To the American government, for instance, important always means oil, sometimes drugs, and now and then strategic military planning. Take your pick."

"I don't know what you're talking about. Let me go and I promise I won't report this to the authorities."

Triple Crossed

Zagaretti kept pacing as if he hadn't heard the man's plea.

"You have some important information, Thad. We want it. There's more than one outfit involved. We know that. The FBI paid your company a visit exactly five months ago, but they also raided the offices of other technological science firms in the Midwest. But of course you knew that, didn't you?"

Thad rolled his eyes at Zagaretti. "I really don't know what you're talking about. Somebody has obviously given you bad information. I'm just a chemist."

Zagaretti stopped pacing and bent over until his face was mere inches from Thad's. He patted him on the shoulder. "Yeah, right, Thad. You don't know nothing from nothing. Say, I'll bet you're hungry, probably thirsty too, huh?" He backed away from Thad and paused before he said, "Of course you're hungry. How rude of me, Thad. I'll have something brought down pronto. What'll it be? Burger and fries? Maybe a steak and baked potato? How about some pizza or a sandwich? You name it, Thad. We aim to please."

"I'm not hungry."

"No? Well, I'll bet you're thirsty, aren't you? How about some coffee?" He grinned. "No booze. Anything but that. We need to keep that chemist's head of yours straight. Now then, what will you have?"

Thad eyed Zagaretti for a long moment before answering. Taking off his rimless glasses, he wiped them on his shirt tail and slipped them back on. His eyes came back to meet his adversary's. "Nothing. Let me go home. That's what I want."

Zagaretti sat back down and his arms dangled over the back of the chair. He turned his Navy service ring on his finger and was silent for a moment. The lines of his tortured expression were etched deeply into his rugged Italian face. He smiled at Thad.

"Tell you what, Hubbard, let's just skip the questions for now and make you more comfortable. I'll have a tray sent down. If you eat, you eat. You don't, you don't. I'll be back."

"What about letting me phone my wife? She has got to be terribly upset by now. In fact she's no doubt called the police. They'll catch you. You have no right, you kidnapped me. The way I see it, you and your friends are in a shitload of trouble unless you let me go."

Nick laughed and puffed on the cigar. He squinted through the smoke, keeping his eyes on Thad as he stood. "Yeah. That'll happen. You must think I'm bug-fucked if you imagine I'm gonna let you talk to anybody on the phone. Your wife doesn't care about you, anyway. Matter of fact, we understand she could have done better than you at the Humane Society. She's probably got a stud puttin' it to her right now. You'd interrupt her, if you called."

Thad jumped up. "You bastard. My Bethany would never speak about me in that manner, and she doesn't cheat on me either. You're a liar."

"Of course I'm lying. Whatever you say, Mr. Hubbard. Enjoy." Zagaretti grinned, turned around and left the room.

• • •

Thad knew that for him to try and understand how mobsters think would be as ridiculous as sticking his head inside a microwave in order to study the relevance of electricity.

He was lying on his back resting when Zagaretti returned hours later. His forearm was draped over his eyes, and he was almost asleep, but he bolted upright as soon as he heard the man's footfalls approach.

"Okay smart guy, I'm back, and this time you're gonna be honest with me, Mr. Hubbard. I'm tired of your shit. I've got better things to do than play your fuckin' head games. There's people I have to answer to tomorrow. They hired me because I get results."

"I told you, I don't . . ."

Zagaretti had started to pace, but then he whirled around and got down in Thad's face. "Shut up, you little weasel. Let me tell you something." He bent down and was only inches from Thad's face when he lowered his voice. "Last guy we had a problem with was back in eighty-two...smart guy like you. We ended up making him cut off his dick at gunpoint." He straightened up and said, "Don't fuck with me, anymore."

"I don't even know what you want," said a trembling Thad. He heard his own voice crack. His mouth was parched.

"I'm going to lay it out for you. You have been working two hundred hours a week on what you claim is nothing?" He unwrapped a cigar, nibbled off the tip, spit it out and lit up before he continued.

"There's two firms in New York, one in Memphis. Some bright guys work there...guys who specialize in energy and oil products. A lot of people got a big stake in what they discovered. So does your outfit in Chicago, only your company has a lot more information than the rest of those big shots, combined."

Thad was silent. He slowly moved his head from side to side, indicating no.

Zagaretti paced again. "Besides that, there's a Chinese guy who travels the

Triple Crossed

world selling his talents for big bucks. Your firm digitized some of his internal stuff, and the hacker got inside without much trouble at all. Piece of cake. He found some pretty interesting material on Carrington Industry hard drives. What would you imagine that information could entail, Mr. Hubbard?"

"I have no idea. I'm just a chemist."

"Bullshit! There's one memo from a CEO in New York to your headquarters in Chicago in which he estimates the cost of keeping the whole project a secret at five billion. The cost of paying people to keep their jobs and their mouths shut alone was estimated at one hundred million, and that was on the low side. You still don't know anything about any of this, eh?"

Thad stared at the floor and shook his head. For three slow beats, time stood still for him. "No," he murmured.

Zagaretti kept pacing. He worked his way over to the bathroom, went in and flushed the cigar butt. When he walked back out, he stepped close to the edge of the bed where Thad was sitting with his head bowed, his hands folded together between his knees.

"You're still lying, Mr. Hubbard. We know what's going on. Carrington Industries has kept a lot of vital information out of the digital storage system. The hacker went as far as he could, then bailed. He covered his tracks and disappeared. He got a cool one mill for a week's work. Not bad. It was risky, though, because he got caught on another deal three months ago and is now sitting in Ossining, New York. Sing Sing."

"I still don't think I..."

"Shut up, Hubbard! Let's cut to the chase. Tell me all you know about Operation Solid."

R.C. Hartson

Chapter Seven

The day was running double time and I didn't have a damned thing to show for it.

I checked my watch before driving out to Oak Park to see Beth Hubbard. After getting nowhere at Carrington Engineering, I called and told her I was coming out. It was looking more and more like our boy, Thad, could actually be missing in action.

It wouldn't take long. Oak Park was only about ten miles west of the city. A warm, late fall breeze blew gently through the window of the car while red and yellow leaves of the maple and elms fluttered chaotically in the wind. A few leaves still tenaciously clung to trees, but for the most part limbs were bare and spidery against the bright sky.

I used the GPS and once there, I drove down Lake Street and turned off to go to her address on Cherry Hill Road. Her red Porsche was parked in the driveway.

Getting out of the car, I heard a lawnmower growling from a few houses away and the rich scent of cut grass mixed nicely with the hint of a smoking barbeque.

The guy who opened the door smiled without warmth, eyes wandering over me. His body language screamed authority with a twist of mean. I had never gotten along with white collar authority. In fact, I was almost obsessed about it and nobody was going to argue with me.

He was a compact man, gray-suited and wearing a white shirt and red tie. He had chiseled features and thick silvery hair. His lips were thin and his nose hawkish. He had a perfect posture that reminded me of a rooster.

I flashed my badge and said, "Cleve Hawkins. Mrs. Hubbard is expecting me."

His voice was low and flat and he made a rumbling sound in his throat which may have been discontent or phlegm. "Yes, sir. Right this way. You can remove your jacket if you want," he said with a phony smile. He heaved an exaggerated sigh that twisted his features into the face of a sad clown as he said, "I will tell Mrs. Hubbard you're here."

I stood with my Bears cap in hand and waited. The meet n' greet guy was gone longer than I thought he should have been, but I knew that the rich kept you waiting so you could feel free to admire all they had.

I eased into an entry hall of carved mahogany paneling. A massive crystal chandelier hung from the second story ceiling. The fireplace had a large round eagle mirror over the mantel. I browsed the artwork on one wall with my hands stuffed in my pockets, not wanting to break anything.

Moments later, Beth Hubbard sashayed into the hall where Jeeves had left me. She walked across the room on high heels in a gait that reminded me of an antelope's.

She looked good, trim and neat with her blonde hair and hazel eyes. She wore some sort of country catalog stuff with a long skirt over high-heeled boots and an ivory, large-sized cable knit sweater. Her long hair was held back with a colorful headband. I think perhaps she had the best posture I had ever seen in a woman.

She extended one free hand and held a drink in the other, a drink that contained a myriad of colors, the kind of drink that needed the shade of a tiny umbrella.

"Mr. Hawkins, thank you for coming out." She pointed to a couple of slipper chairs. "Have a seat, please." She held up her drink. "May I have Carl bring you a drink?"

"No, I'm fine, thanks."

"Oh, of course, you're still on the job, aren't you? How about a cup of coffee?"

"Ah...yeah, coffee would be good. Black is fine. Thanks."

Carl straightened his jacket and moved his shoulders like a boxer who'd just gone four rounds before he went for the coffee. *Nice guy.*

Mrs. Hubbard sat perfectly straight in her chair and sipped from her drink. Her face was composed and soft.

"So, you don't believe my husband is having an affair?" she asked.

"I didn't say that, but if he is, he doesn't fit the usual pattern for a wandering spouse."

"What then? Where is he?"

"I'm sorry, ma'am, but you say that like you expect I would know his whereabouts. Remember, I've never even laid eyes on your husband except for the picture you showed me. I'll have to find him before I can go any further."

"Could it be that his girlfriend is hiding him or something? He could be -- what do they call it -- shacked up with her? Maybe she has hurt him and he can't leave."

I shook my head. "I don't think so, ma'am. In my experience, women having affairs with married men rarely get involved with anything vicious."

Carl brought the coffee in on a silver tray and turned to leave.

"Thank you, Carl." Beth sighed as she studied my face. "I told you, please don't call me ma'am. I don't like that." She got up and shoved her chair closer to mine. "Call me Beth, okay?"

An awkward silence hung for a second or two. I sipped my coffee and listened to the quiet. Finally, I smiled and said, "No need to pick at scabs. If you'll remember to call me Cleve, instead of Mister Hawkins, I'll remember you're Beth from now on. Deal?"

"Yes, I'll try," she said.

I didn't know what she expected, but she looked like a kid who had traveled all the way to the North Pole only to find out that Santa wouldn't grant her an audience. I had an increasing suspicion that she was independent and one of those women whose life was invested with imposing control and power over others. It made me wonder whether her Thad actually ran.

There was another moment of silence before she set her drink down and quietly said, "Should we call the police, then?"

"As a rule, the Chicago Police Department, as well as many other departments in big cities across the country, can't act on a routine report of a missing adult until forty-eight hours have passed since the time of the report. It's been two days. Yes, you can call them now, Mrs. Hubbard...ah, Beth."

Beth shook her head. With her hands pressed against her mouth, she said, "I just can't believe all this is happening to me."

I hoped she wasn't going to cry.

"The reason things are done that way is because most missing people are missing on purpose. They often turn up on their own a day or so after supposedly disappearing. Chicago is a big convention center. Lots of times conventioneers cut loose in the big city. Quite frankly, they shack up with strippers and hookers, they spend a lot of money and are afraid to go home. I'm not saying that's the case with your husband, but...well, you get the idea. There's endless reasons. That's why the cops take a wait-and-see attitude."

Beth slithered closer to me. She turned up the corners of her beautiful mouth in a pseudo-smile. I wondered if she was high. "I guess I'd better call them, then." Her voice was an octave lower than it had been. I tried to ignore her rather brazen move and said, "Yes, we can start with the cops. Meanwhile, I'll try to find him, but I'll need a lot more information."

"Maybe he's in some sort of trouble after all," she breathed. Pausing briefly, she leaned in and rested her head on my chest. Her hair smelled like lavender and the slightest trace of perfume mixed with lovely sweat. I closed and opened my eyes. I felt my heart beating in my chest. Mo's face flashed before my eyes and guilt pricked me like tiny needles.

"I don't think Thad would go near a stripper," she murmured.

"I understand, and I'm not saying that's the case with your husband, Beth." We were silent for a beat. I could have given it up and told her that Thad must have run out on her, but that just didn't make sense, since I wasn't sure.

"I know that forty-eight-hour policy doesn't make you feel any better, but that's where a private investigator comes in, and I'm ready to help with the same fee arrangements we have in place."

She drew back and reclined in her chair. Picking up her drink, she said, "What are you going to do? Where are you going to look?"

"Not sure." I pulled out my notepad and pen. "Does your husband have a work room, a study or something where he keeps a desk?"

"Yes, there's the den, but he doesn't spend much time in it now. He's working all the time, as I told you."

"Can I see that room?"

"Yes, of course." She stood and waved a hand in a follow-me gesture. As I trailed behind her, she glanced over her shoulder and asked, "Are you married?"

"Nope. I'm in a serious relationship."

"Oh, I see. Well, here we are. This is the den."

She was right about one thing. The room, although expensively paneled and decorated, seemed vacated and cold. There were a few pieces of furniture and a large framed picture of the sun hung above a roll top desk located against the opposite wall.

"Mind if I take a look inside the desk?" I said as we approached it.

Beth shrugged. "Of course. Anything that will help."

I rolled up the top and discovered that the inside was as barren as the room outside. There were the usual stationery items, pads, stapler, paper clips and a Mason jar containing ballpoints and pencils. I pulled out the six drawers, one by one. All of them were empty except one that held empty file folders.

I slowly paced around the room, checking for something, anything unusual. Spotting nothing I worked my way out of the room.

"I am supposing your husband has his own credit cards?"

Her expression was a cross between cynical and wrenched. "Sure. He has them all, same as me." She turned the corner and we were back in the parlor.

"All, as in which ones?"

She sighed heavily. "You know. American Express, MasterCard and Visa for sure. He may have more. I really don't know. Why?"

"Listen, tailing your husband to catch him with his fly down is one thing. Rescuing him from gone is entirely another. It's a lot harder to do that than simply picking up after him until I catch him being a bad boy."

"But I . . ."

Raising my hands, palms out like a traffic cop, I said, "When I know the card numbers, I can trace the action. Where they are being used, in other words. I could get the numbers of the cards myself, just like I'll get his plate and driver's license numbers, but you can save me some time. Do you mind if I see copies of the last statements?"

"I guess so, if that'll help. Hold on. I'll go get them." She turned to go.

"Ah, while you're about it, Beth, you were going to give me some better pictures of your husband. I'll take those, too, if you don't mind."

She was good at shrugging, and she did it again. "Sure. Just a minute. That stuff is upstairs."

While I waited, I caught a glimpse of Carl waltzing back and forth from one room to the other. He seemed to be checking me out each time he passed the parlor door.

When Beth came back, she handed me a large brown envelope. "Everything you wanted is in here."

I chose not to check it out in front of her. I needed some fresh air and it was getting late.

"Thank you, Beth. I'll be in touch as soon as possible. Meanwhile be sure to call the cops right away."

"Okay, I'll do that right now."

"Goodbye." I shook her hand, slipped on my cap and headed for the door. Carl was right behind me.

On the way home, I dwelled on what I did and didn't know. I learned long ago that if you wanted to find someone, you can find them even if they don't want to be found.

For some reason, I felt this case had a loose tooth and I couldn't leave it alone.

Chapter Eight

Thursday morning I finished my routine at the gym and drove downtown, heading for the address on West Adams Street where Carrington Engineering was located. I wore my sports coat and a tie. The flap of my coat covered the holstered Glock clipped onto my belt.

It was cool and promising cold. The last leaves of autumn had left their branches and twirled about. Smoke drifted from chimneys along the side streets as the days grew colder and the wind blew in from the northwest, wrapping itself around the contours of buildings, creating small white cyclones that skittered across the parking lot.

After I parked, I stopped at the security guard's nest and showed the guy my ID. The guard was not the same guy I'd signed in with a few days earlier. With reddish apple cheeks and clear blue eyes, he was a sturdy man who looked like he just stepped off a farm in Minnesota. His blonde hair had recently been shaved into a crew cut. His nameplate said Martin Skolnick.

"Dick Tracy, eh?" he sniggered, thinking he was being original.

I was in a good mood and went along. "You probably love *Law and Order*, too, eh?" I said with a smile. He flinched ever so slightly and scrutinized my badge a bit longer.

"Nice," he said.

"I need to talk to your supervisor, Marty."

"That would be Charlie Brightenauer." He picked up the phone on his desk and punched a button. Holding the receiver down on his chest, he said, "You don't have an appointment with him, I take it?"

I shrugged. "No, I'm sorry. I didn't think I'd need one with security." Somebody answered his call.

"Yeah, Suze. Marty down here at the desk. Is Charlie busy?"

I waited with my hands in my pockets while he got clearance and hung up.

"Okay, mister. Mr. Brightenauer will be here shortly. You can take a seat over there if you want." He pointed, grinned and lowered his voice. "Or...we can shoot the breeze about all the action you probably get being a private eye." Wink.

Pretending not to hear him, I said, "I see somebody left their *Sun Times*. I guess I'll sit over there and nose through it, if you don't mind, Marty."

Mr. Brightenauer was speedy. Before I could open to the sports page, he was there, looking suspiciously at me as he maintained a guarded stance.

"Mr. Hawkins? I'm Charles Brightenauer." We shook hands, and he pumped mine like a politician looking for a vote. "Marty tells me you're a private detective. What can I do for you, sir?"

His clothes were plain. Gray slacks, white shirt with maroon tie and a dark blue blazer with the building's insignia proudly displayed over the pocket. I said, "Can we talk somewhere a bit more private, Charlie?"

"Huh? Oh, sure, sure. Come right this way." He led me back to the elevators and pushed the button for the first floor. He explained, "We used to have our office just off the lobby, but the so-called 'progressive inhabitants' put us up on one."

His mouth was drawn into a knot and his pallor was a sickly pearl-gray. A tall, muscular man, his hair was black and full, colored to hide a bit of gray, slicked down, laden with gel, and pulled back fiercely and gathered into a perfect little ponytail that arched downward and touched precisely at the top of the blazer.

We walked down a hallway and entered his office through the third door down. He pointed to a hard-backed wooden chair that sat next to what I presumed was his desk.

"Have a seat," he said.

I parked on the chair while he sat on the edge of the desk, extended his legs, crossed them, and folded his arms over his chest. "Now then, Mr. Hawkins, what have we got?"

"I'm looking for a missing person. Are you familiar with a man by the name of Thad Hubbard? He works for Carrington Engineering on the fourteenth floor?"

"Ha! No, but this is really turning into something, this is."

"Oh? What do you mean by that?"

"Well, two detectives from the police department were just in here yesterday in reference to that same individual, that's all."

"Oh, really?" I felt my stomach clench. "They weren't by chance asking about surveillance equipment, were they?"

"Yeah, exactly. How did you know? I guess it won't do any harm to tell you. They wanted our security camera stuff. You know we don't keep that information on tape anymore. It's all digital, on the camera hard drives."

"And you gave those to the detectives?"

"Yes. Well, I didn't have much choice when they flashed a warrant under my nose, did I?"

"No, no, of course not. Do you remember the names of the officers?"

"Sure." He slid out the center drawer of his desk, pulled out a card and handed it to me. "Here. One of them gave me his card." He glanced at it and handed it to me as he said, "Stockwormer's his name."

I checked the card. "Yeah, I know this guy. Tell me, do you know if they happened to go up to Carrington Engineering at all?"

"Yes. They asked me where it was located, and I sent them that way. Tell me, what in the hell is going on here, anyway, Mr. Hawkins? I mean, so this guy is missing, but it's not like he's Mayor Emanuel or something, right?"

"Well, a missing person is a missing person, Charlie." I smiled. "If it was you, wouldn't you want the cops busting their ass -- pardon the expression -- to find you?"

He suddenly had a hound dog's look about him and his pale face turned pink. "Yeah, I guess you're right," he murmured. "But who is this missing guy anyway? Pretty important, I guess, eh?"

"Like I said, they're all important. I'll be leaving now, but I may be back. Thank you for your time and have a great day," I said. As I shook his hand, I was thinking I would never want him covering my back in Nam or any other tight situation.

I got in my car and drove towards Michigan Avenue and I thought about people I used to know in the Missing Persons Section of the PD. Traffic was heavy. A late model Chevy Blazer was in front of me and caught my eye. Its bumper sticker read, "Heavily armed...and easily pissed."

Playing stop and go, I made my way down State Street going southbound. I kept mulling things over and I realized the cops were thinking along the same lines I was. Mainly, where was Hubbard last seen. His last known whereabouts figured to be his workplace in the Sinclair building on Adams. Perhaps one of the camera's recordings of the last few days would reveal something pertinent to his coming and going. Did he drive his car? Did he take a cab? Did he walk away during lunch hour?

It was a starting point, and I needed something to go with. Maybe there was nothing showing him at all, but I doubted it. The cops were ahead of me on this one, but I had a few more ideas, should I not be allowed to view the recordings.

At the police department, I wanted to see if a few old friends in the Missing

Persons Section had anything they'd share, assuming Beth Hubbard called in. That department would be assigned to the case for sure. I might get to see what was on the hard drives, although the information would certainly be treated as something I was not allowed to see as a civilian.

I was hungry and glanced at my watch. It was eleven-fifteen and I then realized why there was a big gush of people leaving the building at the same time. It was lunchtime.

I pulled into a McDonalds and went inside. While I had a Big Mac and coffee, I pulled out my phone and called Maureen. We'd been staying in touch, but hadn't seen each other in five days. It felt like ten. I was prompted for her department extension and punched it in. She picked up right away.

"Homicide, Lieutenant Andrews' office. Can I help you?"

"I don't know. Can you?"

"Hey, you. I wondered if you'd be calling. Not hearing from you, I was figuring you've been busy or just ignoring me. Which is it, gumshoe?"

"You know I would never ignore you, beautiful."

"Unless something more important came up...right?" She lowered her voice and said, "As long as that's all that comes up when I'm not around, handsome." She giggled.

"Hey, I've got to stop by missing persons right now, but I wanted to see if dinner sounds good tonight."

"Just a minute, I'll check my schedule and see. Can you hold on?"

"No."

"Well, in that case, yes, I would love it. What time?"

"You name it. I'll be free anytime after you get out of there at four."

"Okay, see you at my place at six. How's that?"

"Sounds like a plan. Bye, baby."

"Bye, Columbo."

Arriving at the police department, I went to the Missing Persons Section and asked for Harve Milligan. He had been my go-to guy on a few cases and had a tight mouth that I could depend on to stay closed. Originally from the Nashville area, he was a good old boy who had migrated to Chicago over twenty years earlier. A good, hard-working street cop, he had been in narcotics before he transferred to Missing Persons.

Years ago, when I was working the street in a blue and white with Branoff, Harve had brought me up to speed on the Chicago Police Department's Directive number G04-05 which says the preliminary investigating officer will first verify that the individual is really missing among other things.

If possible, that officer, or officers assigned, will conduct interviews of individuals at the location from which the adult is reported missing. And, if the location where the missing person was last seen is outside of the reporting district, the preliminary investigator will follow up by means of APB (all points bulletins) as well as separate notification to other departments in close proximity to the Chicago area.

Harve Milligan wasn't in the office and I didn't want to press without his help, so I left a note with the receptionist asking him to call me. I left the building.

I was definitely having a bad day. Zero for two. But the way I looked at it, tomorrow was another day. I headed for my apartment to shower and get ready to keep my date with Mo.

• • •

There were a few cars parked on the street in front of Mo's apartment, but I lucked out and found a spot. Her tiny front lawn was neatly mowed and there were shrubs lining the narrow front porch. I pushed the buzzer and she let me in.

She wore a decorous blush of lipstick, but that was all she needed. Beauty was her makeup. She looked ravishing in a beige skirt and black sweater that accentuated her beautiful breasts. Her auburn hair was moussed, tangled and wild. I loved that sexy look.

She stood close and grinned as she fiddled with undoing my tie and at the same time planted wet kisses here and there on my face and neck.

"Whatcha been up to, big boy?" she asked, as I laced my arms around her waist.

"Nothing much."

"Hmmm. What type of nothing much?"

"Missing person thing. His name's Thad Hubbard. His wife, Beth, hired me to tail him. She suspected he couldn't keep his Johnson under control. Trouble is he never came home for two days." I laughed. "She's a real charmer, you know, a gold-digging, spoiled snob, and as it turns out, a real pain in the ass. She's got a broom up hers, I think."

"Well, as you know, missing people can stay missing if they want to. Maybe he left her and moved on. It sounds like you shouldn't be knocking yourself out over it if the wife gets in your way."

"This case was not going the way I thought it would, but I'll find him. You know how it is. You have to believe you are smarter, tougher, braver and more resilient than the person you're looking for."

She didn't reply, but only watched me for a beat. There was no doubt in her face, only rock solid certainty. She smiled as she moved away, perched on the edge of an easy chair and fluffed her hair with her fingers.

"You always manage to handle the ones who give you a snow job and therefore can't be trusted. Do you want a beer? I've got a few Heinies in the fridge."

"Ah, no thanks. Maybe later. Where do you want to eat, beautiful?"

"I hadn't given it much thought, to tell the truth. By the way, I wouldn't believe a word this Beth Hubbard tells you. Your normal bullshit detector has already sounded. You're just not sure why and you'll keep at it until you find out, right?"

"Probably. I'm already into this case like a bad infection."

"You'll never outgrow that blue blood of yours, mister."

She was smiling, but I could see the world slow down for her. It was as if the ceiling had lowered and the end of the hall had receded. She studied me and suddenly stood up as if there was a spring in the chair. She moved close.

"You know," she said, "there's three ages of the American male, lover, youth, middle age, and then...you look so damned terrific."

I eased my arms around her. "I think right now you just need to be held, and I need my arms around you. That works pretty well, doesn't it?"

She nodded and put her head on my shoulder.

"Kiss me," I whispered.

She raised her head and invited my mouth to settle on hers. Parting her lips, she invited the intimacy of my tongue on hers. As with every kiss we had ever shared, I felt a glowing warmth, a sense of excitement. It was a sense of rightness and completeness.

"I need you, Mo," I whispered, dragging my lips across her cheek to her ear.

I kissed her again, deeper and harder, allowing the hunger to grow in both of us. My tongue thrust against hers as I dropped one hand down her back and pulled her hips tight against me, letting her feel my hardness. She groaned deep in her throat as her anticipation begged for more of me.

Breaking the kiss, I leaned back and stared into her beautiful blue eyes.

"My God, I need you, too," she moaned.

She took my hand and led me down the short hallway. We stopped and I pulled her to me again for another kiss, still hotter, deeper, and with more urgency. I held her by the shoulders and pressed her back against the wall. My hands traveled down to the bottom of her black sweater and pulled it up between us.

Triple Crossed

Seeing her breasts, I pulled the cup of her bra aside and filled my hand with her. The need was primal, animalistic.

She gasped as my mouth found her nipple and she cradled my head as I gently suckled it. She lifted her hips away from the wall as I shoved her skirt up around her waist.

"Cleve, oh God, Cleve," she breathed while her fingers dug into my shoulders. "I want you. I want you now."

Then we were beside the bed and I was stripping her sweater over her head. She impatiently pulled at the sleeves of my jacket. In a few rough moves our clothes were off and piled on the floor. We sank down, tangled together on the bed.

Wrapping her long legs around me, she took all of me into her body with one smooth stroke. I felt myself go deep inside, felt her heat and wetness spread across my loins. I filled her completely and perfectly. We moved together like dancers, each of us complementing the other while our passion built like a powerful symphony, building and building to a tremendous crescendo.

When we reached the peak together, we held each other tightly as we murmured words of comfort and love.

We lay in silence for a little bit. The bed and the room smelled of us and our lovemaking and the heat of our bodies. Under it all was the sweet smell of her fragrance and shampoo.

She cradled my face in her hands. "Big guy, you're all I think about. You fill my heart."

I kissed her long and deep. "I love you, Mo," I whispered.

R.C. Hartson

Chapter Nine

Thad Hubbard had been missing for nearly a week. The voices on the six o'clock news blended together with my urge to do something about it, pronto. The papers were covering the story with bold print headers on the bottom of the front pages of both the *Sun Times* and the *Tribune*. The common thread that ran through them all was an urgency that in turn breeds fear.

People wonder how justice is so often denied to those who need and deserve it the most. It's not a mystery. The reason we watch contrived television drama about law enforcement is that often the real story is so depressing, nobody would believe it. TV is the reason the public gets so damned impatient with an investigation that lasts more than a couple of days. The entire country thrives on TV time.

There was another route to take in gaining some traction, and I decided to get with it. Somebody had to see something connected with Hubbard's disappearance.

He was last known to be at his workplace. Beth told me he always parked in a parking garage on Jackson, two blocks from his office, then walked. Somehow I wasn't sure of her accuracy, but if she was right, he had to be included in camera surveillance of the street.

First I checked with the parking attendant at the garage, a guy named Tony who was about five-nine and had a shaved head, dumbbell shoulders, ripped arms and beefy thighs, all mismatched with a high-pitched voice.

After I gave him the description of Hubbard's car, a black 2002 Chevy Monte Carlo, he gave me the lowdown.

"Hey, this is a pay-by-day place, man." He frowned. "If it's the wheels I'm thinking of, my boss, Charlie, had it towed away yesterday. Black 2002 Monte...yep, it's gone."

I handed him ten bucks. "You're positive on this, huh?"

"Sure. We clear this place out once every twenty-four hours. What the hell. If a vehicle is left here four days, we get it towed away. It's at the city impound lot. Check there, I'd say."

Triple Crossed

When I thought about my visit with Beth Hubbard, the more I realized she could spin a spider web and sprinkle it with gold dust to lure you inside and wrap it around both common sense and your heart, all the while making you enjoy your own predicament. But I would get her to go with me and rescue that car so I could have a look inside and out for possible clues.

Friday morning, instead of heading back to Missing Persons at the PD on Michigan Avenue, I left my car in a parking garage on South Franklin and hoofed it straight up to West Adams and the Sinclair building.

Along the way, I noticed some police cameras erected here and there, just as they were all over the city, but none were located close to the Sinclair. Morning pedestrian traffic was brisk and thick, nearly shoulder to shoulder, with people on their way to work. From about a half block away, I stood curbside and surveyed the surrounding buildings. The wind was brisk and crumpled paper coffee cups had lifted out of the trash barrel located just off the curb and were blowing across the sidewalk.

I continued walking a bit further until I faced two buildings located directly across the street from 317 West Adams. When traffic allowed, I slighted the law and crossed to the other side. I noted the numbers on the two structures were 320 and 324. Of the two, 324 was an office building called The Bernard, while 320 was home to an upscale jewelry store. I opted for the office building and went inside through some rotating doors. I hate those things. They should be outlawed.

I smelled coffee and saw a concession stand available to accommodate the building's traffic. It was situated just to the right of a security guard's desk and I bought a cup.

Every office building in the loop must have security of some form, I thought, although it wasn't always that way. Before September Eleventh, very few had full time security in their lobbies. Keeping in mind that nothing is as conspicuous as an attempt to be inconspicuous, I stood there for less than a minute to check for surveillance cameras.

I spotted four before I approached the security guard, a black man with a cheery face. He was a fleshy individual, too big for his uniform. His bulky neck chafed against his collar and his jacket was sprinkled with dandruff. His name plate said he was Leroy Rockford. I moved closer and showed him my badge.

"Hi, Leroy. I'm Cleve Hawkins. Got a minute?"

"Whoa, now...a cop. What can I do you for?" he said in a somewhat rehearsed, but professional tone.

"Well, no, Leroy, I'm actually a private investigator working a case in the area.

I wonder if I could have a word with your boss?"

He looked me up and down and smiled. "Oh, boy. A private dick, eh?" he said, studying my badge and scrutinizing my face. "What's your name again?" he asked as he slipped his hand inside the neck of his shirt and scratched a place on his shoulder.

I shook my head, smiled and made myself look him in the eye. "Cleve Hawkins."

He grimaced and stuffed his hands so deep into his pockets that the top of his underwear showed. "You'll forgive me, Mr. Hawkins, but we have to stay on our toes here. You know, anybody can buy a PI badge. They're bigger and shinier and better looking than a real cop's badge, you know. Ha, ha." When he laughed, I saw that Leroy was in need of some serious dental work. After his obvious insult he said, "Okay, so what, or who, are you here to see, again?"

I smiled. "Like I said, I need to talk to your boss. Sorry, I don't have his name. I was hoping you'd give me that information."

"Yeah, that would be Jeff Dahms. He's the boss. I guess it's okay to take you over to his office. He's never busy anyway. Ha ha." He turned to the frizzy haired older lady working the concession stand. "Hey, Marge...would you mind keeping an eye out. I just wanna take this guy over to Jeff's office. I'll be right back, okay?"

The woman nodded. "Don't get lost, though."

Dahms' office was on the opposite side of the lobby. Leroy knocked a couple of small taps on the door. From inside I heard a muffled "Who?"

"It's Leroy, Jeff. I've got a private detective out here wants to see you."

"Well, send him in."

"This is Mr. Hawkins, boss." Leroy closed the door behind him as he left. The tall man sitting behind a desk had a pencil thin mustache and ears that protruded much too far from his head. He shoved himself up out of the chair so hard, its legs scraped back across the wooden floor.

He was at least six feet with a slight build and a bumpy complexion. He stared at me with serious eyes through the small lenses of wire-framed glasses. We shook hands.

"How may I help you, sir?" His voice was gravelly and deep. His eyes, however, seemed amused, the eyes of a man watching a dog do a trick. He pulled on his ear and made a snuffing sound in his nose as he smiled without warmth.

"Mr. Dahms, I'm investigating the disappearance of a man who works in this general area. I thought perhaps you might help me."

"I'll certainly try. Mr. Hawkins, is it?"

"Yes. I have a few questions, if you don't mind."

"Go ahead, shoot."

"Well, for starters, can you tell me how many people work in this building?"

He smiled for the first time and nodded. "When people ask me how many people work here, I say about half -- but actually, around six-hundred, give or take, I suppose." He gnawed on his upper lip a little.

"Thanks. I just wondered. Now, while I was waiting, I noticed that you folks are using security cameras for the lobby, but I'm wondering if there are more security measures in place for the building. For instance, do you routinely record events occurring directly in front of your place?"

Dahms sighed and hesitated just a bit before answering. "Yes, sir. As a matter of fact, we do cover the front as well as the rear of the building, but I don't understand your interest in this information." His brow furrowed as he said, "What's this about, Mr. Hawkins?"

I removed Thad Hubbard's picture from my jacket pocket and handed it to him. "I'm trying to find this man. As I said, he's employed in this area and he's missing. Maybe you read about it in the papers?"

He shrugged as he studied the picture. "I think I heard about this. Yes, I did read it in the paper, I remember now. He's a scientist or something, right?"

"Good. Well, if you don't mind, I'd like permission to review your videos and see if I might spot the missing man leaving his workplace at the Sinclair Building."

"Oh, you mean this guy they're talking about in the papers worked right over there across the street?"

I nodded. "He's an employee in that building, but he's been missing for nearly a week. We want to be sure he hasn't met with any foul play, so we're checking everything we can in order to locate him."

His face scrunched up in a negative fashion. He acted as though he might be agreeing to a do-it-yourself root canal as he hesitated. "God, I don't know...I could get in trouble for allowing you to see that stuff, you know?"

I pulled my money clip out and unfolded a Franklin in front of his eyes. "I sure would appreciate your help."

"Well, I wonder if the police department might object for any reason. What do you think?" he said as he took the hundred.

"No, of course not. If they want to see your records, they'll be coming by, believe me."

He pushed his chair over to a work table next to his desk, parked in front of a computer and lowered his voice. "Go ahead and grab one of those chairs over there, Mr. Hawkins. Let's have a look." He winked. "We want to help in any way we can," he said, as he logged in. "That poor fellow. Who knows what may have become of him. You never know these days."

"True enough, so let's review the recordings for six and seven days ago. That would be September 26th and 27th, okay?"

"Sure, sure," he said. "Just give me a second here. I need to bring up the recordings for the street views. Those will be the ones you'd be interested in. You wouldn't have any need for our lobby recordings, correct?"

"That's right, Just the Adams Street history will be fine."

"Now, we are looking for your man's face, right? The one in this picture?"

"Yes."

"And we don't know what he's wearing or anything else that might help?" Dahms asked.

"No, sir. We have to spot his face, so if you can go slow with the speed on the recording, that would be helpful, of course."

We stared at the screen. With the head-bobbing mass of pedestrians, the search proved difficult, but nearly an hour later, we did spot Thad Hubbard. He was wearing a trench coat, when he entered the Sinclair building on the 26th of September at 8:36 in the morning. We also saw him leave at 8:22 PM. He was by himself both times. I gathered he must not have left the building for lunch. Beth was right on one count. Her husband appeared to put in long days at Carrington.

On the recordings for September twenty-seventh, however, we scored. After we worked the same tedious process, we saw Hubbard entering the Sinclair building at 8:42 AM. He didn't leave again until 3:46 PM. Then, within less than a minute, two big men crowded in on each side of him. The two wore business suits and fedora-styled hats. As they walked away, one of the men draped an arm over Hubbard's shoulders and said something. It appeared as though they were old buddies. I had Dahms back it up and zoom in on the faces of the three men.

"Hold it, right there, Jeff." I leaned in as close as possible to the monitor. Hubbard's face was filled with surprise, while the two men on either side of him were smiling and talking to him. The camera followed them, their backs at least, for quite a distance until they melted away in the sea of people.

Within the same time frame, approximately fifty feet down from Thad, three teenage boys with backpacks were goofing around and zipping after one another through the crowd. One of them, a Latin-looking kid, climbed up and had his legs wrapped around a traffic light pole. He had his Smartphone facing the crowd of pedestrians a few feet below and he grinned from ear to ear before he dropped

Triple Crossed

down in front of his friends and they took off.

I reached in my pocket, pulled my money clip and peeled off another hundred-dollar bill. I handed it to Dahms. Then I pulled out the USB stick I'd brought with me.

"Jeff, upload that video on to this for me, will you?"

"Certainly, Mr. Hawkins."

Chapter Ten

Thad felt like someone had done a smash-and-grab on his life. Everything had changed so suddenly. One day he had his comfortable home in the suburbs with his beautiful wife Beth and the next he was kidnapped and being held hostage by a crude brute that reminded him of Tommy Hicks, the bully at Thompson Street Elementary School.

He still didn't know the name of the man who was holding him hostage. His name didn't matter, Thad reasoned. It was what the dark-looking stranger was asking for that counted. The Neanderthal said his name was Nick, but Thad didn't believe him.

Zagaretti hadn't been mean in any way. In fact, with the exception of a few flare-ups that ignited his temper, the interrogator was quite congenial. Other times, Thad saw lights of impatience and irritability flicker in the man's eyes.

Thad had managed to hold out and feign virtual ignorance of Operation Solid for as long as he could, but Nick's grilling continued practically non-stop for four days and four nights. To Thad, the time dragged by. It felt more like four months in captivity.

It was always the same man, asking the same questions and feeding Thad information about his capture, little snips at a time. Thad wondered, *Are they going to kill me? No. If he wanted to kill me, he would have done it already. It makes sense, doesn't it? If...if...if... There are no real answers. I wonder what Beth is doing about finding me? Are the cops coming to save me?*

He had alternately moaned and cried. Thad knew a grown man shouldn't cry, but he was mentally and physically exhausted. At times, his hands trembled, stomach acid scalded the back of his throat, and his bowels felt loose. Still, he neither vomited nor soiled his pants.

On the fifth day, the last thing Zagaretti did was make an offer. Thad had sunk into the couch while Nick sat in a stiff wing chair two feet away and one foot higher. He held a tumbler of scotch on the rocks, which he had drained, and he crunched the ice between his molars. He gazed down at Thad with his most sincere grandfatherly smile.

"You've got a beautiful wife, don't you, Hubbard?"

Thad's eyes locked on Zagaretti's. His brow furrowed and he looked at the man with sudden anger. "What has she got to do with this?"

Zagaretti shrugged. "Nothing, I guess...but you're probably missing her about now, right?"

Thad nodded. "Of course, but leave her out of this."

"I'm just saying...you want to get back home to her don't you?"

Zagaretti paused and cleared his throat. "Look, Hubbard, we're just as tired of this shit as you are. We've made a little headway here, but you still refuse to give me the most important stuff. Why is that?"

Thad realized that Nick always referred to his quest for information in terms of "we" instead of "I," which told him more people were involved. Who knew how many there were and how far the information would travel? Who was the intended benefactor, he wondered.

"I have been given the go ahead to cut a deal with you, so listen up," said Nick. "You play along, give me the information we want and I'll personally guarantee your safe return home." He set his glass down and raised both hands over his head, palms out like a cop directing traffic, then crossed his heart. "I swear, I won't let any more harm come to you."

Thad eyed the man suspiciously.

"Ahhh, I know what you're thinkin'," said Zagaretti. "Yeah, we were a little rough bringing you here, but that's all over. You're good now. You notice, nobody has hurt you since you got here, have they? No needles, none of that shit."

Thad shook his head slowly and his eyes locked on a spot on the wall behind the man's head.

"Well...?" Zagaretti's eyes bored into him while he waited for an answer.

"That's true, I guess," Thad murmured. He removed his wire-framed glasses, cleaned them on his shirt tail and stared at the floor between his feet.

"You're damned right, that's true," said Zagaretti. "And I will personally see to it that you continue to be unharmed and are returned to that wife of yours, safe and sound." He paused and bit the tip off the end of a fresh cigar. "Just cooperate,

Thad. Anything else is not worth it." He snickered. "Do you honestly think those big wigs at Carrington give a shit whether you live or die? Where are they now, huh? Have they sent the law to rescue you?" He shook his head, negatively. "This whole damned thing is impossible anyway, if you ask me. So, what have you got to lose? You'll go home and let somebody else carry the load."

Thad propped his elbows on his knees, then squeezed his temples, closed his eyes and reopened them. He stared at a spot between his shoes and felt as though he were drowning. There was a lump in his throat that was so big, he couldn't swallow. His mouth became dry and he grabbed the lukewarm Coca-Cola they'd given him earlier. The pounding of his heart seemed like a jack-hammer in his ears. He realized the end of the ordeal was in sight. He could be free. Clamping his hands on top of his head, he exclaimed, "Shit, shit, shit, shit."

This man is right. What is it worth? To the rich bastards like Cosgrove on the board of directors, the project is the single most important project in the entire world. And maybe it is...that's the problem. This man must be telling me the truth. Why wave meat in front of a caged beast if you can feed him? Why shouldn't I trust him? There comes a time in a man's life when he has to step back and let all the worry and confusion in his life blow away in the wind. I have to say to hell with it and mean it and let the dice roll out of the cup as they will. If these people think Solid is impossible, good. Let them.

"Alright, I suppose you could be right." Thad paused, squeezed his eyes shut anxiously and exhaled loudly, letting his mouth stay open as if he were silently laughing. When he opened his eyes, he looked directly into Zagaretti's.

"On the condition that you will let me go," Thad said, "I will give you what I can. I don't know everything, though. I swear I don't."

Zagaretti lit his cigar. "Rumors, you know. Damned rumors aren't good enough. If what we hear is true, we need some answers that an inside guy like you can supply. We need them now. Not later. Tell me more about Operation Solid, now."

Pointing to Nick's cigar, Thad said, "May I have one of those?"

"Wha...oh, sure, sure." He reached into his blazer pocket and retrieved another cigar. "Here. Let me light it for you." He leaned in, flipped his Zippo open and lit the cigar.

"Let me put it this way," said Zagaretti. "Timing is everything. You know that as well as I do. The deal your outfit is working on, if successful, could bust a lot of wealthy guys, make them broken shit heels overnight. So, we need to know the names of all those corporations involved. Their names and their locations."

He slid off his chair and crouched in front of Thad. Lowering his voice, he said, "Most important of all, we need to know exactly when the newspapers are gonna know about Operation Solid. How far away are all these companies from the final deal, if the whole thing is true, of course? What's the release date? When will Carrington tell the world about it, Thad? I need all of that. People with money need to prepare. Understand?"

Thad still was hesitant before he said, "You were right. We are not the only company involved with the launch." He puffed on the cigar. "We have pooled our resources and manpower to fight off the swindlers and thieves and crooked oil barons." He stared at Zagaretti, waiting for his reaction.

He held up a moment and sipped the Coke. "One of our partner corporations, located in Minneapolis, got raided six months ago. That means, among other things, that the FBI and the government now know the truth. They most likely know the target release date...the entire works. It's supposed to be top secret, though."

"Shit!" Nick said, curling his lip. "Secrets are for people who want to feel good about themselves in the morning. Not for people who care about their country and families. It's a small world, Mr. Hubbard. You should know that by now."

"Nobody knows that better than I do," said Thad. "The discovery of a formula for harnessing the sun's energy to allow the entire world the ability to run motor vehicles twenty-four-seven is perhaps the greatest discovery since electricity. Seems impossible, doesn't it? But you seem to be an intelligent man, Nick. You should know it is going to cause more problems than we can possibly imagine."

The room was silent.

Thad waited for the other man to speak, but Nick gazed at the ceiling, his chin raised slightly, his pulse fluttering in his throat. He leaned forward until he was mere inches away from Thad's face. "And this plan is called Operation Solid, why?"

"Sol is Latin for the word sun, and the plan is certainly solid, wouldn't you say?"

Zagaretti nodded. "Makes sense, I guess. Some Harvard asshole probably lost a lot of sleep coming up with that one."

"I don't know," said Thad.

"Okay, so we know about your corporation in Chicago. We also know about St. Paul. Where are the other four outfits located? And please don't lie to me, Thad, okay? I will have them checked out before you leave here."

"No. I wouldn't do that," Thad anxiously replied. "The other partners are in San Antonio, Texas, Schenectady, New York, Boston, and Boise, Idaho."

"Good. Now the biggie, Thad. When's the rocket going to blast off? When's the big parade?"

"Huh?"

"When will a press conference be held to announce Solid?"

"Oh, but I can only tell you what I have heard. As I told you, rumors, remember? I don't know everything."

"Okay. Give me what you've heard, then. The date?"

"I was told January first, New Years Day, 2020."

"New Year's Day? You sure?"

"I just told you. That's all I know."

Nick stared at him for a long time before he finally said, "I'm not going to get my ass in a sling over this, Hubbard. Everything you told me better be right. Because if it ain't, and I find out, your ass is grass and I'm the fuckin' mower. You'll be one dead chemist."

"Yes, of course. I'm telling you everything." He hung his head and said, "I feel dirty for giving it to you." He slowly looked up and said, "When will you let me go home?"

Zagaretti puffed his cigar. "Just sit tight. I have to clear this with some other people, first."

"But, you told me you would personally make sure I..."

"Yeah, settle down. I'm gonna keep my word. I just have to inform some people that you've cooperated. Then I'll arrange your transportation back home, okay?" He patted him on the cheek and smiled. He started to offer his hand, but Thad looked at it like it was smeared with shit and declined.

"Be right back," said Zagaretti.

Triple Crossed

. . .

Upstairs, Zagaretti made some phone calls. When he was done, two and a half hours later, he checked his watch and called a Holiday Inn near Newark. The time had changed and it had gotten dark early. It was only five-thirty.

"Yes, give me room 231, please," he said.

The man on the other end sounded sleepy when he answered, "Yeah?"

"Toad, it's me. We're all done here. I know you guys been antsy over there for the past few days."

"Few? Yeah. How about five...five days now, what the hell?"

"Hey, you been comfortable, right? Good food, plenty of booze, broads. What the hell else could you ask for except your payoff, right?"

"Yeah, we're okay. I'm just itching to bitch. It ain't bad. You should hear Walker, though. He's been moanin' like a fuckin' baby. The guy's like a stopped-up toilet that keeps backing up on the floor.

"Fuck him. Listen up. This last job, there can't be no fuck ups. It's got to be clean as a whistle too. Be here around midnight. Don't be late."

R.C. Hartson

Chapter Eleven

Things were moving too damned slow. After reviewing the recordings with the security chief, Jeff Dahms, it appeared as though Thad Hubbard had been taken for a ride, and his life, for whatever reason, was probably in jeopardy. Worst case scenario, he was dead. The newspapers reported that Carrington executives were sick with worry and had offered a hundred-thousand-dollar reward for any information regarding their missing chemist.

My mind sifted through a laundry list of things I needed to do as fast as possible. On the video I had discovered that a young man may have inadvertently taken a picture of the two men who escorted Hubbard away from his office building when he left work.

I was out two hundred bucks as a result of the pay-per-view with Dahms, but I would recoup that with my expense billing to Beth Hubbard, whether she liked it or not. I was thinking, with her financial status, she wouldn't care one way or the other.

Anxious to look more closely at the stuff I had on the USB drive and get organized, I put my Dodge Charger through its paces as I drove back to the office with a head full of "what if's" and "why's."

The Missing Persons Section at the PD had been at the top of my list, but now, other more important matters jumped to the head of the line. I had to track down that Latin kid with the SmartPhone. He was key. Hopefully he had captured the faces of the two men in question and saved the images. I also had to visit the city impound lot to get a good look inside Thad's Monte Carlo. I had to put a tracer on his credit cards. I didn't want to make Beth Hubbard privy to anything just yet.

I decided to call Jeebers. I hadn't seen him in nearly two weeks and I hoped he would answer his phone.

After I grabbed a twelve-inch meatball sandwich from Subway, I headed over to the office. I found Deckle sitting on the steps puffing on a cigarette. Being on his toes as usual, he barely noticed me until I almost stepped on his bony leg, draped across the steps.

He jumped up. "Hey, Cleve! Glad to see ya'. I didn't think you were ever comin' back. You been gone for nearly three days." His thick brown hair was matted and he reeked of booze.

"Yo, Deck. What's happening, partner?" I said as I inserted the key in the lock.

"Nothing going on, nothing at all, Cleve. I been watchin' the place real good. Nobody's been here to see you. Nobody's been here but me all the time."

"Good man," I said as I opened the door and Deckle followed me inside. The air was stale. "What say we open a couple of windows, my friend?"

"Sure thing, Cleve. I got it." When Deck was wound up, he was a barely contained dynamo of energy that required constant movement, but he had a nose for eats. His bloodshot eyes settled on the Subway bag on my desk. "Uhh, you need me to run for some donuts or anything?"

"Not right now, Deck. Tell you what, I'll split this meatball sub with you if you'll go ahead make some coffee. I've got some urgent stuff to take care of."

He clapped his hands together like a kid at Christmastime. "Sure thing, Cleve. You know me, I can handle that. I make good coffee, don't I, Cleve?"

"Yeah, Deck. You go ahead now. Get it done."

I booted up my computer and dialed Jeebers' number on the land line.

He answered on the first ring. "Yeah?"

"Hey, Jeebs, what're you up to?

"Hang on."

The rustle of paper sounded like static over the phone. In the background the sharp clack of billiard balls smacking together was lost in the distant wailing sounds of Bob Seger's "Night Moves" on the jukebox. I heard Jeebers muttering to himself while I waited.

"That you, Cleve?"

"Yeah."

"You caught me sitting on the crapper, but I'm done. Hold on. Gotta wash my hands."

I heard running water. I couldn't help smiling as I pictured him.

"Okay, what's up?" he mumbled.

I could think of no response, except to laugh and ask, "What's the zip code on Mars?"

"What? Why?"

"Because that should be your zip code, buddy."

"Yeah, funny man." He paused and I heard the paper towel machine cranking.

"What ya' got, smartass?"

"Where are you? I mean, what bar?"

"I was just grabbing a cold one at Neeley's place on Rush."

"A little early, isn't it? You sound like you've been smoking wacky tabaccy."

"Not really, but it's not a bad idea. I think putting people in the cage for smoking is bullshit, but there's no doubt in my mind that long term daily use is a recipe for CRS, otherwise known as Can't Remember Shit."

"Sounds like that place is jumping already," I said.

"Nah, this joint don't jump. It limps. Neighborhood old shits, ya know? What the hell, it's way past noon. You need to get a life, my friend. Neeley's is an okay joint. In their defense, they serve strong drinks and decent red meat." He paused and I heard the bathroom door slam shut behind him. "You checking up on me, pal?"

"Hell no, buddy. Remember, I told you I might need some help sometime?"

"Yeah"

"Well, if you're not busy, that sometime is now. I've got a lot on the board. I need all the help I can get from you, or I'll spend a lot of time sitting on my ass. Any chance you can swing by here tonight? Take a cab. Don't drive."

"Shit! I can drive, but I'll take a cab, I suppose. You mean now, right?"

"Yeah, soon as you can make it. I'll fill you in when you get here."

"Ahhh, I'll head your way soon as I finish the beer I got sitting on the bar. You're over on Wells, right?"

"Right. See you in a few then."

I realized the temptation of opportunity for Jeebers to drink lured him like a crooked finger and a seductive smile. I had the same urges and could fall back into that groove myself if I didn't stay busy. I caught myself. Who was I to ever lecture him about drinking? Shit, that would be like warning Satan about his overdue library books. I slipped the zip drive into the computer and started scanning.

Deckle was sitting in his hard-backed chair watching the coffee drip into the pot on top of the filing cabinet. "Here, Deck." I used my pocketknife to slice the sub in two and handed him half. "Chow down."

"Thanks, Cleve." He took a big bite out of the sub, but continued to stare at the coffee maker with marinara on his face. "The coffee's almost done, too," he croaked. He put down his sub and sanded his chin with the Subway napkin I handed to him.

Jeebers walked through the door about twenty minutes later. He was wearing an ill-fitting blue blazer over a collarless black shirt and gray slacks. His clothes had the worn and rumpled look of a thrift store sale. He was squinting a lot and swaying from side to side and he smelled like his clothes had been doused in Budweiser.

We shook hands. "Semper Fi, Marine," I said.

"Same to you, jarhead. Hey, buddy, what's the difference between a jarhead and a pig?"

I shrugged. "What?"

"A pig won't stay up all night trying to fuck a jarhead."

We both laughed. "How about a cup of coffee, Jeebs?"

"Yeah, might as well. Coffee sounds good."

He ran a hand through his hair and shifted his weight from one foot to the other while staring past me as if he were looking at his own past, just beyond my right ear. He slid a cigarette out of the pack in the breast pocket of his shirt and lit it.

Deckle gave us both a cup of coffee. Jeebers sipped his loudly, smacked his lips, frowned as though swallowing vinegar and then plopped down in one of the client's chairs in front of my desk.

"Good to see you again, Jeebs. Where you laying your head these days?"

"Ah, I'm renting an efficiency over on Chestnut. Second floor. College kids, two guys and two chicks, are living downstairs. I never have to worry about oversleeping at that place. Toilets flushing, people yelling and stomping around. All their morning kitchen smells work their way upstairs. Coffee brewing, bacon frying. Jesus! Glad it's just temporary. Drives me nuts."

Jeebers leaned in closer to the desk and lowered his voice. "You should see this one babe that lives there. A woman can only be so beautiful. I tell you, Cleve, if your dick doesn't go on autopilot when a broad like that one walks by, you need to get a refund on your fuckin' package."

He tapped ashes off his cigarette into an empty paper coffee cup on my desk. "What in the hell is going on, you need me so soon? Who died?"

"Nobody died yet that I know of, but remember that client I told you wanted me to tail her husband? She thought he was screwing another woman on the side?"

"Yeah. I remember you said something about her. Why? What happened with that deal?"

"Her old man has come up missing and to tell the truth, I think he's history."

"You mean as in *dead*?"

"Yeah. He hasn't been at work or home in a week. His wife called missing persons downtown. I've been doing some snooping and got a copy of a video here.

Shows two assholes, looking like bookends, walking on each side of him. It sure looks to be an abduction. Now, with a week gone by, I'm sure it's even more than that. Trouble is, I can't ID these guys' faces."

"So, you're fucked."

"No, not necessarily. I'll show you this later, but there's these three young guys, goofing off, playing grab-ass, you know, zipping in and out among the crowd of walkers on Adams. Then, one kid, a Latino, jumps up on a traffic light pole and he's taking pictures of the crowd with his SmartPhone."

"No shit, what the hell...?"

"Who knows? So I'm thinking the kid might have their faces, up close and personal, on that phone of his." I pulled out the zip drive and held it up. "The cops don't have this stuff as far as I know. I'm not giving it to them either, know what I mean?"

"Yeah. Don't blame you there."

"Maybe later, but not now. I want to work the case my way, not have Andrews and his guys telling me what to do. You and I both know when you involve yourself in these things, you assume a measure of risk. There always comes a point where we turn it over to the cops, but then the risk expands. Will the cops blow it? Will my client be helped or hurt? Will justice be served? These are always questions. The answers are not always clear, either. They're often unknown, even after the fact, right?"

"Yeah. That makes sense, but do you really think you'll ever find that kid again? I mean talk about a long shot." His eyes drifted towards the coffee pot. "Shit, I need another cup."

Deckle grabbed the pot and refilled his cup.

"That's where you come in, Jeebs. I need somebody down on Adams to spot this kid. I've got the security tape from the building and it shows these kids' faces real good. I'll show you the tape and you can take it from there. We'll take turns, you one day, me the next, and so on. I'm thinking it won't take long before we spot him and go from there. I've got other stuff to do with this case, too, so this would free me up to handle some of that. I'll have more for you too. The money's right on this one for sure. What do you say?"

"Funny you should mention Andrews. I hit him up for a comeback job last week. I still have my shield from L A. He's going to let me know. I wouldn't mind going back as a D One."

"Good deal, Jeebs. I'm glad for you, but this can keep you working until something pops with the department, right?"

Triple Crossed

Jeebers considered that for a moment and stared out the window, pulling at his lower lip. He glanced at Deckle, who was headed for the john. "Can you trust that one?" he murmured.

"Him?" I said. "That's my pal Deckle." I lowered my voice. "He's a gopher I've sort of adopted...or the other way around. He has an IQ of about eight, but he'd eat thumbtacks with a spoon if I told him to. When I'm here, he's as happy as a fish with a new bicycle."

Jeebers shrugged. "Good guy to have around, I suppose."

"That he is. Anyway, Jeebs, you know yourself, as a cop over the years, how many times have we seen the file drawer slammed shut on too damned many unsolved disappearances? They usually involved people who had no voice and whose families had no power. For the rich bastards, it's a different ballgame all the way around."

Jeebers nodded like he was buying in. He slid back into the chair and sipped his coffee.

I said, "Private detective stuff is similar to cop work in many ways. You keep listening and watching and nothing much makes any sense and you keep listening and watching and then something appears -- a pattern, a clue, a break -- maybe just the small end of something you get a hold of and begin to tug. That kid with the backpack is my only thread right now, and if I could locate him, I'd begin to pull on it. This shit requires basic instinct, but it seems I'm searching around in the dark through fog for my little thread these days, to be honest."

Jeebs shrugged as he stood. He reached out and shook my hand.

"We've got a deal, jarhead. Right now I gotta get some sleep, but I'll see you here in the morning. That okay? What time?"

"I have to hit the gym around six. How about eight? Then I'll buy breakfast at the diner on North Avenue."

He said, "Awful fuckin' early, don't you think?"

On the way out the door, he brushed the cigarette ash off his sleeve and shook his head. Looking my way, he added, "You still work out, too? No shit? You're a demanding son of a bitch, ya' know?" Then he was gone.

R.C. Hartson

Chapter Twelve

Toad closed the cell phone and flipped it over his shoulder onto the bed. He stood up, tugged an earlobe and headed for the bathroom.

"That was Zagaretti," he said over his shoulder.

Walker was smoking a cigarette as he sat in a plush easy chair staring at the *Doctor Phil Show* on television. He slumped low in the chair, staring for maybe a minute before he reached for the remote, rolled his eyes and clicked the set off. "How much time we got?"

"He wants it done right away," Toad replied. "Means we've got to get moving tonight." His voice was an echo until he edged back out of the bathroom while fiddling with his tie. "Go get ready. And get your shit out of your room while you're at it. We're not getting a bellboy. We'll carry our own." His words were blunted like those of a drill sergeant, but came out much like a whisper, as though they were filtered through wet sand.

Walker groaned as he pushed his frame up and out of the chair. "Shit! This means we're not gonna' go to Trump's place tomorrow, like we planned."

"Hell, no. After we pick up the pigeon, we're headed for Camden. Fuck the casino. Between the casinos and pussy I've blown too much green already." He paused and said, "You too, from what I seen."

"Nah. Who's keeping track, anyway? Fifty grand apiece for this job will make us fat again, so I'm not sweating it, ya' know? I suppose we still have to wait until we get back to Chicago to get our money, though, right?" He glanced at Toad and saw his partner's face was quiet, his eyes empty.

It bothered him that Toad had the habit of turning his whole head as he glanced around, like an owl on a tree branch. Walker knew the look well, but, never was sure what his partner was thinking.

"That's right," said Toad. "Cosgrove has our payday. I told you, forget Zagaretti, okay?"

"Yeah, it'll have to be okay, I guess." He paused. "Give me about twenty-five minutes. I've gotta take a shower and finish packing my shit. Chill out for a few, okay? I don't want to be feeling jumpy with this shit going down. Why are we using Camden, by the way?"

"Because, it's the perfect spot. If the world had an asshole, it would be Camden. Now, just get a move on," Toad growled.

Walker ground his cigarette out in an ash tray, took the box of Good n' Plenty he'd been munching and left.

When Walker came back, Toad had his right foot up on the bed and he was strapping a Velcro holster with a .25 caliber pistol to his ankle. He wore a double-breasted black suit and a gray shirt with a bolo string tie knotted up tight. His black hair was combed straight back and accentuated his big nose, which came straight down from the bridge with no curvature at all. Dropping his heavy foot back on the floor, he said, "You got your piece on you, right?"

Walker laughed. "Is the pope a Catholic? Never leave home without it." He patted the left side of his chest. Even though he thrived on gun smoke and blood splatter and never showed remorse for his participation in a contract, he had both deep-seated fear and respect for Toad.

Walker wore a pink tie and a pale blue shirt with white cuffs. His brown hair was long on top and trim on the sides and made him look taller and his face more lean.

"We gonna eat before we make the pick up?" he asked. "I'm hungry enough to eat the ass end out of an elephant."

"Yeah, we can stop," said Toad. "We'd just as well eat first. Won't have time once we're rolling."

Walker suddenly lowered his voice as if someone else might be in the room other than the two of them: "You got any toot left from last night? I sure could use a little snort before we leave?"

Toad rolled his eyes, slowly reached into his coat pocket and handed him a seal. "Hurry up for Christ's sake. We gotta go."

Walker quickly shoved the sanitized water glasses off the drink tray sitting by the two cup coffee maker. He rolled up a ten-dollar bill, laid out three lines and snorted two of them. He glanced over at Toad, waiting by the door.

"You want this last one?" He snuffed through his nose again to catch the full benefit of the drain.

Toad shook his head. "Not now. C'mon, will ya?"

Walker shrugged, bent over, snorted the last line and grabbed his suitcase.

Toad's phone vibrated on his hip just as he started to open the door and he answered, "Yeah?" He stared at the floor while he listened. "Now?"

He glanced back at Walker, who had dropped his suitcase and stood staring at Toad with inquisitive eyes and a furrowed brow.

"Okay. Sure, no problem. Yeah. Well, we expected that." There was a long pause before Toad finally said, "Yup, be there within two hours, long as traffic don't hold us up." He shook his head as he hooked the phone back on his hip and looked at Walker.

"Zagaretti again. They got the guy cold already. He admits he jumped the gun a little. Anyway, they hyped him full of crack plus the tranquilizer. Kicked his heart all to hell, I guess. He ain't breathing no more, anyway." He snickered. "They jabbed the poor bastard's arms with the needle nine different spots so it looks like he was really on the shit."

Walker said, "It was up to me, I'd put one in his mouth, one in the forehead, and one in the ear. When I pop 'em, I shut all their motors down. They can forget about life support."

"Uh-huh, but this ain't our show. And Zagaretti wants to move everything up, by the way."

"What? You mean now?" said Walker. He grabbed his suitcase again. "When in the fuck are we supposed to eat?"

"Hey, I told you. I'm damned well starving too. Let's just skip through a Burger King for now. We'll chow them on the way and have a steak later, after the job's done. C'mon, pull that door closed behind you."

• • •

The slum neighborhood in Camden, New Jersey, was quiet. The sky was dark, the moon obscured by cloud cover. By the time Toad and Walker found the area of large stone houses that had gone to trash, it was after three in the morning. There were few cars on the road, or so it seemed.

Toad drove their black Buick LeSabre through an area where cornerstones bore spray-painted gang slogans and paint blistered from window trim. There were very few streetlights. Some of the houses had been torched or abandoned and were boarded up. The street was lined with broken-down, single car wooden garages and overflowing bashed-in garbage cans. Various clutter, debris, newspapers and bottles were scattered about in what resembled a post-apocalyptic world.

"Talk about shitty neighborhoods. This is one fucked up part of town," said Walker. He puffed on his cigarette as his eyes swept the area on both sides of the car.

Triple Crossed

"Seen worse," said Toad.

"Where? On the fuckin' moon?"

"You ever been to Detroit? Put that cigarette out and roll down your window. We'll be stopping, pretty quick."

The two men were silent for a moment. The dash lights and hum of the big V-8 were reminders of their presence in the night.

"Zagaretti's guys took care of cleaning our pigeon's pockets?" said Walker.

"Done. He ain't no amateur, ya' know."

"I didn't say he was, did I?"

"You got your gloves?"

"Check. Right here in my pocket. And I'm not allergic to latex. Ha, ha!"

"Okay, listen up. We can't waste any time with this shit. I pull up and stop. We move. No bullshit. Slip on the gloves. We both lift his ass out of the trunk, roll him out of the plastic. You toss the plastic back into the trunk and we're gone, got it?"

"Got it."

. . .

The room was quiet where a man named Charlie Schuster slept with a tattered New York Jets blanket over his shoulders. The only light was provided by a corner streetlight, but it was awfully dim where it trickled through some cracks in the boarded up windows facing the side of the abandoned house next door.

The floor was worn linoleum, but a poorly cut rug of orange shag, like something the Brady Bunch would have considered too garish, covered the far quarter of the room. The place stunk with the smell of sour sweat, cheap wine and fried onions.

Charlie was a small man, about seventy, with a hard-boiled look. He had pasty, delicate skin and layers of tiny wrinkles around his eyes. His mouth was small and petulant, his teeth tobacco stained and uniformly leaning on their neighbors.

Having no home of his own, he had been nesting comfortably on the bottom floor of the gutted apartment building as if he were the landowner.

Charlie was tired that night and he didn't want to get up, but something woke him. What was it, he wondered. A car door closing? He felt groggy, but he grunted and pushed himself up off the mattress that lay on the floor.

Fumbling around in the pocket of his ragged field jacket, he found the crumpled pack of Camels he had bought with his bottle money. Squeezing his eyes shut, he continued to listen. He heard nothing further and he was about to light up when there was another unfamiliar noise. Maybe those pot-smoking Mexican kids were back, he thought. Charlie didn't want to hide, but he would have to if it was them. He didn't want any trouble. It couldn't be the cops. Cops didn't care about any of the shit on this street.

Deciding to investigate, Charlie held his breath as he trudged across the rickety linoleum floor that flexed under his feet. He bent over and put both eyes up against one of the cracks and saw two men, one short and heavy, one broad and tall. They were unloading something from the trunk of a sedan. That was nothing new. People dropped their trash down here all the time, just as if it was a landfill.

The October air was sharp and cold, and the breath of the two men came out in cloudy puffs. Charlie's eyesight was not that good, but he could tell that it took both of them to lift whatever it was out of the trunk and drop it on the ground.

Charlie's breathing quickened and he felt his heart thumping in his chest. He was afraid to move. He was witnessing more than a garbage drop, he thought. Who was that out there, and what had they dumped, he wondered.

Both of the men crouched down for a moment or two. When they straightened up, the tall one wrapped something in his arms and then threw it back into the trunk and snapped the lid shut. Meanwhile the shorter, heavy man took a few steps towards Charlie's building, but stopped about twenty feet away. Charlie felt as if he was going to choke. The man had his hands shoved in his pants pockets and appeared to be checking Charlie's building, but checking for what?

Finally the man turned and walked back to the sedan where his companion stood on the passenger side of the car with his door open.

"Okay, let's go," said Toad in a near-whispering voice. Both car doors slammed shut and the sedan rolled back out onto the street without any lights whatsoever until it was well down the street, two blocks away, and Charlie saw the left turn signal blink.

Charlie started breathing again. He was glad it wasn't those Mexican kids, but first thing in the morning he would check out the garbage those people left behind.

Triple Crossed

Chapter Thirteen

Eight days had passed since Thad Hubbard disappeared. The case seemed to be dragging, with little in the way of leads. What began as a simple stalking job had become a pregnant mystery.

The weather in Chicago was changing, not only from one day to the next, but from fall to winter. The sky was gray and overcast with thick clouds the color of aluminum. There was no sun and it was cold.

Jeebers spent Monday and Tuesday prowling West Adams, keeping an eye out for the kid who scaled the light pole with the SmartPhone.

It was one hell of a sad situation when all I could pin my case on depended on that teenage boy.

Jeebers went to work in the Loop after we spent the better part of Saturday and Sunday browsing the images I had on the USB I'd gotten from Jeff Dahms. I wanted to be sure he knew *exactly* who we were looking for and I directed his attention to the specific segment that captured the two men who resembled stereo bookends escorting Thad Hubbard away from his office building. Jeebers broke out his glasses and moved closer to the screen.

"Ha! I didn't know you wore glasses, Jeebs."

"I don't. My nose does." He put one of the ear hooks in the corner of his mouth and let the glasses dangle. "Hey, I can see. These are just for insurance," he growled.

"Insurance?"

"Yeah. I don't wear 'em very often, but they do help when I get serious about seeing shit close up, and before you ask, no. I don't wear them when I'm eating pussy."

I laughed. "Okay," I said. "Let's get down to it. Here's our man, Hubbard, leaving the Sinclair Building. Now, I'm going to start freezing the frames for you. There he is." I pointed. "See, there's Hubbard. He's the short guy that looks like a CPA or librarian." I looked sideways at him. "Well, doesn't he? I mean with the small round face, glasses and all?"

"Looks like a bookworm, alright, and short too. He should sue the city for building the sidewalk so close to his ass. What did you say he does for his company?"

"He's a chemist, works in the lab according to the CEO, Carrington. Now, get a good look here." I pointed. "You see these two heavies swoop up alongside Hubbard?"

"Jesus, yeah. Where in the hell did they come from? First, you don't see them, then they're on both sides of him. They sure as hell must have been laying for him."

"Yeah. Now try to concentrate your eyes on all that clusterfuck of pedestrians. See the three kids dodging in and out like assholes, bumping into people? There. See how that one clipped that old woman right there?"

Jeebers eyes narrowed slightly, and he looked at me sort of sideways as if squinting into the sun. "Yeah, yeah. Don't pause it again, partner, okay? Let the thing go so I get the flow of all the action. You keep fucking me up with this stop and start shit."

"Okay, I just need to pause one more time. Just a second. There! See the kid climbing up on the pole with his SmartPhone aimed at the crowd. You see him?"

"Yeah, I got him. He's got shoulder length brown hair and tan skin. Shit, with your close up, I can even see that small fuckin' scar above his right eyebrow. Damn, that's good, Cleve. And I see he's sportin' a silver earring in his left earlobe. Yeah, I got him good."

"Okay, he's our guy. I have a hunch, with that backpack, he and his friends were on the way home from school that day. Probably one of those vocational shops paying rent in the Loop."

Jeebers stood and stretched his big arms out to his sides. I got up, too. "Ah, shit," he said. "This should be a real grin, keepin' an eye out for a snot-nosed kid who probably cuts school three days a week."

"Hey, this is all I've got right now." I patted him on the back. "Good luck, partner. Keep me posted. If you spot him, flash your badge on him and call me, right away, okay?"

Jebbers saluted me. "Aye, aye, chief."

. . .

Though I've still got a lot of buddies downtown, I try not to bother them any more than I have to, but there have been times when they've saved me a ton of red tape and legal bullshit that can have a tendency to roadblock the path to simple answers.

While Jeebers was handling the lookout downtown, I snooped for other key information. Checking with AT&T, I found that Thad Hubbard hadn't used his cell phone in nine days.

Next I called a friend of mine who works at the First National Bank. I gave her Thad Hubbard's name, social security number and account numbers for his American Express and Visa cards. I told her I wanted to know about any activity whatsoever on his cards for the past thirty days. I also told her I wanted to know if Hubbard had applied for or received any other cards during the past six months.

Her name was Priscilla Schott, but I called her Schotzee. She asked me who the hell did I think I was, calling up after such a long time and asking for all of that. I told her I was the guy who had two front row seats to see Garth Brooks at the United Center. She asked if tomorrow was okay or did I want the information by nine that night.

Schotzee called me back within a couple of hours. Hubbard hadn't used his credit cards in the past ten days. Prior to that, he had never gone two days without using one of the cards. The record showed that to be the case for more than five years. He paid for everything with a card, hardly used cash at all, most likely because he couldn't deduct business expenses. Most all of his charges were for business, with the exception of FTD florist charges for roses he'd sent to his wife Beth on occasion.

I decided my next stop should be to see Harve Milligan at the Missing Persons section downtown. As a matter of policy, the unit cannot act on a routine report of a missing adult until forty-eight hours have elapsed after a report is filed. Most missing people were missing on purpose and often turned up on their own a day or so after supposedly disappearing.

However, for the concerned and sometimes hysterical loved ones, who feel that forty-eight hours is too long to wait for a search to begin, Detective Milligan would suggest my name as an alternative. At four hundred dollars a day plus expenses, I often locate the so-called missing individual inside of an hour with a simple credit card trace.

Milligan wasn't in the office when I had stopped a few days earlier, but he was that day. I found him in his assigned cubicle, busy playing FreeCell on his computer.

His eyes flicked on mine. "Jesus! Don't sneak up on me like that," he gasped.

He wore a white shirt and a rust colored knit tie with a Windsor knot. A brown tweed jacket hung on the back of his chair. His slacks were charcoal and he wore cordovan loafers. I knew he was carrying a piece, but couldn't tell where it was.

Harve was a smiley faced individual and his eyes lit up when he settled down. I knew him to be a drinker, and in the harsh light his skin was reddened and chapped. Small acne scars ran down his cheeks and across his neck.

"Sorry, Harve...how's it hangin'?"

"Huh? Hell, I didn't know it was supposed to hang, Cleve."

"Still got it in for the Captain, eh?"

He lowered his voice. "Yeah, I don't trust that prick. If he told me the time, I'd want a second opinion, know what I mean?"

"I guess so. Hey, do me a favor. See what you've got on one Caucasian male named Thaddeus Hubbard, will you?"

"Why? Is he somebody special?"

"He's the husband of a client of mine. His wife hired me to catch him playing hide the weenie, but he hasn't come home for the past week or so. She was going to call in on it a few days ago when the forty-eight was up."

Harve swiveled around in his chair and scrolled through some lists on his computer. "H. This would be H, yes, Hubbard, Hubbard. There he is. Hubbard, Thaddeus B. He was reported by his spouse, Bethany Hubbard on October fifth." He pointed to Hubbard's picture. "Hey, isn't he that big shot from Carrington? It's in all the papers. He's your guy?"

I leaned in. "Yeah, that's him, alright. I don't suppose you have any leads on his whereabouts?"

"Nada. According to this, the case is under investigation. Outcome pending." Harve clicked a few more times and brought up another screen. "Were you aware our guys confiscated a surveillance hard drive from the security department at the Sinclair building two days ago? Stockwormer and Rodriguez caught the case, by the way. It's been over a week since he disappeared. You know what that means as well as I do, Hawk."

"Yeah. That's why I'm desperate."

"Well, worst case scenario, Hubbard is found with a gunshot wound or his head bashed in. That's one thing. The killer could have been anybody, but if he disappeared with no sign, then whoever snatched him knew what they were doing, and that's another thing entirely. You don't find those kind of guys sitting around in a Starbucks, a button man who knows how to organize it and carry it out clean."

"You got that right. All the more reason, I want his ass in my sights, pronto."

Triple Crossed

"Careful. These are goddamned dangerous guys, Cleve. Not like movie stars, not all muscled up with torn shirts. A lot of them are pretty small guys, neat, quiet. You'd think you could smack them around like rag dolls, but you'd be wrong."

"Thanks, Harve. I knew stopping by to talk to you would cheer me up. What did Stockwormer see on the hard drive, by the way?"

Harve shook his head and smirked. "No can do, Cleve. Sorry, you'll have to locate this guy on your own as far as that goes. I can't say. You know that. He's bound to turn up, though."

"Sure," I said. "I understand you not wanting to give me that info, Harve. I'll find him alright. Hell, I'll just stick my head out the window and yell 'Hey Thad.' That will probably work."

I turned to leave and he said, "Hey, can I buy you lunch? They've got great burgers 'n fries a few doors down."

I looked at my watch. "Sure, why not. I suppose I should eat."

He began to slip on his jacket when his phone rang and he answered, "Detective Milligan."

He grabbed a pen and started scrawling on a yellow 8 X 11 legal pad on his desk. "Yes, we've got that one. Yes. No sir, this is the first I've been notified." There was a brief pause. In the silence, I was sure I heard my watch ticking.

"Yes, sir. I imagine you have most of it, but I'll get the file over to you right away. Yes, sir. Okay. Right. And I'll notify Stockwormer and Rodriguez, too. Yes. Thank you, sir."

When Harve hung up his eyes flicked on mine.

"What?"

As he plopped back down in his chair. "Your man's not missing anymore."

My heart skipped a beat and a shot of adrenaline cut through me like a knife. "They found him?"

Harve nodded. "That was Andrews in Homicide. They found Hubbard alright. Lying face down in an alley way the hell over in Jersey. Dead as dead can be, Hawk. He was easy to ID. His wallet was in his pants pocket."

R.C. Hartson

Chapter Fourteen

After Harve Milligan informed me of Thad Hubbard's demise, I called my friend Phil Andrews at the Chicago Police Department. A former homicide detective, he was promoted to Lieutenant and had taken over the department after the fiasco when serial killer Kris Branoff was offed.

Andrews was doing a good job from what I'd heard.

Remembering Phil from way back when, he hadn't been a bad street cop. Okay, not a terrible one. He might have picked up a roll of fifties on the floor of a crack house that didn't make it back to the evidence lockup, he may have acquired a few used guns that scumbags didn't need anymore which found their way to some gun shows in Iowa, but he'd also put a lot of bad guys behind bars. Overall, given the opportunities, and the stresses, Phil Andrews wasn't a bad guy.

My girlfriend Mo was his personal secretary and answered his phone.

"Hi, Mo. It's just me. Are you clear for dinner tonight?"

"I don't know, stranger. I'll have to check my date book and see whose turn it is tonight."

There was a beat.

"I'm smiling, but I fail to see the humor, as a famous man once said."

She giggled. "Of course, I'm free. Well, not free, but reasonable, for a studly detective I know. What time?"

"I'm not sure, but right now it looks like seven-ish. That okay?"

"Seven it is, Tracy."

"Sounds good. Is Phil in his office?"

"Yes, you caught him just right. He was busy a minute ago, but the two guys that were in there are gone now. See you later. Hold on." The phone buzzed once and Andrews picked up.

"Hi, Phil, this is Hawkins. How's it going?"

"Hey, Hawk. Everything's about the same. You know, ten new cases for every one solved. What's up with you?"

"Not much. I was just informed that you've got a report on a vic named

Triple Crossed

Thaddeus Hubbard...supposedly found somewhere in New Jersey. Is that accurate?"

"Hold on, I got some new stuff in. Let me look here." I heard the rustle of papers. "Yeah, just got that one. Here it is...Hubbard, Thaddeus Hubbard. He's not listed as a homicide yet. It's pending further details. Why? What's he to you?"

"He's the husband of a client. His wife hired me to follow him eight days ago. She thought he was screwing around on her, but as it turned out, he never came home. Missing Persons has had the case for the past five days."

"Oh yeah, I see that on the daily log. Anyway, like I said it's not my case yet. I can tell you this much though. A homeless guy contacted the Camden cops in New Jersey after he'd found your guy spread-eagled in an alley. He had his wallet and all his ID, including credit cards, on his person, too. Good thing he was a pretty honest homeless dude, know what I mean?"

"That's for sure. He was probably too scared to touch the body, but he could have skated with the whole wallet. Know the cause of death yet?"

"Nope. There's nothing firm on that. The coroner's still doing his thing over there in Newark. That's evidently where they process the local has-beens."

"Nothing at all? Was it gunshot?"

"Nope. There's a great big question mark on this prelim report that was faxed to us. Physical trauma is ruled out altogether. What the hell? What kind of work did he do, took him to Jersey, Cleve?"

"Good question. He worked as a chemist for an outfit downtown, Carrington Engineering. Ring a bell?"

"No. But now that you mention Carrington, I realize they're the ones that's been screaming in the papers about a missing employee. A big shot, I thought. This must have been their guy then?"

"Yeah, that's him. He'd been working on some sort of top secret project according to what Carrington told me about a week ago. But how or why Hubbard got to Jersey is beyond me. Anyone informed the next of kin yet?"

"No. Take it easy, buddy. I told you, it's not my case yet. Probably Missing Persons will tell his wife. My sheet says the vic was married to Bethany Hubbard, formerly Bethany St. James of Oak Brook."

"Correct. She's my client. Well, you've got my numbers. If you get anything else on this guy, will you let me know?"

"Sure, Hawk. I've got to run. I'll try to catch you as soon as I get something."

"Thanks, Phil."

• • •

This whole thing was tying me up in knots. I felt like the world was zooming ahead without me. Thinking Jeebers might have some good news, I called him on his cell phone. He answered on the first ring.

"Yup."

"Hey, Jeebs. I'm figuring you didn't spot the kid, eh?"

"You'd be figuring right. Tell you what, though. We need to get his face on paper, know what I mean? Blow up that image from the recording somehow. Call in one of the tech people from the department, if we have to."

I heard his Zippo snap shut as he lit a cigarette and exhaled. "There's a shitload of kids running around down there between two-thirty and three-thirty in the afternoon. If we had a picture of the kid, we could ask around. Maybe one of them would ID him for us."

"Down there?"

"Yeah, down on West Adams."

"I figured you were still there. Where are you now?"

"Oh, I'm having a cold one at Streeter's on East Chicago. Why don't you get over here and join me?"

I felt the blood instantly throb in my temples, but I said, "No, I can't do it, Jeebs. I've got a date with Mo tonight."

"What time?"

"Around seven, but I have to go . . ."

"Seven? What the hell, you've got plenty of time before that. Where are you?"

"I just left the Starbucks on North State. Why?"

"Well, come and get me. My car's in the parking garage. I might as well leave it there for now. Pick me up and we can talk some of this shit over before tomorrow. We need to regroup and relax a little."

Jeebers still didn't know about Hubbard and I realized we should get together. Maybe he was right. "Yeah, okay. I'll be right there. Give me about fifteen minutes. Traffic is a pain in the ass this time of day."

"Ha! All day, every day, you mean. See you in a few, jarhead."

I had second thoughts, but the truth was, I wanted a drink. Not a lot, just a couple of shots with a beer back, I told myself, Just enough to cool my jets and absorb the new wrinkle with Hubbard's death.

It was 4:47 p.m when I pulled up to the curb in front of Streeter's Tavern. Outside, the sky was gray and the wind was blowing in off of the lake.

Triple Crossed

Jeebers opened the door on the passenger side and leaned in. He took his car keys from his pants pocket and spun them on his finger. He smiled, and I saw the familiar alcoholic glow shining in his eyes.

"I changed my mind," he said. "Let's take my wheels and park yours across the street. I'll drive. "

"Why? What difference does it make? Come on. Get in. We're pissing off the traffic behind me."

He jumped in and slammed the door. "Okay, but just follow my directions since you want to drive. Head west."

"Where in the hell are you taking us?"

"Don't sweat it, Sam Spade. Just drive. We're going where nobody knows our faces. I want to relax, not have everybody spotting me as a cop. Jesus, Cleve, sometimes you remind me of my ex wife. Too many fuckin' questions."

I headed west on Division and about ten minutes later I was definitely wishing I had passed on getting a drink. While I drove, I gave my friend a quick rundown on Hubbard's body showing up in New Jersey.

He was as amazed as I was.

"So, those two assholes that snatched him on Adams," Jeebs mused, "carted his ass all the way to Jersey? What the hell? Plenty of John Gotti's buddies are from that neck of the woods. Jersey City is the mob's playground."

"You've got that right. Makes one wonder, doesn't it?"

"Damned sure does. I was you, I'd leave this one alone now. Let the cops do their job."

"Nah. I can't do that. This one's eating me alive."

Meanwhile, the area was looking more and more depressing. Plenty of buildings were burned out. The windows on the Seven Eleven were covered in posters for the Power Ball and Mega Millions tickets while the neighboring storefronts were all covered over in plywood.

"This is bullshit, Jeebers. You're bringing us into what's got to be one of the worst fuckin' neighborhoods in the city."

He leaned back and laughed. "Nah, this ain't bad. Go ahead. Pull over just past this light. See, the bar's right over there on your side, right next to the check cashing place."

"The Hole?"

"Yeah, that's it. Come on, where's your sense of adventure, flatfoot? Park right there." He pointed to an opening ahead of two other cars.

I had to laugh as I pulled over and parked. "You are one crazy sonofabitch,

Jeebers. Of all the places you find to relax...what was wrong with Streeters, anyway?"

"Ah, Streeter's is for pussies. All the cops hang out there. Is that where you want to relax, pal?" He slapped me between the shoulder blades.

We stepped inside the place with Jeebers in the lead and waited a few seconds for our eyes to adjust. The Hole was aptly named. There was an extreme degree of bar darkness among the high-backed booths, the better to attract adulterers, I figured. There were only a few freestanding tables, six stools at the bar and a small stage on the other side of a dance floor. There was a jukebox by the back wall. A mixture of about eight older men and women were in the place and they huddled in booths except for two guys situated at one end of the bar.

The place was obscured by a billowing fog of cigarette smoke and it smelled of fried onions and body odor plus the unmistakable stink of marijuana was in the air.

Electronic dance music with a Latin beat blared from the jukebox and there were two flat screens high on the walls, one over the bar showing a silent soccer game and kick boxing. We sat at the bar.

Jeebers poked me in the shoulder with his mammoth fist. "I know this joint isn't too classy, Hawk, but they have all kinds of beer, the pizza is excellent and we're anonymous, know what I mean?"

The bartender eased down from the other end where he had been talking with the two guys who looked like castoffs from Hells Angels. One had narrow shoulders and small ears that were tight against his scalp. The hair at his temples was silver-streaked. He either could have been a boxer or gotten kicked in the face by a horse.

The other man was maybe six-seven with long blond hair and a chubby pink face. Under thirty, I thought. He had a wallet connected to his belt with a brass chain, wore heavy motorcycle boots, and put out a vibration. His overdeveloped, steroid-pumped muscles made him look like he needed a bra. He had probably been a thin guy once, but as time passed he became fat until the only remnant of his former self was his neck.

Both men stared at us as we took our seats.

I reached in my pocket for my money clip, but Jeebers pushed my hand away. "Nope. This was my idea. I'm buyin,'" he said.

The bartender had now made his way down to us and I glanced at him as he leaned with the palms of his hands on the bar, waiting.

"What'll it be, gents?"

Triple Crossed

I was running on too little sleep and too much stress when I flashed a half-assed smile at the guy. "Okay, give me double Jack with a bottle of Heinekens back. And my friend here needs a drink, too. Give him somethin' to perk him up." Then, I added, "But not Viagra. We've been fucked enough for today."

Jeebers nodded at the guy. "Everybody likes ass, but nobody likes a smart ass, right? How's it goin', Randy? Gimme a double Beam, and make mine Bud on the side."

After Randy set up the drinks, I faced Jeebers and said, "Here's to those who do, to hell with those who don't, and better luck tomorrow for all of us." We touched glasses and chugged down the doubles like water. The beers sat for a moment untouched.

The whiskey went down into my stomach like an old friend, in a way that made me feel warm and confident and sexy at the same time. Then it spread throughout my body and deadened, like a woman closing my eyes with her fingers as if she were whispering to me that the world was a good place in spite of it all.

. . .

Five doubles later, two hours had passed before I had thought of looking at my watch. It was almost eight-thirty *Oh shit! Mo will be pissed. Maybe I should call.*

That thought melted away as Jeebers said, "Hey. You notice those assholes at the end of the bar been staring us down?"

"Yeah, I saw that. Fuck 'um," I held my shot glass up and said, "Here's to you, Marine. Semper Fi and down the hatch."

Jeebers continued to play eye-fuck with the two bikers. "I swear, those ugly sonofabitchs haven't taken their eyes off of us since we sat down, Cleve. What the hell you figure's their problem?"

I glanced over there and then back to Jeebers. "And I say, fuck em."

He lifted his face, indicating we shouldn't ignore them. The skin twitched under his left eye, as though an insect was walking across it.

"You were always a good cop, Jeebs. The best I ever knew. But you're crazy, my friend, always have been. Working with you is like being around a guy with nitroglycerine for a brain." I playfully tapped his cheek with my fingertips. "I'm in a shitload of trouble now with Mo, thanks to you, buddy."

"Bullshit. You need to chill, Hawk. She'll be okay. This is what it's all about. Right here. Time out. Fuck that cop blotter. We always deal with the problems after the fact. We only catch the assholes by chance and accident, either during the commission of their crimes or from snitches."

He paused briefly.

"Shit, because of forensics and evidence bullshit, most of the crimes street thugs commit are not even prosecutable. In the long run, jail is the only place the perps feel safe from their own failures. And we're running out of room there."

I glanced over his shoulder and said, "You know what, you're right. Those assholes down there are troublemakers. I'm going to find out what their problem is."

"Nah, you were right. Let it go."

My head of steam was building, though, and I made my way down to the end of the bar.

I remember seeing Randy, the bartender, with his hands in the air, palms out as if he was the victim of a stick-up.

"Hold on now," he called out. "I don't need no trouble in here. Hey, fella...I'm talking to you."

I wasn't sure who he was talking to and I didn't care.

I stopped about two feet away from the two eye-guys. "You guys got a problem with me and my partner?" I heard myself ask.

They both smirked and the one with the long, scuzzy hair looked at his buddy and said, "You smell pig shit, Cal?"

His buddy sniggered. "Yeah. I thought I did, but now I'm sure of it."

I gritted my teeth and said, "I'm a coward. I don't like confrontation." With that, I clobbered him with a short left hook that landed under his right eye.

The other guy jumped up and clubbed me with his right. I took most of the blow on my left shoulder and upper arm, but even so, it rocked me and my arm hurt.

I stepped inside him real quick and busted him three times before he finally dropped. He tried to rise but another blow sent him down face first.

The few women sitting in the booths shrieked.

Beside me I heard Jeebers yell, "Aw shit," as I nailed the other guy with the same left hook, then a straight left on the nose. Blood splattered everywhere and he went sprawling.

The bartender screamed, "Knock it off! Hey! I said knock it off!" He grabbed a mop from someplace and began to swing it at all of us.

My friend shoved me aside and pounded the other guy's face and gut with both fists in rapid succession until he dropped to his knees. Then Jeebers kneed him in the chin and that man was done.

Triple Crossed

The first guy got back up and I delivered a crunching straight jab to his face. I felt his nose flatten under the impact. When my fist hit facial bone, he went flying again, landed in a corner and seemed to be down for the count.

We were both breathing heavy and Jeebers said, "I guess we'd better shag ass out of here."

"I guess you'd be right," I said as I tossed a twenty on the bar and followed him out the door.

About three minutes down the road, I looked at my friend and said, "Why did that feel so damned good?"

He breathed a heavy sigh and answered, "The bottom line is we all get to be dead for a real long time."

R.C. Hartson

Chapter Fifteen

I stirred awake in the morning to white noise, like a television turned up on high volume with no picture on the screen. Stripping off the clothes I was wearing when I passed out on the couch, I took a shower and let the water beat down on me as I rested my forehead against the moist tile wall.

My breathing was usually slow and steady, like the tick of a clock, but as I thought about how I'd stood Mo up, it was erratic and too fast, like a wheel freed from a car and bouncing out of control down a mountainside.

Shower done, I struggled through putting on fresh clothes, combed my hair and slipped on my nylon shoulder holster and blue-black Smith and Wesson revolver. Grabbing my gym bag, I headed for the door, but suddenly stopped and stood in silence for a moment.

Dreading the thought of working out, I decided to blow it off. I tossed the bag back in the living room and walked out. It wasn't the first time I had cheated myself.

As my day unfolded, everything I touched seemed to have sharp edges and thoughts of "I'm sorry" ran rampant in my throbbing head. My world had become an unforgiving place where images of mistakes made had not evaporated with sleep.

It was an experience I was all too familiar with, but would not soon forget. I screwed up and couldn't shake the guilt. *I'm a used up jarhead and alcoholic flatfoot with no tread left on his tires. How will I get her to forgive me this time?*

The sun was white overhead, as if a flashbulb had just gone off, and it seemed as though the trees were void of birds and shade. I tried calling Mo, but got her answering machine. I knew she wouldn't have left for work yet. It was only seven-fifteen. Too early. I sat behind the wheel, breathing hard, unable to move, feeling apart from my own body as if this had just happened to someone else. My heart pushed into my throat and it felt larger than a clenched fist.

Mo knew it was me, but just wasn't answering. I decided not to leave a message, as if I blamed her. I could have waited a while and called her at the department, and ordinarily I wouldn't hesitate to do it, but not under the circumstances. I couldn't put her on the spot like that. It could mean certain relationship castration if I tried. I'd call her later at her apartment and see if I was still getting the answering machine treatment. I figured if I did, I wouldn't chicken out. I'd tell her I was sorry, if nothing else.

I had enough to keep me busy until she cooled off enough to let me explain. *What will that explanation be, asshole? I don't think "I'm sorry" will cut it this time, Hawkins.*

Stopping at the Seven Eleven, I saw that I still had bars on my cell phone and called to check with Jeebers.

He answered with his usual, "Yeah."

"Hey, buddy, how are you feeling this morning?"

"Great, no problem. Why?"

"I don't know. Let's just say I'd expect you to at least have a headache, snot on your eggs, or something."

"Nah, I'm good. How about you? Did you mend the fence with Mo? I'll bet she's pissed."

"No, not yet. Too early to call," I lied. "Listen, I've got that USB of that kid with the phone. I'm stopping by Staples to get a couple of copies made. Where can I meet you before school lets out?"

"No can do. Sorry, buddy. I've got some of my own shit to cover today. I'm afraid you'll have to take this thing over by yourself for a few days. Something has come up, plus I've got another interview with Holson in personnel about getting reinstated. Remember I told you about that?"

I was somewhat floored at Jeebers' complacency, but didn't let on. "Oh, yeah. You did mention something like that. Well, no problem. I'll be okay, but stay in touch, partner. Let me know how you make out with Holson, okay?"

"Sure thing, Hawk. Catch you later."

I stopped by Staples on North Wabash and managed to get two different pictures of the teenager, one head shot, and one from a distance showing him up on the pole with the SmartPhone in hand. The copies were blown up as big as was possible and even though the enhancing made them a tad blurry, I felt sure that the boy's features were distinctive enough for a positive ID. I was confident that if I spotted him, I'd know it was him.

It was close to noon when I made a call to the Missing Persons and got through to Harve Milligan. I asked what he had on Thad Hubbard, if anything, and he said, "I'm not supposed to let anything out yet, Hawk, but as far as I'm concerned, you can look at everything I've got...which isn't much. Hubbard's body was shipped back here from Jersey yesterday. I'm expecting the Medical Examiner's Report anytime now. Outside of that...oh, I forgot to tell you, old man Carrington himself called in a day after Beth Hubbard reported her husband gone. He sounded genuinely concerned, if you know what I mean."

"Hey, Harve, one more thing. Do me a favor and get a Release for Inspection at the Central Impound lot on Wacker Drive, will you?"

"The pound? What the hell for?"

"Just covering all my bases. I want to check the inside of Hubbard's Monte Carlo."

"Makes sense, I guess. Yeah, I can do that. Just have Nettie call me when you get there. He's the guy in charge at the gate. Let me know what you find. Good luck, pal."

I didn't really know what I expected to find when I got there, but you never know. I figured maybe Thad had left something behind that would help me understand what he had gotten himself into. However, except for the usual yard dust on the outside, the vehicle was spotless.

The glove box contained the owner's manual, registration and proof of insurance, plus some coupons for Burger King specials and a brick-hard package of Dentyne gum. I also found papers tucked above the visor on the passenger side. Three sheets, stapled together, referenced the entrance fees and so on for a golf outing at The Oak Park Golf Club. The trunk was empty except for the spare and standard tire changing tools. In short, a dead end.

After that waste of time, my stomach had healed enough and agreed to take food, so I stopped for lunch at Perry's Deli on North Franklin and ordered one of their ultimate corned beef sandwiches on rye with a cup of coffee to wash it down. I had been thinking about Mo again and again as the day wore on. Guilt has a strange way of chewing on your head.

After lunch, I headed for West Adams Street. Around two-thirty I found a place to park and waited for the teenage after school crowd to materialize within the hour. I stood off to the side, just to the left of the Sinclair Building. I had the pictures in my pocket and the kid's face embedded in my brain as I watched the pedestrian traffic move back and forth along the wide sidewalk.

There were plenty of kids zipping in and out with the flow. Most of them had backpacks, just as I'd seen on the USB. I sidetracked one young man with black curly hair and a bad case of acne. He was wearing jeans, a denim jacket, ratty-looking sneakers and surprised eyes when I flashed my badge. If he had looked

Triple Crossed

closely, he would have realized I wasn't a cop, but he was rattled. I edged him gently off to the side and sort of crowded him up against the wall of the building.

"Hey, man, I didn't do nothing," he whined and tried to pull away. "What's going on?" His dark eyes registered fear.

"I didn't say you *did* do anything wrong, did I?" While he pondered that, I said, "I want to ask you a few questions, is all. What's your name?"

He pulled his arm free of my hand and backed up a foot or two before he answered, "Eduardo."

"Eduardo, what?"

He hesitated. "Eduardo Castro. Why?"

I kept my eyes locked on his as I fished the pictures out of my coat pocket and held one up.

"I'm looking for this kid. You know him?"

Eduardo nodded. "Maybe I do. So what?"

"Here's the deal, Eddy." I paused. "Okay if I call you Eddy?"

"Yeah, I guess so." He studied me and said, "What you want with him?"

I edged forward and closed the gap between us. "Listen to me. It's very important I talk to this guy. Believe me, he's not in any trouble. I just need to ask him a couple of questions. Help me out here, will you?" I handed him a ten spot.

He took the money and grinned. "As long as you're sure it won't get him in no trouble. That picture isn't a very cool one, man, but it looks like my friend, Jesus." Fumbling around in his pocket, he pulled out a SmartPhone. His fingers clicked on this and that, and scrolled, and there was Jesus in a clear head shot. He said, "Is this the dude, man?"

I felt an adrenaline rush as I took the phone and studied the picture. "It just might be, Eddy. Jesus who? What's his last name?"

"Figuroa."

"Jesus Figuroa? That's it?"

"Yeah, man. What did he do?"

Handing the phone back to him, I said, "I just told you, he's in the clear, didn't I? So how would I get to speak to Jesus, Eddy?"

His eyes flicked back and forth for a beat and he craned his neck to look at the stoplight, near the crosswalk, at the end of the block.

"Man, Jesus just left school with me a little while ago. He's in my shop class."

"So, he should be here, is that what you are telling me, Eddy?"

He nodded. "Yeah, I guess so. Follow me, mister. Just remember, I don't want no trouble."

"No trouble. You have my word." I stayed right with him as we shouldered our way through the late afternoon crowd. Less than a minute later, I spotted Jesus standing on the curb waiting for the light to change.

Eddy magically disappeared just before I tapped his friend on the shoulder and showed him my badge. "Come with me, Jesus."

He looked surprised. "What? Hell no, I won't. Who are you? You got the wrong guy. I didn't do it, whatever it is. I ain't done nothing." He gave me a mean stare that was supposed to make the marrow in my bones harden, I guess. "I ain't going nowhere with you, mister." A pack of Camels was sticking out of his jacket pocket and he reached for one.

He was a good-looking Latin kid, but his ears were a little too big for his narrow face. He had a missing tooth on the upper left side. The gap was prominent. He showed me his everyone's-out-to-get-me eyes. "Why you got to be hassling me, anyway?" he said.

"I didn't say you were in trouble, did I, Jesus?" I circled my hand under his arm and guided him over to the wall of the building. "Okay, let's just get out of the way of these people for a minute so we can talk." We moved together and I said, "I just need some information, Jesus. Maybe you can help me out." I flashed a twenty under his nose and his brown eyes widened.

I pulled out the pictures from Staples and showed him the one with him up on the pole.

"See this? Take a good look, amigo. That's you up there on that pole, isn't it?"

He glanced at the picture, then back at me. "Yeah, so? I ain't breaking no law there, man?"

"No. None that I know of, but you were taking some pictures with your phone. right?"

He hesitated at first, then said, "Yeah, and like I said, so what?"

"This was about ten days ago, give or take, right?"

I could see the tension in his thin shoulders and feel the anticipation that crowded the air around him. His uncombed hair flopped in tangles around his face as he answered.

"Yeah. I guess so. I was screwing around taking shots of my compadres. Anything wrong with that?"

As we talked, the sun slipped behind a dark cloud and a few scattered raindrops fell around me. I hardly noticed.

"No, Jesus, nothing wrong with that at all. But, here's the deal. There were two very bad hombres in the crowd of people you were aiming that phone at. We need to ID them and we need a close-up of their faces in order to do that. You most likely have them right there on your phone."

Jesus stared at me. A smart-assed grin spread slowly across his face. He began to light up a Camel, but I slapped it out of his hand.

"What's so funny, Jesus?"

"Man, I uploaded that stuff onto YouTube that same night. I always do." His voice had become small and flat. "It was just a goof on my friends, like I said." He paused and reached for another cigarette. "Wow! These guys are real bad asses, huh?"

I nodded. "You could say that." We were silent for a beat. "Any chance you still have it on that phone?"

"Oh, man, I don't delete any of the good shit. Here, I'll show you. While he scrolled he grinned and glanced sideways at me. "You ain't got another one of them Jacksons in your pocket do you?" Raising his hand like a traffic cop, palm out, he continued, "I mean if I got what you want on here, I could use a little more first aid. Know what I mean?"

"I'm fresh out, Jesus. Don't push. Let's see what you've got."

He brought up a video that showed everything with unbelievable clarity from his vantage point up on the pole. There was less than a minute of it, but he had captured plenty of action. Heads appeared to be bobbing up and down, and then, there they were, all three men. Thad and his captors, one on each side of him, preparing to round the corner into the parking garage. Their faces were crystal clear.

Thad's expression was one of shock and fear.

R.C. Hartson

Chapter Sixteen

Loneliness is a perfect excuse to drink. But trading the quiet confines of my apartment for a bar stool could lead to a dead end. Sooner or later it would catch up with me. I might as well put a nail gun to the center of my forehead and pull the trigger.

I sat in my office with my feet on the desk, pondering my latest screw-up, and studied the way my name looked backwards through the glass window of my office door. My eyes wandered to a stain on the wall which marked the stubborn seepage of a suspicious, but unidentifiable liquid. I realized that the women's rest room was one floor above. The landlord already knew as much, but didn't seem to care.

I had to get busy with the YouTube images I'd gotten from Jesus as soon as possible, but getting anything done after five was practically impossible. I would wait and attack it first thing in the morning by going downtown to look at mug shots. I felt certain that the two thugs who accompanied Thad that day would have rap sheets as long as my arm.

I also knew the real reason I couldn't function as I should. I couldn't shake the guilt of my fuck up with Mo. She was the kind of woman who could be a friend as well as a lover and I had hurt her big time with my selfishness.

I needed to talk to her, but couldn't bear another negative rejection from her answering machine. Sometimes it's best to just stick your head in the gorilla's mouth, I guess, so I decided to go to her place and face the music. Hopefully Mo would at least hear an apology.

I hadn't been very good company for Deckle and he had left an hour earlier. I decided to lock up and go home.

There was one message on my answering machine--Jeebers had called. I decided to deal with him later. I took a shower and decided I didn't want to go too formal so put on jeans, a black pullover shirt and a light leather jacket that hung down over my .38. Too bad there wasn't something available to hide the shame plastered on my face.

I sensed that offering to take Mo out to dinner would be a stretch and would simply look like another bullshit move. But I was hungry and decided to grab a Market Fresh Rueben at Arby's on the way over to Mo's apartment.

When I pulled up to find a place to park, large cirrus clouds hung heavy with the promise of rain. Forks of lightning danced along the horizon and I hoped it wasn't an omen for my visit.

In front of her building, her postage-stamp lawn had already started to turn pale with the coming of winter. The flowers in the flowerbeds looked wilted, most likely from an early frost, and the wind swirled and scattered the dead leaves that lay in a heap alongside the curb. Somewhere nearby a dog barked.

Her apartment was on the second floor, and there was a hand-twist bell on the door. I had to ring it twice before she answered. She looked great in black slacks and a white angora sweater with her gold earrings and modest gold necklace. I could see the uncertainty in her face, like someone about to light a candle in a storage room that smells of gasoline. I paused for a moment and looked at her amazing blue eyes.

"Hi, Mo."

"Hello, Cleve." When she spoke, I heard shallow, raspy breathing, as if she were trembling with excitement.

Her arms were crossed over her chest, her lips pressed tightly together. She gave me a look that would boil cheese.

"No, I'm not going to do this anymore," she said as she started to close the door. I blocked it with my hand.

"Wait, Mo...please...please. At least give me a chance to apologize. I know I was wrong. There's no excuse this time. It's all on me. Please let me come in for a minute. Really, I can't live with myself, baby."

Her eyes narrowed. She looked at me sort of sideways, as if she were squinting into the sun.

"This is nothing new, Cleve. I've heard it before--too many times." Her eyes widened and she rested her hands on her hips. "You call me, ask me out to dinner, then leave me sitting at home wondering whether you're dead or alive. What kind of bullshit is that?"

"I know. I just wanted to..."

She leaned forward, biting down on her lower lip. Her eyes were wide and fixed on me. Tears suddenly formed in her eyes and rolled down her cheeks and she raised her hand like a traffic cop and shook her head.

"I don't want to hear it, Cleve. I just can't anymore." She grabbed a fistful of Kleenex from a box sitting on the entry table.

There was a long pause of sinister silence and in that moment I felt like a damned fool as she slowly turned and left the door ajar, allowing me inside. She lowered her head, and I could no longer see the tears, but I could see her shoulders shake. I'd seen the look before, much to my chagrin.

Her eyes lifted up to me, her chin shook a bit, and then she clenched her jaw just before the muscles in her face appeared to relax.

Our eyes met, our hands touched, our lips smiled, her brow wrinkled. I said, "I'm so sorry, Mo."

I looked at the earnestness in her face and wanted to hold her. Putting my arms around her back, I cupped one hand on her neck. I rubbed my cheek against her hair and squeezed her tight. After a moment she gently pushed me away and moved to the kitchen table. I closed the door and followed her. She dabbed her nose with the Kleenex, sat down at the table and pointed at a chair.

"Sit."

I didn't say a word as I sat across from her. She sipped from a can of Diet Coke. It was her favorite, and I watched the way her fingerprints stenciled themselves in the moisture on the can. A minute or so passed and her eyes were now nearly dry, though she still held the Kleenex in both fists, clenched in her lap, just in case.

After a long pause she said, "I don't want to know what happened last night--I really don't. I suspect I know, anyway."

"I can explain . . ."

"No, Cleve. No, I just need to know that it will never happen again. Not that way. No phone call...nothing? You will never do that again." She put her hand on her chest as if to calm her beating heart.

I nodded and tried a comforting smile for her as I slipped out of my jacket and reached across the table for her hand.

"Are you still working the missing person case?" she asked.

"Yes."

"Doing any good?"

"Yeah, as a matter of fact I just caught a break today."

"That's good." There was a long moment of silence. "I ran into Harve Milligan in our office. He mentioned that he had seen you a couple of days ago. There's a lot of coverage by the media on this guy, you know."

"Yeah. Did Harve tell you they found the body over in New Jersey?"

"Yes."

"Sounds like it's going to be a cop only deal now, huh?"

Triple Crossed

"No. Not really. I was hired by Hubbard's wife to find him, and I won't be satisfied until I find out how, and why, her husband died."

Mo smiled. "You'll never change, will you?"

"What do you mean?"

"You know what I mean. The only person who doesn't worry about you is you, Cleve. You are so damned hard-nosed when you get a case, you hang on like a pissed off pit bull. You were the same when you worked homicide."

I shrugged.

We stared into each other's eyes with a look of inevitable intimacy. It was something beyond my ability to describe or to resist.

We stood up at the same time, then circled the table and wrapped our arms around each other. She murmured into my neck, "I worried, Cleve. Please promise me you won't ever hurt me again like that."

"You've got it, Mo. Never again." I looked into her eyes the way you do when you want to make sure the person you're talking to doesn't just hear you, but believes.

I heard my hoarse voice say, "I love you, baby."

"Oh, I love you, Cleve," she said, then looked deliberately into my eyes. "Too much," she added.

With her eyes locked on my face and a pout on her mouth like an adolescent girl, she removed her earrings and necklace and laid them on the table. She pulled her sweater up and over her head and unhooked her bra and let it drop from her breasts. Unzipping her slacks, she pushed them and her panties down over her thighs and knees and stepped out of them. Then she pulled the pins from her red hair and shook it out over her shoulders.

Her eyes never left mine.

Things began to move lightning fast. I put my hand behind her head and kissed her. She kissed me back. It wasn't eager--it was ferocious. I felt the stirring in my loins and my phallus began to swell. With one arm around her back, I managed to slip the other under her knees and pick her up. Her mouth never left mine as I carried her to the bedroom.

I pulled the covers back and gently lay her on the bed. I kicked off my shoes and began stripping the clothes from my body. Seeing her naked body stretched out before me gave me a rock hard erection.

I knelt on the bed and let my lips trail down along her breasts, her stomach. She was lightly scented with perfume. I kissed between her legs and she moaned, gently calling my name.

"Oh, my God! Cleve! Cleve!"

When I entered her, she sucked in a huge mouthful of air followed by a hissing sound as she clenched her teeth. She lifted up her hips to take in all of me. She was strong and gentle and graceful, all at the same time.

It was a wild ride in the beginning and then the rocking and rolling morphed itself into a slower rhythm that was even stronger and I knew life was not right without that kind of passion.

I was barely moving inside her, but she tightened up around me and I surged deeper. She seemed to swell around me as we began to move faster and faster again, trying to get closer.

First she climaxed and then the two of us came together. I felt myself melting into her and we were both whispering, "Yes, yes, yes, yes, yes, yes." When she climaxed, she bit me, scratched me and pounded me on the back with her clenched fist as hard as she could.

When we were spent, she turned on her side, revealing her breasts and a smile. I caressed her breasts, shoulders and hair while staring into her eyes. She reached up and pulled me down into a long, passionate kiss.

I held her in my arms and lay my head on her pillow. I smelled her perfume and sex and our sweat.

After a while I knew Mo had something she wanted to say. She smiled and moved a strand of her hair behind her ear and rolled toward me. One of her breasts pressed against my biceps.

She wetted a finger and circled one of my nipples in a distracted way and said, "Want to go again?"

Chapter Seventeen

I was half asleep when I felt Mo kiss me on the forehead before she left for work. After I heard the front door shut, I lay there with my eyes closed listening to Springsteen's "Dancing in the Dark" playing on the classics station she'd left on in the bathroom. I smelled the coffee and wanted some, but stayed on my back for a while and thought about the night before, not only our fantastic lovemaking, but more than that, how truly lucky I was for having her and her forgiveness. I felt revitalized.

Slipping my boxers on, I traipsed to the kitchen for a cup of coffee. The weather people were talking about cold weather moving in, but they didn't know when it was supposed to come. I eased over to the living room window and looked at the street below. There weren't many cars parked along the curb. Everybody was at work. The trees lining the street were, for the most part, barren and twisted, like broken fingers in the air, but the sky was blue, with no clouds. Good, I thought, another beautiful day.

I had a lot to do.

The sun was still bright when I headed for the office around eight-forty-five. I pulled down the visor, but still couldn't keep the brilliance out of my eyes. Traffic was heavy as usual and I had plenty of time to think about everything I had to do. Topping the list was a stop at Staples to get enlargements of the two men's faces in the YouTube segment. I was hoping for clarity more than anything else. I needed decent quality to use in order to view mug shots at the police department. It took balls to snatch a man off a busy street in broad daylight and I concluded that the two men must have rap sheets listing their prior offenses. This definitely wasn't their first rodeo.

At Staples I had the pictures on the USB enlarged and I couldn't have been happier with the result. The two eight-by-tens were a bit fuzzy, but they were clear enough to ID. I headed for my office.

It was unusual to not find Deckle on the front steps. It wasn't the first time, however, and I was sure he'd turn up. I unlocked the door and picked up the mail that had accumulated on the floor below the mail slot. All bills, no doubt.

The office had been shut up for nearly a week and I opened a window facing Wells Street in order to dilute the stagnant air. After I made a pot of coffee, I sat at my desk and pawed through the mail. Around nine-thirty I called the police department and asked for Ralph Bidden, an old friend and the detective in charge of the Criminal Identification and Investigation section.

Bidden was a sharp individual, and I was glad *he* was the go-to-guy handling the processing and storage of mug shots. Even though I wasn't with the police department any longer, he always treated me as if I were still one of the guys. The switchboard put me through immediately and he answered on the first ring.

"Detective Bidden."

"Hey, Ralph. it's Hawkins. How ya' doin?"

"Hawk? What in the hell have you been up to? I haven't seen you since that last deal with the serial killings."

"Yeah, it's been a while, that's for sure. I'm still playing snoop, you know. Gotta stay busy. I need your help. If you can spare the time today, I'd like to stop by."

"Depends...what time?"

"This morning, actually. I've got something pretty hot."

"Well, Captain Silvers has called for a section meeting at two-thirty, but I'm fairly clear up to then. Get your sorry ass in here pronto,"

"Thanks, Ralph. I'm on the way."

I parked in the Chicago Police department's guest lot and walked inside. I had a friendly chat with the policewoman in the glass cage and was buzzed through to the back of the building. I badged my way back to the Identification Unit, a room that was a maze of ugly steel desks the color of dirty putty. Most were covered in paperwork. Notes, news clippings and photographs were taped to walls and cabinets.

I found Bidden in a cubicle. He was staring inside a brown paper bag and rolled his eyes with disgust when he looked up and saw me.

I said, "Looking for a clue in there, detective?"

"Nah, just looking at what the wife packed for lunch today. I'm thinking of eating early because I'm starving to death, and she's got me on this new food-free diet. Low carbs. What the hell's a man supposed to eat, for Chrissakes?"

My cell phone rang and I answered it. "Hawkins."

"Cleve, this is Stoney over at the Medical Examiner's. You wanted to be informed when we received Mister Hubbard's remains. The body was delivered here yesterday afternoon after I left for the day. We'll be doing an autopsy as soon as his next of kin verifies him and so forth."

"I believe that kin would be Bethany Hubbard, the wife."

"Yeah. The lieutenant said the deceased's wife would be calling, and she did, just a little bit ago, as a matter of fact."

"Did she say when she would be down, Stoney?"

"Sometime today is all she said. She's going to call before she leaves home."

"Okay, buddy. I want to try to be there when she arrives. I'm in the middle of something right now, but I'll call you back. I appreciate the heads up."

"No rush. This stiff isn't going anywhere."

"Thanks, Stoney."

I hung up, and before I could continue with Bidden, a female detective sidled up beside me.

Jill Albers had worked in the homicide division when I was there. She was not one of my favorite people, but she knew Mo. She was quite a gal. She wore pinstripe suits, silk ties and an enormous chip on her shoulder. Many of us suspected she also wore a jockstrap. I remembered she usually had three or four women clustered around her. She was gossip central and I always tried to ignore her.

"Well, hello, Cleve Hawkins. I haven't seen you in forever. What are you doing here?" She was wearing a gray calf-length skirt and a matching soft gray v-necked blouse. Her fists rested on her hips. I guess she'd learned how to act nosey and pleasant at the same time by watching old Doris Day movies. She smiled a lot. In fact, she was much too pleasant and smiled way more than she should have.

"Hello, Albers."

"You been behaving yourself?" Even her voice annoyed me.

I smiled and said, "That's like asking if there's any washroom graffiti that shouldn't be on a Hallmark card."

She giggled. "What's this I hear, you and Maureen are getting married?"

Ralph overheard, "You getting hitched, Cleve?"

"No. And Albers, you're watching too much Oprah."

"Ha! Just asked," Albers responded. "And why must you always be so angry, Cleve? When I first got assigned to Homicide, Maureen described you to me. That was while you were still riding in a blue and white, wise guy."

She wasn't done. "Mo said you were a guy with big shoulders and a bigger heart, sort of rugged with blue eyes and a small scar on your forehead. She thought that was sexy, although, I can't see it myself. I think you're just a stick of dynamite with a short fuse."

She paused and I turned to Bidden.

Albers went on, "I heard you blew a perp out of his socks is why you're not there anymore."

I glared. "Easy does it, officer. Before you climb on the cross you might consider this. It was not a premeditated deal."

"Yeah, I know, so now you...what? Work divorce cases, chase ambulances, maybe handle payroll theft?"

"Excuse me, Jill."

Ralph spoke up. "For Chrissakes, Albers, if you haven't got enough to do, I'm sure I can find something for you."

Albers shrugged and eased away from the cubicle. I took the pictures out of the envelope and laid them on his desk. "I've got a couple of ugly assholes here that I'm hoping you can match up and give me some names to go with them."

He picked the pictures up, one by one. "Ha! This one looks like a bullfrog, doesn't he?" He paused. "What makes you think I've got mugs on them?" said Bidden, as he put on his glasses and studied them.

"Nothing but a hunch that they are from here, to be honest with you, Ralph." I went on to explain the entire Hubbard deal and where I'd gotten the pictures.

"Man, did you catch a break with that kid, huh? Shit like that never happens, ya' know? This is still one hell of a long shot, Hawk. Of course, you know that."

"Is the Pope a Catholic?"

Bidden scooted his chair closer to his desk and tapped the enter key on his computer. "Well, let's roll them." With that, he typed something in and began to scroll from page to page. It was like slowly thumbing through a loose leaf notebook.

"They're paged in alphabetical order, not that it matters," said Bidden. "With two of us, we should be able to spot them pretty quickly if, in fact, they are in the system. Maybe we'll luck out. They might be progressive offenders."

"Ralph, I'm still not sure what was actually involved here. As I told you, I still haven't got a positive handle on why Hubbard was kidnapped, and now he's dead."

"Sounds like a homicide case to me," he said as he continued to scroll through the pages of some of the ugliest people God put on this earth, and yet others were nice-looking, everyday Joe types that one would not expect to be a part of the book.

"What in the hell is your stake in this, Hawk? We may be looking at one hell of a lot of mug shots before we score. You realize that, right?"

Triple Crossed

"Yeah. I'm afraid so. As you can see with their pictures, the two guys don't look like your run-of-the-mill street thugs."

Bidden continued to sift through screen after screen and said, "Who knows? Just because they were wearing ties doesn't necessarily mean you're looking for business types."

We looked at pictures for nearly forty-five minutes when Bidden suddenly stopped scrolling and looked up at me the way you look when you open your front door and see it's a Jehovah's Witness.

"Lookee here at what we've got." He pointed to the screen and I leaned in to scrutinize the face he pointed to.

He stood up now, waiting for me to pull the string.

"Holy shit! That's one of them, isn't it?"

"Think so. Let me isolate it and see what we've got." He clacked some more keys and we had the dope on the guy. Bidden read aloud:

"Keith Parker Alcott...originally from St. Paul. Small-time dealer, moved to Chicago five years ago when he got tired of the twin cities cops busting his balls." Bidden paused, then said: "We got him on assault and possession of cocaine. He went away for a year. When he got out, he got busted two more times, looks like for holding, but it was small amounts of marijuana so he was cut loose. His sheet is a lengthy one, partner. We lucked out."

I slapped Bidden on the back. "Good work, Ralph. I owe you big time."

"Yeah, well, I can't do any more for you right now. I've got that meeting coming up."

"That's okay. You've given me a start. You think you'll be able to get back to it today?"

"To find the other guy, you mean?"

"Yeah, if you can?"

"Okay, I'll give it my best shot. Call me before five and I'll let you know. How's that?"

"Sounds good." We shook hands. "Thanks again, Ralph."

On the way out, I stared at Jill hard enough to stop her heart, and then I left.

As she passed, she gave me the finger. Obviously she thought I was number one.

Chapter Eighteen

After the Italian salute from Jill Albers, I put on my jacket, grabbed my keys, stopped at the candy machine for a pack of Chuckles, and drove north towards the medical examiner's office. I did a lot of thinking on the way.

I knew all along that this had become police business and I was no longer a cop. By pursuing it, I was flirting well beyond the bounds of what was legal. For one thing, I was withholding evidence. I had no intention of stopping just yet, but I had made up my mind that if I did make significant progress, I'd turn everything I had over to Lieutenant Andrews at the police department.

However, now that Thad Hubbard was dead, I wanted to find his killer or killers. His wife had originally hired me to detect possible acts of infidelity by her husband. In other words, she thought he was screwing around on her. But then it became more than that when he went missing and she had hired me to find him.

Back when I took the case, little did I realize my next meeting with Beth Hubbard would be at the City Morgue, where she was coming to identify her husband's body. When I got there, I parked and paused for a moment to enjoy the almost-noon morning with its bright sunshine and irregular shadows near the entrance.

The medical examiner was longtime City Employee, Orville Stone, known to everybody as "Stoney." Originally from Alabama, he was a cheery, good ol' boy with a morbid sense of humor, but more than qualified in his field. Twenty-two years to be exact, and anyone could take what he said as gospel.

Stoney could not be described as having a neck like a fireplug. He had no neck at all. His jowls and chin seem to grow straight down into his shoulders. His starched shirt and gold collar pin didn't help his appearance either. The man had a voice that sounded like he swallowed a plug of chewing tobacco.

He was wearing a white smock when I found him sitting behind the huge mahogany desk of which he was so proud.

"Hey, Stoney. Thanks for the heads up earlier. I appreciate it. Has the Hubbard woman called since we talked?"

Triple Crossed

"Hey, Hawkins." His fingers on top of the desk pad were as thick as sausages, the nails broken down to the quick. He shook my hand, but didn't ask me to sit down or even look at me directly. He simply clicked a fingernail against a paper spindle, as though he were involved in an abstract thought.

"Yeah, she called, said she would be here at one-thirty or thereabouts. I like that, prompt and courteous. I think she's stalling. But they all do when it comes to seeing their loved ones with a tag on their toe. We still got about a half hour or more before she gets here. I suppose you want to visit the deceased before she arrives."

"Yeah, if you don't mind. Have you come to any conclusions without the complete autopsy?"

Stoney sighed and stood up.

"Andrews from Homicide called earlier and I told him, just like I'm telling you. One, the man is dead. Two, it wasn't a gunshot or a knifing. Could be poisoning of some kind, I suppose. Lots of needle marks on his arms. It sure as hell wasn't natural causes took this man from us. Of course, when we cut him open, we'll see what's what. Come on, follow me. And don't touch anything."

I followed him as he waddled down a shiny linoleum floor to a set of split doors and then we passed through a second set. His shoulders seemed to swing to and fro with each step and our footfalls echoed in the hallway. A wooden bench about eight feet long sat against the wall.

Stoney finally stopped in front of a heavy steel door and casually reached into the pocket of his smock. Pulling out a jar of Vicks, he said, "Here. I think you'll appreciate some of this under that private eye nose of yours." He grinned. "Put this mask on, too, Hawk."

I saw the large plate glass viewing window just to the right of the door. It was curtained on the inside.

Inside, the room was cold, but even the frigid air couldn't prevent the smell of death. The stench was an entity, a presence. It was invisible, yet it forced its way into the senses.

Stoney led me inside to a stainless steel table and pulled back the sheet covering the body of Thad Hubbard and dropped it over his genitals.

"Like I said, the guy is dead."

"Yeah. I think we can dispense with the funnies, Stoney."

"What?" He looked at me with a straight face. "Just stating a fact, detective. Don't be so touchy." With that he rotated one of Hubbard's arms so the underside was showing. "See these red dots all up and down here?"

He pointed. "Them's needle marks, my friend. A lot of them, too. If I was to guess, I'd say your pigeon was shooting up. Exactly what, who knows? Could be crack, heroin, Draino...God only knows today. Could be anything."

Stoney's cell phone played "Taps" and he answered.

"Stone." He listened and I watched him yank the sheet back up on Hubbard's body as he spoke. "Yep. Okay. She by herself?" Then pausing he said, "Okay, send her back." He snapped the phone closed. "Bethany Hubbard is up front. Sheila's bringing her back right now."

"This is the worst part," I said.

"Yeah, but it all depends on how you look at it, I guess. Slicing him open ain't no picnic." He positioned the table by the viewing window and we both went out into the hall to meet them.

We waited a few minutes until a medical assistant named Sheila Buford brought Beth back as far as the first set of double doors. We met her there.

Wearing a blue-and-white vertical striped blouse and a navy skirt, Beth's heels were black and tall and registered her quickened pace with their clacking on the hard floor. As she moved closer, I noticed a tiny silver necklace with a diamond pendant on her long neck. She had put on some makeup, dabs of smoky eye shadow and mauve lipstick that went with her engagement ring, roughly the size of a walnut.

She had a jumbled look of intense denial, of desperate hope and of shock. The look would soon change to something much, much worse. I wished I were in a position to just tell the woman her husband must have run off with another woman.

When she looked at me, her face was pale, her mouth trembling. "Oh, Cleve. What in the world happened to my Thad?"

Stoney waited barely a moment before he pistoned a hand out and said, "I'm Orville Stone, the Medical Examiner, Mrs. Hubbard." They shook hands and he said, "Follow me, please."

I stood with Beth outside of the curtained window while Stoney went through the door to his lab. A few moments passed before the curtains were drawn. Stoney then slowly pulled the sheet down, exposing Thad Hubbard's body down to the waist.

Beth threw her hands over her mouth and said, "Oh my God. Thad. It's really him. Thad!" She splayed both hands on the glass and sobbed. "I don't know why, but I was hoping so much it wouldn't be true."

She curled herself into me and I guided her to the bench.

Triple Crossed

Her face got red and squeezed up. Tears began to roll down her cheeks. She clasped both hands together in her lap and lowered her head as if she were studying her grip and she began to sob. I put my arm around her vibrating shoulders and watched while she kept sobbing at her lap. For a moment the vibration changed to a whole body shake. I fully expected her to run.

Then the shaking subsided and she put her head on my shoulder. She was still breathing rapidly.

"It will take time, but we will find out what happened. I promise you that, Beth."

She considered that for a moment and then threw back her head and made a Virginia Slims-husky laugh. She bit her lower lip, caught herself and stopped doing it. For a moment all expression left her face. Then she gave me a look that was both frightened and defiant.

"You were supposed to follow him. This wouldn't have happened if you had been following him like I hired you to do, would it?"

"Beth, that's just not the case. Look, I never really had a chance to tail him. We both know that."

Stoney stepped back out into the hall. He had a clipboard with him. "Is that man your husband, Mrs. Hubbard?"

She nodded. "Yes. What killed him? I didn't even see any blood. Was he shot?"

"No, ma'am."

"Well, what then?

"We still have to conduct an autopsy on your husband. He was found out of state and the cause of death is yet to be determined. You will be contacted as soon as it is complete, I assure you. Now, if you would please sign these papers, I would appreciate it."

Beth took the clipboard and while she signed, he said. "Those are releases stating that you have in fact identified your husband. Someone from the police department will be contacting you for further information. I may call if I have any questions, too. Do you have any further questions right now, Mrs. Hubbard?"

Beth shook her head. The crying was obviously over.

She shrugged as she stood, and I watched as she pulled a pack of cigarettes and a lighter out of her purse. I stopped her when she began to light up. "Not in here. If you're ready, we can go outside."

"Damned right. Let's go, before I scream."

We headed for the door, I aimed and shot Stoney once by dropping my thumb on my forefinger and left.

We walked side by side on the way out to the front of the building. Outside, Beth lit her cigarette and blew a huge plume of smoke in my face.

"Smart guy. You were so smug. You promised me you would find my husband and now he's dead." She turned away and stared off in the distance.

"Beth, I really..."

"Never mind. How long will it take them to figure out what killed my Thad?"

"I'm not sure, but I would guess three days at the outside. Can I drive you someplace?"

She continued to look the other way. "No. Carl will pick me up." Suddenly she whirled back around. "I want you to find out who killed my husband, Mister Hawkins. Will you do that?"

"I'll try, but you do realize that this is a police matter. And I am no longer a cop."

"So? What difference does that make?"

"I can only do so much, but I promise I will do all I can. You just be sure to tell the police department that you have asked me to continue on the case."

"Yes, okay. God, how I hate this whole mess. Why me? Why?"

"You mean, why Thad, don't you?"

"No. I meant, why me?"

Her eyes were still pleading with me when Carl pulled up to the curb in her Mercedes.

My phone vibrated on my hip, and I grabbed it.

"Yeah."

"Hawk?"

"Yeah."

"This is Bidden. I've got a present for you, snooper. Maybe change that foul fuckin' mood of yours."

"Yeah? Lay it on me, Ralph."

"I found your other perp. Name's Walker, Benjamin Charles Walker. He's a Chicago alumnus. Pulled all his shit in Illinois, looks like. Did four years for armed robbery back in 2010. Liquor store in Evanston. He's got a long sheet that includes theft and smuggling of firearms among other felonies. You look in the dictionary under criminal, you'll find this clown's picture."

"Good work, Ralph. Fast, too. I didn't think I'd hear from you for a couple of days, partner."

"Yeah, my wife says I'm too damned fast. So, when you coming in to see this guy's snapshot? I won't be here after five-thirty. Old lady's folks are coming over for supper."

"I'm on my way, Ralph. See ya' in a few."

After I'd pulled out into traffic, I'd gone about four blocks when I noticed somebody in a maroon sedan who appeared to be following me. I knew I was jumpy, but kept an eye on the car to be sure it wasn't my imagination.

R.C. Hartson

Chapter Nineteen

I'd played this game of cat 'n mouse enough to know whoever was tailing me had to have picked me up long before I stopped at the morgue.

The afternoon was slipping into early evening, and the sun was dropping into the western sky when I turned right and headed for Lake Shore Drive, noting that block after block, the maroon sedan continued to follow.

He had to brake now and then in order to keep his distance when cars in front of him turned left or right. I knew the driver either was a real amateur or just didn't give a shit whether I spotted him or not.

I traveled west four or five blocks while he stayed back about five to six car lengths. It was a late model Chrysler. The right front fender had a big gash in it like a twisted smile. Although I couldn't make out the driver's face, I could see he was wearing a baseball cap and wasn't alone. Somebody was in the passenger seat with the visor flipped down.

I drove a few more blocks north and decided to head back toward the police department by doubling back around. If my plan worked, I wondered what my tail's reaction would be when I pulled up behind him. Swinging wide to the right, I headed south on State, hung a tight left, then another three blocks and came back traveling south on Michigan Avenue.

The light at Harrison was red and while I was stopped, I checked all my mirrors, but no longer saw the Chrysler either in front of or behind me. How in the hell did that happen? I banged the heels of my hands on the steering wheel. I didn't know how I'd lost the sonofabitch, but he was gone.

The big question was *who* was tailing me. And *why?*

I continued on to the police department, parked in the cop's parking lot next to the cruisers and went inside to see Bidden. He was putting his jacket on.

"Hey, Hawk. You made it in time. Good. I was just getting ready to make like the donkey peddler and haul ass." He grinned. "You look rattled and flushed, pal. You and God have a lover's quarrel?"

I wasn't in the best of moods, and I used the good old-fashioned crime solver technique. I shut my mouth and let the other party continue.

"Well, if you're looking for sympathy, buddy, you'll find it in the dictionary between shit and syphilis." He reached into the center drawer of his desk and pulled out a brown eight-by-ten envelope. Showing me the mug shot of the man named Walker, he said, "There are two pictures here. I'm giving you good copies -- one of this guy, Walker, I found today, and the other one is that first guy we fingered. Name's Alcott."

"Thanks, Ralph." I studied the two pictures for a moment.

Bidden cleared his throat and said, "I'm not telling you what to do, partner, but I think it's time to get Andrews involved and have them put out a BOLO on both of these assholes."

I slid the pictures back into the envelope. "I'm not so sure that's the way to go with this yet, Ralph. The "Being on the Look Out" program sometimes backfires. You know that. These guys think they've gotten away clean, so we have to get all we can before every paper starts printing misleading bullshit. A BOLO gets everybody all fired up. They'll do that soon enough, know what I mean?"

He looked me in the eye as he closed his drawer. "I'm being straight with you, Hawk. Obviously, you've got a lot of time invested in this case, but if I were you, I'd let it go."

I shrugged. "You're not me." I shook his hand and smiled. "Thanks for the help though, Ralph. I appreciate it."

He shook his head, ambled to the door and waved. "I know you do. See you around the campus, detective. Be careful."

I left and walked to my car, but caught myself looking all around for that Chrysler. I got in, rolled down my window and studied the pictures of the two men who had kidnapped Thad Hubbard.

They looked like Mutt and Jeff. Alcott, with a balding head, fat face and no neck. Bidden had been right. The guy resembled a bullfrog. The information sheet said he was five foot seven, two-hundred-and-twenty pounds. He was short and fat, just like Mutt in the comics.

Walker, on the other hand, had a narrow, horse face, short black hair, and a long neck with an over-sized Adams apple. He was six foot two inches tall, one-hundred-sixty pounds. Definitely Jeff.

Their last known addresses were there, but I was sure they were only listed for the benefit of their probation officers and they had long since moved elsewhere without reporting. Probably out of state. Walker lived northwest, in Wheeling, and Alcott had an apartment in the western suburb of Aurora. The information was more than five years old, but still, the addresses would be a start.

True enough, I'd like an all points bulletin out on the two men, but I had an idea that might not give me the plate number of the car they had been driving. If they were smart, they had gotten rid of the one they had driven to kidnap Hubbard, but there was a strong possibility the kidnappers had parked underground that day in order to handle Hubbard with the least amount of attention.

My day hadn't been a good one. It seemed as though it was turning out to be one of those days where I couldn't find my ass with both hands, but I had one idea I'd been toying with. It was past six in the evening and I would probably be wasting my time, but I decided to stop by the parking structure located around the corner from The Sinclair building on West Adams.

Getting in and out of the Loop at that hour would be hairy for sure, but I was pumped, especially after being followed by those two unknowns earlier. They had given me the slip and I was definitely pissed off about it as I edged along in the bumper-to-bumper rush hour traffic. Served me right, I guess.

The yellow arm of a gate stop was down, blocking the entrance to the parking garage. The attendant was a squirrely guy about forty, all bad skin and jutting bone. He was pale, with wispy gray hair and caterpillar fuzz above his lip. A couple of ripe zits loomed large on his forehead. On the back of his left hand he had a tattoo of a blue snake with green eyes. He wore a cheap gold chain around his wrist and "PAULY" was stitched in red above his shirt pocket.

Perched up on a high stool behind the counter, he inhaled a cigarette and squinted at me. Sucking on his teeth, he nodded to me and said, "Ten bucks an hour. How long you gonna be?"

"I don't plan on parking. Just need to ask you something."

"What did you say?" His voice was somewhere between a whisper and a growl. He flicked his cigarette and it sparked in an arc when he tossed in into the road.

"Hey, Pauly, I'm a little worried about my car. I need to know if you have good security here, partner. I don't want anything to happen to it, know what I mean?"

He smiled. "Yeah. That would tend to tighten your testicles, huh?"

"Well?"

"Well, what?"

A new bronze Cadillac pulled up behind me.

"Security, Paul. Do you have camera surveillance, for instance?"

"Cameras? Oh, yeah, we sure do. We've got cameras all over this joint. Got you covered on every floor." He paused and raised his eyebrows. "You want to park it now, Mister?"

"No. One more thing, my friend. Who's the boss and when is he here?"

"Hey, man, I don't know. There's more than one guy owns this place." He handed me a card. "Call them, if you want. But, you've got to move it now, bub. I got cars lining up behind you."

I handed the guy a ten. "Keep that for your help. I'm going to pull forward and circle around to get out, okay?"

"Yeah, whatever. Go ahead." He stuffed the ten in his shirt pocket. The guy in the Caddy gunned it and moved forward.

After I worked my way out of the Loop, I headed for my office. The late afternoon was humid and my head was throbbing. I hadn't eaten since breakfast and I decided to stop at Glenn's Diner on Clark Street. The thick smell of fried country ham wafted out the front door when I approached. The place wasn't very busy and I took a stool at the counter.

The waiter was a tall, pale man who looked as if he were about to be shoved out an airplane door. He was a meaty guy with a mustard stained white apron. There was a cigarette parked behind his ear. I picked up the menu, studied it for perhaps thirty seconds and decided on two Chicago Dogs and a cup of coffee. I devoured the hot dogs. I was starving.

While I nursed my coffee, I looked at the card that Pauly had given me. "Caliber Enterprises, Inc. Contact: Charles Gretsch Jr." There was an e-mail address. I wondered what other enterprises Caliber included.

Checking my watch, I saw it was nearly seven. What the hell. I pulled out my SmartPhone and punched in the number.

I was kind of surprised that anyone answered, but a guy did. He had the kind of booming voice that makes you want to hold the phone two inches from your ear.

"Charles Gretsch, please."

"This is Charlie. Who's callin'?"

"Hi, Charlie, my name is Hawkins, Cleve Hawkins. I'm a private investigator looking for some information. I thought you might be able to help me."

"What? Who did you say you were?"

"Cleve Hawkins."

"A private eye, you say?"

"Yes, sir."

"I don't see how I could help you. Did my ex put you up to this shit?"

"No, Charlie. I was just over at your parking facility on West Jackson and

Pauly gave me your card."

"Why did he do that? What do you want?"

My hand was clenched tightly on the phone, my temples throbbing with a level of anger I hadn't been ready for.

"Your man was only trying to be helpful, Charlie. Anyway, here's the deal. I've been hired to track down a guy who came up missing, and he was last seen in the company of two men who I suspect parked at your place. I wanted to know if I could have a look at the recordings from your surveillance cameras. Maybe I can spot them and their car."

"Hell, I don't know. I never been asked this shit before. Is it legal?"

"There's nothing illegal about it, sir, I assure you. Do you save the recordings from each day or week or what?"

"Well, yeah. I keep everything for sixty days. I got two other places besides that one on Jackson, ya' know, and my insurance company says I have to keep them recordings in case somebody has a claim of some kind, ya' know what I mean?"

"Yes, sir, and this would be on there sometime about two weeks ago. I'd be glad to make it worth your while, if I could have a look."

"No, you ain't gotta' pay me nothin'. I don't work that way." There was a long pause before he said, "Somebody's missing, I want to help. Your name is...what did you say?"

"Hawkins, Cleve Hawkins."

"Yeah. Hold on a sec, will ya'? Let me get a pen and paper."

"Sure."

He wasn't gone long.

"Okay. I'm back and I'm writing. That's Hawkins, right?"

"Yes, sir. Cleve's the first name."

"Yeah, well, you can quit calling me sir, okay? Call me Charlie. How do ya' like that, Cleve?"

"Fine, Charlie."

"Okay, you got an office, a phone number, somewhere I can reach you, Cleve? Boy, there's a name for you. Cleve, huh?"

I didn't reply.

"You there?"

"Yeah, Charlie, I'm here." I gave him the number of my SmartPhone as well as the one at the office.

"Okay, Cleve, so let's make a deal. I'm clear tomorrow after eleven in the morning. I'll call you if that changes. Otherwise, I'll still call and give you directions so you can come by my place after lunch, say one o'clock, and we'll see what's what. That okay with you?"

I thought that was a lot of unnecessary bullshit, but the payoff could be worth it and I said, "That'll work just fine, Charlie. See you tomorrow and thanks."

Maybe the day wasn't such a bust after all.

R.C. Hartson

Chapter Twenty

Beth Hubbard staggered as if she had been struck. She reached behind herself, found the armchair and sank into it.

Her dark blonde hair was pulled back and fixed with a matter-of-fact tortoise shell barrette. With just a touch of makeup, no perfume, her thick brown eyebrows drawn low and menacing, and her mouth held in a tight slash of blood red lipstick, she looked rougher than usual.

She closed her eyes, massaged the lids and exhaled long and slow.

Carl Cosgrove, her "live-in assistant," approached and was standing a few feet away when she opened her blue eyes. She studied him with a level stare. He wore tan slacks and a short-sleeved blue shirt with daisies printed on it. The back of his neck was pitted. His hair, thin and gray, was cut short, lightly oiled and clipped.

Beth saw the smug look on his face as he gazed around the room and took a big drink from his tumbler of vodka. The ice made a clunking sound against the glass when he sat it down.

"We've got a problem," said Beth, raspy, borderline terrified.

Taking a seat on a matching chair in front of her, Carl rubbed the backs of his hands, his coarse skin making a whispering sound. A smirk crept over his face as he saw impatience and irritability flicker in her eyes. "Okay, so what's got your panties in a twist, now?"

"Don't talk to me like that," she hissed. "You don't seem to care that things are turning to shit."

The muscle in his jaw locked. "Hey, I'm tired of hearing about what could have been, should of been. You begged me to handle this whole deal, and I did. In fact, I did everything just the way you wanted. Now, because things didn't work out perfectly, you want to bawl and bail. Well, not this time, sister. Shit happens...what's done is done. We're moving on."

She could see the color rising in his neck and she hesitated before she said, "Please pay attention, Carl. This Cleve Hawkins has turned out to be a real pain in the ass. I should never have hired him. That was a bad idea." She paused. "Okay,

Triple Crossed

my fault, I know, but you agreed with the plan and now I can't get rid of him."

"Yeah, but at the time we *all* figured it was a good idea just to keep you looking clean when your old man disappeared. It worked and I told you, don't sweat Hawkins. He's a loser who can't find his own dick with a pair of salad tongs. He's a joke. Why do you think he's not a cop anymore? Nobody listens to him. The man's a nobody, a fart in a gale."

"But you said he's nailed down mug shots of your men, Toad and Walker."

"Yeah. No problem. Toad and Walker are pros. They hang together like shit and stink. One goes down, they'll both go down, but they're up to speed and they won't cave. Besides, worse comes to worse, they can be eliminated too."

"See, Carl, you scare me with that kind of talk."

"Scared? You? Hey, I remember when you had a taste for cocaine and cowboys, both of which you supposedly gave up when you got hitched." He grinned. "But that taste has not necessarily gone away, has it, Mrs. Hubbard?"

She shook her head. "That wasn't necessary, you bastard." Wringing her hands, she said, "I don't want anything to do with it anymore." She flicked a hand that said *You and your people are flies.*

"Listen, Toad and Walker have got it covered. They even got a couple of other guys to follow Hawkins for a couple of days while he's been snooping. Alright, the man's as persistent as a pissed off Pit Bull, but we think he's reached a dead end." Carl blew a puff of smoke. "Toad says Hawkins spotted the guys tailing him, by the way, so they had to back off."

"What?" Beth said, her hand going to her lips.

Carl held up his hands like a traffic cop. "There you go again. See, I shouldn't tell you some of this shit. You get bent out of shape too easy. I told you I'll handle everything and I will. The boys will just put a new tail on him in a couple of days. He's ready to hang it up. You haven't heard from him since that day at the morgue, right?"

"Right."

Doubt passed like a shadow over Beth's face. She stared at the floor and murmured, "Thad wasn't supposed to die. I feel terrible about that." She stood and edged her way over to the living room windows. The sun was disappearing on the horizon as she dabbed at her eyes with a Kleenex and watched a strong breeze scatter the few leaves still on the trees. The color of the lawn was a dull, depressing shade of brown that wouldn't change until spring. More depression to coddle.

"You said the people in New Jersey, or wherever, would just get the information they wanted and bring Thad back." She whirled around to face him.

Her voice sounded shaky. She suddenly looked as though she were drowning, her eye shadow running, her cheeks wet: "You killed him," she yelled.

"Hey, bullshit, girl. Not me!" Carl said, looking stung. Painting himself innocent was an art he had mastered.

He loved playing the big shot, putting people in their place, handing out favors to people, crewing a cigarette into his mouth, firing it up with a Zippo, snapping the lid back tight, like he was the man in control. He was a quick study in contrasts, successful but badly dressed, intelligent but plain-faced, smiling but vicious, mild-spoken but sharp-tongued.

"Well, you had it done," she said.

"I didn't have a damned thing to do with any killing," he growled. "I repeat, *I didn't kill anybody.* You'd best watch that smart mouth, baby. This whole thing was your idea from the get go. If you weren't so fucking needy and greedy..." He paused. "You know I'm not used to taking orders, but I did what you told me. Now, *Do not* fucking make me regret it."

His gaze wandered along the painting-laden walls, his breathing audible in the silence that followed. He finally said, "Your old man had an accident. An accident, get it?" He turned his head away as though avoiding his own words. "Look at it that way and you'll be fine." His face was without expression, his eyes empty. He put his hand inside his shirt collar and picked at a mosquito bite on his shoulder. "You need to settle down. No shit."

Beth hated his attitude and she felt betrayed. She put her hands on her hips like an angered school principal and looked sideways out the window as though the room were too small for the level of anger she needed to express.

"An accident, hell, that's more bullshit! I cannot, and will not, pretend it was, you bully. Thad is dead and we both know it wasn't an accident."

Carl sniggered as he stood and made his way over to stand beside her. "Don't pretend you cared that much about him, baby. Come on, get over it. You'll be fine." He caressed her shoulder with his fingertips and brushed his lips across the back of her neck.

She turned. "What the hell do you expect, Carl. He was *my husband* after all."

"Ha! Your meal ticket, you mean."

Beth slapped his face with a resounding smack. "I said don't talk to me like that!" She stepped back. "And, if you don't stop touching me, I'll get somebody I know to break off your hand and cram it up your ass."

Carl glared. His mouth hung open as he grabbed her by the shoulders. He snorted like a broken diesel.

Triple Crossed

"Damn you! Don't ever do that again, you spoiled little bitch."

She pulled away and turned her back to him. Sniffling into a Kleenex, she continued to stare out the windows and thought the red leaves that now blew out of the maples and oaks were no more an indication of a person's mortality than the nature of the people. When they disappeared, they would be quickly replaced by others whose likeness to them would barely show that a transition had taken place.

Yes, Carl is replaceable, she thought, but not yet.

Carl waited for her to retaliate, but she didn't. She gazed down the street, her chin raised slightly, her pulse fluttering in her throat. There was silence for a beat until she finally turned to face him again.

"I'm sorry, Carl, but everything is falling apart and I'm feeling so damned helpless. I'm afraid. Don't you understand?" She wrapped her arms around herself and her whole body trembled.

It got Carl to stare at her straight on, deadpan, before managing a kind of a smile. "Come on and sit down, baby. We'll talk."

She followed him into the study and rested her butt on the edge of the desk.

"Okay, let's take it by the numbers," he said. "There's nothing that can't be fixed. You've just gotta chill out and relax, though. I told you, I'll take care of Hawkins. What else are you worried about? The cops?"

"I don't know…I mean, I'm not sure."

"Well, I'm saying, don't worry about the cops either. There's no fuckin' way they could be on to us. I got it figured, after the autopsy, they're gonna write Thad's death off as a drug overdose."

She slid a cigarette out of a pack of Slims that lay on the desk and said, "I wondered about the autopsy report and I actually called the police and asked who was handling the case. When I was done, I hung up and worried they'd trace me, worried I'd get a call back. But it never happened."

"No, and it won't." He leaned in to give her a light. "Police lines don't have caller I. D. so people won't be inhibited about giving tips."

"Oh." She let herself look confused. A fairly simple task, Carl thought.

He nodded and winked at her as she exhaled a plume of smoke. He waited and watched her tap the cigarette in the ashtray, twice, three times. He leaned back in his chair and held her eyes for a few moments, looking to see what he might find there.

"What else have you got?" he asked her.

Beth picked up a green folder that had been lying next to the computer with CEI in an elaborate design on the cover. She showed Carl the stock certificates and statements from Carrington Engineering Industries which were inside.

"I went on the computer and looked up the Stock Exchange and found Carrington's web page through Google. I knew most of what they had, but anyway, it told me what we already know. We have to unload our 52,000 shares of oil stock before the bottom falls out. And it will, as soon as word gets out about Operation Solid and goes public. Those oil barons are going to be jumping out windows. 1929 all over again."

"I told you. I'll handle that through Zagaretti," Carl said. "We're good there. They've got all the information they need, thanks to your husband." He lowered his voice as if harboring a secret. "Zagaretti is connected to The Outfit, and that makes it like Free Parking in Monopoly."

"Yeah...so you said." She edged over to his chair and sat on his knee. "I'm banking on that. Literally."

"Yeah, Nick Zagaretti is also a lawyer, so we have to accept the fact that he's opinionated and full of shit." He grinned. "Personally, I think he could probably sell central heating to the devil, but he's legit with our deal and we need him."

Beth placed her cigarette between his lips and watched him draw and let the smoke drift out of his mouth.

"Thanks, Carl," she said, biting her lip, as she leaned into his chest.

Triple Crossed

Chapter Twenty-One

The next morning I phoned Charlie Gretsch after I finished a seven a.m. workout at the gym. I'd had my usual few minutes of flirty banter with the owner's wife, Jessica, before I put on my gym shorts and running shoes. I ran three miles on the treadmill and followed that up with three sets of dead lifts, bench presses and curls. After a quick shower, I headed for the office with my day mapped out in my head.

Charlie had given me directions, instructing me to come by his place in Winnetka at ten. It would be a twenty-minute drive at most. That allowed me plenty of time to grab some eggs and take care of some loose ends before the meeting.

The sun was bouncing its first rays of the day off the restless waters of the lake shore when I headed there. The mid-October air was brisk, the humidity gone. I expected any day I would find frost on my windshield and I was already wearing my trench coat and fedora.

I found Deckle sitting on the top step smoking a cigarette. He sat, bent over, forearms on his knees, head hanging down, but jumped up when he saw me parking at the curb.

"Hey, Cleve!" His body swayed as he stood up. "Am I glad to see you. I counted three days, and I was starting to wonder if one of those boogie men got you." He tapped the ash off his cigarette and raised it to his lips for a drag.

I brushed past him and climbed the steps while pulling out my keys. "Nah. I don't sit still long enough for them to put a hurt on me, Deck. You know that."

I unlocked the door, snapped on the lights, stepped over the pile of mail and hung up my coat. Deckle was right behind me. He gathered up the mail, put it on the desk and grabbed his favorite hard-backed chair.

Holding the coffee pot up in the air, I glanced at him.

"Yup. Want me to make us some coffee, Cleve?"

I grinned. "You think you remember how, eh?"

He laughed at that, a cross between a bark and a snort. Snot ran in an elastic string from his nose to his chest.

"You're teasing me right, Cleve." He shuffled over and took the pot with a shaky hand. "Darn right, I got it."

"Good man, Deck. I know I can always depend on you. Go ahead, make it good and strong, okay?"

"Oh, sure." He rolled his eyes. "I know that's the way we like it, Cleve."

From being closed up so long, the room was hot and stuffy. I sat in the swivel chair behind my desk, turned the air conditioner vents toward my face and opened the mail. I knew I had to pay my monthly rent for fear my desk and other office necessities could be moved to the curb. I paid the rent, a couple of other urgent bills, sealed the envelopes and gave myself a mental high-five for the accomplishments.

I noticed Deckle bent over, with his eyes and nose within an inch of the pot as he waited for the coffee to finish brewing. I decided to call Mo and I'd just started to punch in her number at work when Deckle straightened up. His eyes widened as he scrambled for the door. It was not a strange action on his part so I decided to go ahead and grab a cup of coffee. I figured he'd be back shortly.

I was worried I didn't spend enough quality time with Mo. She was always on my mind, chewing at the edge of my consciousness. I needed to call.

My neighbor in the office next door, Chad Deskins, hustled vacuum cleaners for Vector Corporation, and although I didn't see him very often, he poked his head inside my door and said, "Hey, Cleve, I hate to tell you, buddy, but your pal, Deckle, just did the rainbow yawn on the sidewalk out front."

"Oh, shit, really?" I stood and Chad stepped back as I crowded past him. Deckle was swiping his mouth with the sleeve of his coat. We both shook our heads. Chad said, "Sorry, man."

Pushing that vision aside, I went back to my desk and hit Mo's number on my speed dial. We hadn't seen each other in nearly a week and when she answered, just the sound of her voice excited me.

"Lieutenant Andrew's office."

"Hi, Mo."

"Hey, stranger." She lowered her voice when she said, "Please don't tell me we are canceling tonight."

"No. All clear on my end, I just wanted to confirm the time in case you had to work late."

"No sir, Columbo. My place at six-thirty. I'll let you escort me to Harry Carey's if you like."

"Sounds good. See you then. If anything comes up, I'll be sure to call."

Triple Crossed

In a near whisper she said. "Don't let anything come up before you get to my place, slick."

I laughed. "Later, baby."

Deckle stumbled back in just before we broke the connection. He was still wiping his mouth as he took a seat. It was hard to see how the man functioned with his bleary red eyes and trembling hands.

"Sorry, Cleve. I must be catching a cold is all. I didn't want to get sick all over your floor, know what I mean?"

I nodded, pulled some money out of my pocket and peeled off five bucks. "I have to run, Deck, but I'm betting you haven't been eating right since I last saw you. Do you and me both a favor. Get some hot food in your stomach after a while, will you?"

He reached for the fin with a trembling hand and feigned a smile. "Yes sir, Cleve. You know I will. Thanks, Cleve. I sure will get something to eat, I promise." He turned and scurried out the door, leaving me to wonder where he would spend the night, and, if he would, in fact, get food or another pint.

. . .

Charlie Gretsch lived in a rich-looking colonial located on a narrow paved road. The flower beds along the front of the property were weedless and appeared to receive daily care. Between them and the road, the long wide lawn was thick and well cut. The driveway was crushed white rock. Hundreds of mums bordered the driveway and the perimeter.

I pulled in and parked in a driveway that led to a three car garage. A Cadillac Seville and a late model Mercedes SL were parked side by side on the apron.

There was a porch-like overhang at the front and a front door recessed in a wide alcove. A single door, it was at least nine feet high by four feet wide.

I got out and using the walkway, passed late-blooming flower beds of impatiens and red and pink mums. I used the gold-covered knocker and waited for somebody to answer the door. A breeze blew in from the west, scattering leaves and bringing a chill. It flirted with the tail of my trench coat.

An elderly, white-haired woman came to the front door. She was leaning on a cane and I guessed she was in her sixties, an unpleasant woman with a sour face and shrill voice.

"What do you want?" she demanded.

I showed her my badge. "Good morning, ma'am. I'm Cleve Hawkins. I have an appointment with Mister Gretsch for ten o'clock."

She stared at me for what seemed like a long and unnerving time before Charlie slid in behind her like magic.

"I've got it, Sis." He waggled a bent finger at the woman.

"Come on in, Hawkins." He stuck out his hand and we shook. "Charlie Gretsch. Don't mind my sister. She's a bit superstitious and cautious. Come in."

"Hello, Charlie. No problem." I stepped into the entry hall and scrubbed my shoes on the mat. His sister disappeared. An enormous hairy cat sat on the hall table. It made a noise like a squeaky toy and jumped to the floor with a thump.

Charlie was a small man about sixty with a hard-boiled look and small, mean eyes. He looked like a 120-pound opossum. He reached inside his jacket, dug out a Winston cigarette and dangled it from his lip. He had a brush mustache, and I noticed his nicotine-stained fingers when we shook hands. There was also an $8,000 gold Rolex watch on his left wrist and a $3,000 Wesley Barron pinstripe suit on the rest of him. He wore a Kangol cap of all things. Later he would tell me he had been wearing soft Kangol caps as long as he could remember. "Longer than Samuel L. Jackson had been wearing his backwards," he said.

The foyer was rich and opulent with chandeliers, polished wood floor and oriental rugs. On one wall, cursive gold letters painted on a mirror spelled the name Gretsch.

Charlie led the way and guided me down a short, but wide hallway into a den with lots of light stained pinewood paneling and dark green paint on the walls. A pair of mahogany tables sat back-to-back on one side of the room, each fully equipped with computers, copiers, phone-fax machines and the usual clerical clutter. I had to admit I was somewhat impressed.

He pointed to an easy chair in front of a long oak desk. "Have a seat. How about a cup of coffee?" He pointed to a setup placed on a silver tray on one side of the desk.

I smiled. The offer instantly brought my earlier time with Deckle to mind.

"Yes, thanks."

Charlie stood and poured two cups. "Cream or sugar?"

"No, black's fine."

"So, Hawkins, before we start, can I see your ID? A badge or somethin'? Not that I don't believe you, understand. It's just...well, let's just say I conduct things with caution."

"Sure." I reached in my coat pocket, pulled out my wallet and showed him my shield.

Triple Crossed

He scrutinized it and, satisfied, said, "Good enough," as he sat in a swivel chair behind his desk. "I can spot a cop a mile away, you know. It's in the way they walk, in the eyes, in the mustache. You...you're not a cop."

I grinned and said, "I see."

"So tell me more about this kidnapping. You say it happened in my garage, Cleve?" He grinned. "That name sure gets me. Cleve. I like it. In fact, if I had a kid, I'd probably name him that. Ha, ha." He allowed himself a smile.

I was anxious to stay on track. "Let me make a long story short, Charlie. I've got two guys on tape escorting the kidnapped man down Adams, turning to the left and I think they took him to a vehicle parked in your Jackson Street garage on Friday, September first. If I'm right about that, we might be able to track them by the make, model and license plate number. You say you keep the recordings filmed by cameras in your place, is that right?"

He sucked his teeth and nodded. "Damn right. We keep them sixty days. I'm nobody's fool, and I don't lie, like a lot of assholes." He hesitated before saying, "Like the Catholics. Are you Catholic, Hawkins?"

"No."

"Good. Nutty Catholics," he grumbled. "Only know how to do two things, screw and beg forgiveness. Can you believe it? My daughter is gonna marry a Catholic next spring. Ha!" He frowned and continued. "My ex is all for the marriage. You think that don't boil my nuts? I can't stand the lying little prick. I just know the wedding's gonna be a puke fest."

I nodded as he exhaled smoke through his nose.

"Anyway, people come around claiming all sorts of shit. Schemers, you know? Telling me shit has been stolen from their cars or saying somebody dented their fenders and on and on." He waved a hand in disgust and paused. "Hell, I even had one idiot wanting me to keep an eye out for his wife, who he claimed was screwing her boss in the back seat of his Lexus. Like, I care. Me and my partners have to stay on our toes, alright."

He took another long slow drag on his cigarette. "Sometimes the bitching is legit, but not very often." He leaned across the desk, lowered his voice and winked. "I've got records to back us up, no matter what. Fuckin' vagrants are the problem. They go into our places to piss in the corners and try all the car doors there in search of change. Assholes."

I jumped at the chance to get a word in: "It's great that you stay on top of things, Charlie. How difficult will it be to access the date and time I just gave you, then?"

"Hell, no trouble at all. Come around here. We'll take a look." He flipped open a laptop that sat on his desk and I edged around to stand on his right. While the laptop was booting up, he said, "That was at our place on Jackson, right?"

"That's right. Where are your other locations, Charlie?"

"Ahhh, we've got one on Randolph and another over on North Dearborn. We've got other investments, too, but these parking structures are the biggies. A real pain in the ass, though. If it wasn't for the good money, I swear, I'd get out of the fuckin' business." He paused briefly and looked up at me. "Sorry about the language. I've got an incurable speech defect."

"No problem. Go ahead with what you're doing."

He navigated the mouse and brought up programs, then locations, and finally under "Jackson Street," found a heading titled security and service.

"Okay, here we are." He clicked a few more keys. "And we want the video for September first, you said, right?"

"Right."

"What time of day was it? We can shorten this up a bit, ya know? We'd be here the whole fuckin' day otherwise."

"Yeah, our records show it was 3:46 p.m. when our man left work at the Sinclair Building, so I would say right around 4:00 p.m. -- give or take a few minutes either way -- would be very close to the time you want to bring up."

"Good. That shouldn't be a problem then and I hope we find the guys you want are on our property. Let's see."

Charlie fast-forwarded the video and stopped ever so often to check the time in the lower right corner of the tape. He wasn't too swift on the computer and the time seemed to be dragging by.

"There. Look! See that guy? He's taking a piss by his car. Told ya. Sonofabitches can't wait 'till they get home." He continued to move the video ahead and then stopped. "Okay, here we go. Here...see the time is saying 3:45 p.m. That should do it. Have a look," he said as he sat back and lit another cigarette.

I hunched over his shoulder and watched.

"Here," he said as he pushed me aside and slid off the chair. "I got the right place. Why don't you sit here? Hell, I'll get out of the way. You know who you're looking for. I don't."

I was lucky, I guess. It didn't take long before I hit gold. Thad Hubbard and two men, one on each side of him, passed in front of a camera by the entrance. They disappeared into the garage and were headed for the garage elevator when I lost sight of them. But the recording continued until nearly twelve minutes later

Triple Crossed

when I saw one of the men paying the parking attendant. He was the same guy who looked like a bullfrog in his mug shot.

They were driving a blue Buick LeSabre, but I only saw two men in the car. That meant one was missing. Thad Hubbard must have been in the trunk. I watched as they pulled out and spotted their Illinois plate. I paused the video.

"Got 'em!" I turned to Charlie and handed him a USB device. "Here, Charlie. Do you mind giving me a copy of this video?"

"Hell, no." He stubbed out his cigarette in a king-sized ashtray and said, "I'm just glad I save shit like this. Let me sit down there. I'll copy it right now."

"Thanks, Charlie."

My heart was as heavy as an anvil in my chest and I knew more than ever, I would have no peace until I found the killers of Thad Hubbard.

R.C. Hartson

Chapter Twenty-Two

I thought about stopping at the Redhead on Ontario for a drink. I hadn't had any booze since Sunday and I could feel the fight going on within me, the longing for a little buzz, the urge to get out of my head, smashing up against the vague feeling that something had been accomplished and that it would be a shame to throw it all away.

When I worked homicide, I'd believed I was happier without a real life. The job was a safe place. I knew what to expect. I knew who I was, where I fit in. I've never been good at any of that without the badge, even the PI badge.

When I got back to my office, I found three visitors who had the balls to let themselves in without me. I doubted they were in need of my detective services. One was sitting in my chair with his feet up on my desk. He stared hard at me. I resisted the urge to shudder.

Another had his back to the wall near the filing cabinet. He stood there looking like something out of a Raymond Chandler novel. His long coat had the collar turned up, his hands were stuffed in the pockets and an old fedora slouched down over his forehead.

The third, younger-looking guy, had a round face splattered with freckles and zits. He had a military hair cut that didn't help his look at all. He straddled my extra chair, the straight-backed one that Deckle favored when I wasn't busy. The kid was pathetic. He looked as menacing as Howdy Doody on a bicycle.

I realized Deckle was nowhere to be seen. Not that he was supposed to be there, but it was rare not finding him sitting on the front steps. A lot of blood rushed into my face and I felt a jolt of adrenaline zap my chest. I wanted to kick some ass.

"You're Hawkins, right?" the one in my chair growled.

"Damn it to hell. You bust in my place to lean on me. At least you could read the lettering on the door. No...I'm Harvey Quaginfrigger, Accountant...Hawkins is three doors down. But be careful. He doesn't care for inconsiderate assholes putting their feet on his desk."

Triple Crossed

His thick eyebrows climbed his forehead and he stood quickly. He was a big man, like all bouncers and leg breakers tend to be. He had a bald head shaped like an egg and wore a black leather jacket, as did the kid.

"Nice jackets," I said. "Was K-Mart having a sale? Two-for-one rat skin?"

Baldy seemed to be in charge and frowned as he said, "I'll cut to the chase."

"Yippee." I said as I edged behind my desk and pushed within a few inches of where he sat. He grinned, stood up and stepped back. I saw the bulge of the gun he wore on his right side. I eased into my chair and flicked my eyes at the other two.

The young one with the military haircut wore dark sunglasses. He stood cocky and sure, popping gum as he looked at me.

The clown by the filing cabinet smirked and sighed as he demonstrated the perfect slouch.

Baldy didn't say anything as I inched my hand under the desk, not far from the right-hand drawer.

"I'll spell it out for you," he said.

"Good. Let me know if you need any help."

He glared. "You keep being a smartass and they'll be cleaning you up off of Wells Street with a mop."

I nodded. "Could you say that one more time, only slower, and squint your eyes? You'll look more badass that way."

The young one snickered.

"Shut the fuck up," snapped Baldy.

"Young dudes these days. Hard to train, huh?" I said.

"It's like this. Your services are no longer required on behalf of Mrs. Bethany Hubbard."

"Really? Says who?"

"Don't push it, Hawkins. You have no idea the kind of people you're pissing off with your fuckin' snooping."

"That's where you're wrong. I know who I'm pissing off, and pissing on, for that matter. You're getting near the top of that list, my friend. Would you like me to write a note for you to take back to whoever pays you for this shake-em-up bullshit?"

Baldy looked at me, his eyes narrowed and he said, "Joey. . . "

The young kid stood holding a gun. He had to be Joey. The older guy with the fedora pushed himself off the wall. They both walked toward my desk.

"Hold on," I said, reaching for my yellow legal pad and a pen. I did so with my left hand, using my right to open the drawer. Picking up the pen I reached in the drawer for my .357. "So, let me get this straight." I started to write. "First, I need to stop checking into the disappearance of Thad Hubbard. Second, keep my mouth shut. Is there a third part I have to remember?"

I heard the stomping of feet outside my door but couldn't stop Deckle before he barged in. Freckles held the gun loose by his right leg. Deckle stopped after two steps inside. His head swiveled from back and forth and settled on me.

"Oh, hi, Cleve." His eyes jerked from side to side. "Sorry, my man. I didn't know you was busy. Real sorry."

"Who's this bum?" said Baldy.

"A good friend of mine coming to visit." I winked at Deckle and waved towards the door. "He was just leaving, weren't you Deck?"

"Yup. I'm goin'." He stumbled backwards and then, after quickly righting himself, said, "See you later, Cleve."

He left the door ajar on the way out. Howdy Doody kicked it closed.

The fedora thug began to reach into his jacket. I grabbed the Magnum and pointed it dead center on the bald guy's chest. He swallowed and stood still, breathing hard.

"Drop the gun, kid," I said. My eyes flicked over each one of them. The young man smiled, but soon the smile disappeared. He let go of the gun. It clattered to the floor.

"Okay, I don't appreciate the B&E you boys pulled here today. I should call the cops. I've got office hours like everybody else. Call next time before you come. Now, all of you walk out the door and go away. I'll need to fumigate the place after you're gone."

The one with the shaved head spit on the floor and tromped out. The Boston Blackie guy smirked at me as he followed the leader. The kid was still standing like a deer in headlights, unsure whether to leave his gun or not. I waved my piece signaling him to the door in order to help him make up his mind. He said, "Fuck you," and turned and left.

I looked out and spotted them getting into a late model black Cadillac. I set the .357 on my desk. I couldn't make out the tag number, but knew they'd be back. Question was, who did they work for and why were they trying to muscle me?

I learned a long time ago if a detective gets tunnel vision on one aspect of a case, he runs the risk of missing crucial pieces of the puzzle. You can't know where everything fits if you can't see the big picture. Given enough time it would come into focus, but I was running low on patience.

Triple Crossed

. . .

When I got to Mo's place, she regarded me from her front door with a certain resignation as I got out of the car. She flicked a cigarette butt out into the bushes while she waited to greet me.

She was wearing jeans, tan sandals, and a pink peasant top with a white ribbon threaded through the top. The front of the blouse hung straight down from her breasts. She wore a delicate turquoise necklace that chimed with her eyes and a knit sweater was draped over her shoulders. I leaned over and kissed her on the neck through the the doorway. Moths spiraled in from the night, hungry for the light.

"My mother warned me about guys like you. She said they only think of one thing."

I whispered into her ear, "Your mom was right."

"In that case, come in and make yourself comfy, Detective Hawkins." She placed a palm on the nape of my neck and ruffled my hair with the tips of her fingers. It sent a shiver all the way down to the small of my back.

"I can't believe I actually have you to myself for a while," she murmured before touching my upper lip with the tip of her tongue, just a flick there and then gone.

We fell silent until she eased out into the kitchen and poured herself a glass of wine. Over her shoulder she said, "I've got a Heine in the fridge if you want."

I shook my head. "No thanks."

"Good," she said as she moved over to the couch and patted a place for me to sit. She lit a Virginia slim and exhaled a puff of smoke. I joined her on the couch and settled in, my eyes never leaving her beautiful face. Sitting as close as possible, I slid my hand around her waist.

Patting my hand, she said, "You haven't been by the station in a couple of weeks. Are you still working on that case involving the dead chemist?"

"Yeah." I leaned forward with my forearms on my thighs, "Hey, you want to go get something to eat? We can do Harry Carey's if you like?"

Her eyes widened. "Don't change the subject, Tracy. Answer me."

I smiled. "I asked if you wanted to go out and get something to eat."

She leaned in, kissed me full on the mouth and murmured, "Nice thought, but to tell the truth, I'm only hungry for you, big guy. Seriously, I'd rather spend all this time alone, with you." She smiled. "If you're really hungry, I've got plenty of left over this and that in the fridge."

"Okay. Thanks, Mo."

She studied my face. "You look rattled. What gives? What's been going on? I heard you're still working for that Hubbard woman. Her husband was found dead. So what's left to do?"

"He was murdered, Mo."

"Then, that's homicide. Andrews's job, Cleve. Besides, the talk is Hubbard overdosed on cocaine. So let the coroner and the cops sort it out."

I was surprised. "Who told you that? I thought the results of the autopsy weren't available yet."

"Until today. I knew you were still close to the case and wanted to tell you when I saw you tonight. I'm not supposed to let stuff like this out. It could mean my job. You know that. Listen, Andrews never really got the case on his desk because it wasn't officially classified as a homicide. Now, the cause of death has been confirmed. It appears he was a closet coke addict who went on a binge. He overdid it. End of story."

"But that's bullshit, Mo. I know he was murdered and I've got good leads on who was involved. I can't just drop it, you know what I mean? Three animals came to my office this afternoon, just before I came here. They were telling me to drop it or else."

"What?" She stubbed her cigarette out in the ashtray and set her glass on the coffee table.

"That's right. Told me to drop the Hubbard case. And by the way, they had guns. Now more than ever, I can't let loose, Mo."

"Oh, no. This means you really won't stop, will you?" I read the disappointment in her face.

"No. I can't." I looked into her eyes. There was a lingering silence between us. "You know with me you get exactly what you're looking at, Mo. I'm a flatfoot at heart, a straight-line cop in a cheap J.C. Penny's suit. I'm a walking, talking stereotype who eats junk food and drinks too much. I don't run marathons or compose poetry in my spare time. If I have a question, I ask it. People don't always like that, but fuck 'em. Pardon the language. Another bad habit I won't soon get rid of. I'm knee-deep in bullshit half of the time…and I don't even mind the smell anymore."

Triple Crossed

She regarded me through wet eyes. "And you'll never change either."

"Mo, I'm used to people dying. Drug dealers kill each other over money. Junkies kill each other over dope. Husbands and wives kill each other out of hate. There's a method to the madness. But when something like this happens, I try to make some sense of it. I've tried to make my choices with the idea that I made them for the greatest good. Sometimes people have suffered in the process, but I make the decisions for the right reason. That should count for something, shouldn't it?"

I knew the need for reassurance was clear in my eyes.

"I know you do the best you can," she said. She stood and so did I.

She stared at me for a moment and whispered, "You're a good man, Cleve."

Half a smile curved my mouth. "Please say that again."

"You're--"

I touched a forefinger to her lips. They were soft and wet. "No...just my name. Say it again."

I moved my hand to cup her face. A single tear slid down her cheek as the word slipped from her lips on a trembling breath. "Cleve..."

I lifted my eyes to hers. There was a level of sadness to them that seemed to have no bottom. I stroked her red hair. I bent my head and pressed my lips to hers as desire swept through me in a warm rush.

Her hands came up slowly and rested on my forearms. Her mouth trembled beneath mine. Accepting. Wanting. Needing. Her tongue touched mine.

The kiss lingered. Time suspended. I lifted my lips a scant inch from hers and whispered, "Mo." I gathered her into my arms as carefully as if she were made of glass. When I raised my head again and looked in her eyes, she said "Make love to me now, right now."

She led me to her bedroom where the ghost of her perfume clung to the air and the sheets. Pieces of her lay scattered on the dresser. Earrings, a watch, a green velvet hair band. The lamp on the nightstand glowed amber. The light bathed her skin as I undressed her.

We didn't speak. Everything was said with a touch, with a look, a shuddering breath, a trembling sigh. When I entered her, it felt as though my heart had stopped. As we moved together, it beat like a drum.

Urgency was in command. There was the need, the heat, the pure passion. One melded into the next and back again. The feel of warm and wet, hard and soft. She came under me, her release actually scalding, then got on top of me and did it again, her breath drawing slowly in and out. When she came again, it was on a crescendo of hard-caught breaths and the desperate sounds of need.

When I finished, it was like a bolt of lightning and my body jerked and jumped with the climax. I thought I cried out, but wasn't sure.

I never stopped kissing her, even after we finished. We lay entwined and Mo fell asleep in my arms. My lips moved over hers, against her cheek, on her hair. I thought, we have this. We have now. Even if it's all we ever have, I didn't have anything else that's worth a damn by comparison.

Exhaustion swept over me like a blanket and I closed my eyes and fell asleep.

Chapter Twenty-Three

The next morning I left Mo asleep and on my vacated pillow I put an orange and a note that read "Breakfast in bed--love you--will call later. Tracy."

It had been nice to fall asleep with her in my arms and to wake up with her there. To do that more often would be a great idea. Not that I craved something permanent or a legal hook-up. Neither of us wanted that for many reasons. Rules and regulations had changed our expectations and issues of trust in a lasting relationship, and not for the better as far as I had witnessed.

Guys like me never quite learn that real love doesn't always come your way, and even when it does, it can always change its mind and walk away. Who knows? But as soon as I became more settled in my life outside of the job, and more satisfied with myself, maybe stability and a normal relationship would be possible.

I thought back to the first day I saw Mo, a face right off of a Hollywood glossy from the days of black and white and Veronica Lake. I somehow knew that what lay beneath those looks was a mystery worthy of any of the great detectives, real or fictional. That drew me in as much as her looks. I wanted to slip into her secret door and see what made her tick.

Early morning was a soft, sweet dream on the horizon to the east of the city. There were narrow strips of purple, orange and rose waiting to come into bloom like a sky bouquet. A brief overnight rain had cleared out, leaving the air fresh with the promise of Technicolor blue skies.

At quarter to six it would have taken me no time to get downtown. By quarter to seven the trip would take twice as long. I negotiated a lane change around a snot green Pontiac Firebird doing twenty with a white-knuckled bald guy at the wheel. Iowa plates, lost without a cornfield on each side.

It could be worse. By quarter of eight the roads would be bumper-to-bumper and so slow I could read the Tribune front to back before I got to my destination. Heavy trucks, their engines hammering, crept past me, air brakes hissing.

I had decided it was time to bring the cops into my investigation even though I still didn't like the idea. Whether the case was considered a homicide or not, I would need their help in putting out All Points Bulletins on the suspects, Alcott and Walker. If it weren't for my being a department alumnus, the cops definitely wouldn't give me the time of day. But I still had a lot of pull at the Department. They were people I knew I could count on without them doling out a ration of shit. I had only hesitated because I knew how these things could get screwed up with too many hands on the file.

Deciding to declare it a no-work-out day, I stopped at Gus's Diner on the south side for breakfast. It was a cop hangout and I knew a lot of the guys who ate there. It wasn't because I liked that many cops, but because I could eavesdrop, pick up the mood of things on the street, catch a bit of gossip that might prove useful.

With a run-down, filthy fifties exterior, the place had ignored the face of progress, recession and everything else that might have changed in the forty-plus years it had existed. The years would come and go, but tradition kept the cops, including me, coming to Gus's, and the place was always busy.

Old Gus was rarely around early in the morning. He could sleep in because he had reliable help in his employees, including Bill "Hap" Woodward, who had been with Gus for at least fifteen years. Hap was the counterman, a fat guy waiting for retirement or a heart attack. He looked to be a twenty-eight inseam with a forty-two waist. His hair was long and slick and matched his sparse gray goatee. I could never tell if he was trying for the stubble look or just forgot to shave. He nodded when I walked in and sounded like Marlon Brando in *The Godfather* when he said, "Mornin', Hawk."

"Morning, Hap. What's going on?"

"Nadda. Same scramble, different eggs, another buck-fifty an hour." He took out a pack of spearmint gum, selected a stick, unwrapped it, and folded a piece into his mouth. "You lucked out. There's a vacancy right over there." He rolled his eyes and jutted his jaw at a booth.

I shrugged out of my coat, ambled over and slid into the booth. Heaving a big sigh, I tried to idle my motor down. I felt as though I'd been revving into high gear. Things were beginning to come together with the case, but ever so damned slowly. As time passed, it had gotten too stale.

I thought about the people tailing me the other day and more than that, the three clowns who'd broken into my office. Enough was enough. I needed to know who or what I was up against. I felt like an amateur and the clock was ticking for me to close the case.

I picked up a copy of yesterday's *Sun Times* that had been left on the bench opposite me and checked to see if they left the sports section. I hadn't gotten far when I was slapped on the back by a heavy hand.

"How ya' doin, Hawk?"

It was Jeebers. He scooted in on the other side as we shook hands. At six-three or four, but linebacker broad, his body took up space the way a tank takes up space.

"Hey, Jeebers, what in the hell have you been up to, partner?"

He reached in his topcoat pocket and pulled out a badge and discreetly flashed it. "I'm baaaaaack," he said, reminding me of Jack Nicholson's "Heeeere's Johnny" line in *The Shining*.

"Hey, good deal, Jeebs. I'm glad for you. Back in homicide?"

He nodded. "I was stubborn. Told the Captain, it's all I know."

"And he swallowed that bullshit, eh?"

"Is that the voice of authority, Cleve?"

"Fuck you, Jeebs."

"Is that a no or wishful thinking?"

I chuckled. "Nah, that's great. You're a good cop. Andrews will be damned glad he took you on. Have you met him yet?"

"Tomorrow morning. I've got a one-on-one with him."

"I've got to admit, you're looking great since I last saw you," I remarked.

"Yeah, well...you know." He smiled nervously and his thin moustache crawled over his upper lip like a worm as he muttered, "I'm off the sauce, buddy. Have been since shortly after that fiasco we had in The Hole. That was just plain nuts, ya' know?"

"Yeah. I have been laying off booze myself. Ya' know, during my tour with homicide, I watched a lot of good people straddle that awkward line between normalcy and the reality of violent crime disrupting their lives. I never thought much about it as a rule. I wasn't a social worker. My job had been to solve the crime and move on."

Ginny, the waitress, stopped at our table. Another one of Gus's fixtures, she had freckles on her nose, unruly ash-blonde hair and green bulb earrings the size of Yule ornaments. A bit heavy on the makeup. "Well, look what we have here...Mutt n' Jeff," she chirped.

I watched her pour our coffee. Her hands were strong and rough from work, yet feminine and beautifully shaped. She pulled a pencil out of her hair and set the pot on the table.

"Hey, Gin. It's always nice to be remembered so fondly," I said. "How about three poached on English muffins, sausage links and home fries."

"You got it." She glanced at Jeebers and winked. "How about you, good lookin'?"

"Left your glasses at home again, huh, Gin?" I said.

"Give me three over medium. And that means no snot on 'em," Jeebers said. "And I'll have some of those home fries with a ton of onions. Skip the meat. It's fattening."

Ginny turned to leave, but winked and said. "Two fat free breakfasts coming right up."

I leaned in and told Jeebers, "I've got pictures of the two perps who drove off with that chemist, Hubbard, but I have the feeling my source was lying to me about something. In fact, there's a whole lot of lying going on with this case. I think something smells with the story I've been getting from Hubbard's wife, too."

"People lie to the cops all the time, and not just bad guys or the guilty. Lying is an equal opportunity activity. Innocent people lie," said Jeebers. "You know that as well as I do. Mothers of small children lie. Pencil pushers lie. Blue-haired grannies lie. Lying to the cops seems to be embedded in the human genetic code, partner."

"They're all lying sacks of shit. That's my sweeping generalization for the day," I said. "Career criminals act guilty even when they haven't committed the crimes they had been hauled in to discuss. They know damned well they are guilty of something."

"People even lie with their body language. Or try to." I said. "Yet that's seldom as successful as the verbal variety, right?"

He nodded.

"The USB I got from this guy, Charlie Gretsch, showed a late model Buick LeSabre, but everything was so dark in the underground tier of the parking garage that the grainy shadows covered the pictures the security camera captured, making it damned near impossible to make out the plate number. The bastards had parked at the end of the row, next to the wall, in a spot too dark for most people's liking. Nose out, poised for a quick getaway."

"Bad break there," said Jeebers.

"Yeah, but it was definitely an Illinois tag and began with the letter H and had two numbers, an eight and a two. Not much to go on for sure, but I figure it's better than nothing."

About ten minutes later, Ginny was back with our food. "Here ya' go, fellas. Them eggs look alright?" She poured another cup of coffee for each of us.

Jeebers smirked. "What would you do if we told you 'no,' Gin?" He was already putting ketchup on his potatoes, popping the bottom of the bottle with

Triple Crossed

the palm of his hand.

"I'd hate to see you boys wearing them, know what I mean?" She eyed Jeebers. "Behave, handsome." She flounced off with a smile on her face.

"Anything else going on?" Jeebers asked.

"I went to see my friend Lynie MaClam at the DMV and asked her to start digging and research it the best she could and get back to me ASAP. You know her. She's an intelligent woman with a good soul, and I know that if anyone can build anything with so little information, she will be the one."

Jeebers swiped some fries through a puddle of ketchup on his plate. "Sounds like you've been as busy as a two peckered Billy goat."

"Yeah. I've also done my homework and found no recent employment records for either of the suspects, Alcott or Walker. None filed by any employers for the state. They could have given me addresses if the assholes were using their real names. They didn't show up in the property tax records, so they were probably renting. I got addresses from Ralph Bidden in records, but they're three years old. I'm going to check, but I doubt I'll find them still there."

"How about tax records?"

"Well, I couldn't get directly to the records. I've got a friend who could, but I hesitate to use her when I don't have to. I don't really need to know how much they were claiming they made. I'm just trying to find them. I'm on my way now to see Andrews. I'm hoping to get him to activate APBs on both of these clowns."

"Good luck with that."

We both finished eating and were nursing our coffee when Jeebers tossed a twenty on the table and stood to leave. "Give the rest to Gin, buddy. I've got to run. You still got the same phone number, right?"

"Yeah. Good seeing you again, Jeebs. Stay in touch."

"Yeah, I'll do that. Always good to see my friends are still in the game." He shot me with his thumb and forefinger. "Let me know if I can do anything, okay?"

"Thanks, Pal, and good luck."

. . .

In spite of my involvement with the Hubbard case, I found that Mo was on my mind more than ever before. For some reason, I hated to admit it and wished I could have lied to myself, but there it was. I'd been in love with her for the better part of five years and had never done anything about it because I wouldn't allow myself to try.

I hit Andrews' number, knowing Mo would probably answer.

"Lieutenant Andrews' office."

"Hi, Mo. It's me. Is Andrews free for the next hour or so?"

"Oh, hi, me. There's nobody in his office right now except him. Let me see something here." There was a pause for a moment until she continued, "And it doesn't look like he's expecting anybody until after two. But let me warn you, proceed with care. He's in a bad mood today. Earlier he was looking as if solving a murder would spoil his day so I'd tread easy, if you know what I mean."

"Thanks, babe. I'm on my way."

When I got to headquarters and entered the hall, I looked up and down. It was deserted for the moment at least. The building often gave that impression, even though the place was full of cops and criminals, lawyers, city officials and citizens. I went to the water fountain, got a drink and badged my way back to homicide's inner sanctum where Mo greeted me.

She looked sexy as she leaned against the side of the desk, her hair spilling down behind her like a waterfall. She gave a low whistle and smiled. I smiled back. There was a long silence as we flexed our facial muscles. I wanted to plant one on her, but knew too many eyes were on us.

She nodded towards Andrews' office. "He's all yours, Tracy." She lowered her voice and said, "I forgot to tell you thanks for the breakfast by the way."

I winked and continued to cross the Detective Division bullpen, aware of the curious glances as I deflected any leading questions with a stone face.

One wall was dominated by a huge calendar dotted with round colored stickers. I knew red was for open homicides, black for cleared cases, orange for open assaults, blue for when they closed. All neat and tidy.

Andrews had his computer on and the telephone wedged between his shoulder and ear when I tapped on his door. He was a good cop in his late fifties, about five feet, ten inches with a ruddy complexion and sandy hair, thin on top. He saw me, hung up the phone and waved me in.

"Hawk."

"Hey, Lieutenant. You got it under control in here?"

"Oh, hell yes, Hawk. You know you can't let the motherfuckers get you down." He stood and shook my extended hand. "Have a seat. Yeah, there's something new every minute." He waved a piece of paper in the air. "Here's a new terminal domestic situation. Get this. A common law wife claims she got tired of the hubby raping her every time she was passed out drunk -- after eight years of it. She stabbed him in the face, chest and groin with a busted vodka bottle."

Triple Crossed

"Wow. Absolut murder, eh?"

He snickered. "That was bad, man. Yeah, but can you imagine? Jesus!" He dropped back into his chair, crossed his arms over his chest and leaned back. "How have you been, Hawk?" He belched loudly. "Shit. Sorry, partner. I skipped breakfast, filled up on burgers for an early lunch." He flushed pink. "Damned onions."

"Good stuff, anytime," I said.

"Yeah, well, it's tough. Right across the parking lot's that White Castle. You can smell those beautiful sliders with the onions fried on 'em, seven in the morning." He paused and leaned forward. "So, what can I do for you?"

"Makes me hungry, loot, but anyway, you may have noticed I've got my hat in my hand. I need a favor and I'm sure it will help you out in the long run, too."

He smirked. "I'm listening."

"You're familiar with the case on this victim chemist named Thaddeus Hubbard?"

"Yeah, well enough so I know it's not mine. It's been determined a drug overdose killed him. Stone says it's a sure thing. DNA search is still ongoing, though, but otherwise it's cut and dry."

"I don't think so. In fact, I've got some potent information that may prove Hubbard was, in fact, murdered. I need APBs put out on two suspects."

Andrews studied me briefly and said, "Really?"

He slid his chair back and went through a couple of desk drawers, took out a file, pulled some papers from a wire tray on top of his desk and grabbed the binder that I hoped was the "murder book" that contained notes, Polaroids and everything to do with the Hubbard case, except his own personal notes.

He handed me a thin file folder and said, "Have a look. This is it for now. It's all we've got including the autopsy. You know something we don't? Let's have it."

Chapter Twenty-Four

While I began to browse through the Thad Hubbard file, Lieutenant Andrews sat on a corner of his desk on one haunch, as he always did. "Can I have Maureen bring you a cup of coffee, Hawk?"

I looked up from the file. "Yeah, sounds good, LT."

Andrews was an older cop, lean and hard-looking, with a shot of gray through his thick hair. He picked up the phone and said, "Hi, Mo. Would you please bring us some coffee?" He hung up and edged back around his desk to slouch in his swivel chair.

"You know, Hawk, I transferred in here from St. Paul four years ago and as you know worked under Kris Branoff for a year or so. I understand why you left the department, but I have never really gotten much of a lowdown on your background." He grinned. "I understand you were one hell of a good cop. Help me out, if you don't mind. Fill me in."

"Hmmmm. Well, not much to tell, really. I had been at it eight years out of seventeen with the Chicago Police, started at the seventh precinct in blue and whites, went to Violent Crimes and then Homicide for six. In less than eight more years I could have retired on half pay. I'd only be forty-five."

"Hell, I'd take that any day," he said.

"Uh huh, and then what? Corporate security someplace? No, not for me. I decided to stay in the game with private practice. What I know is how to investigate a homicide, how to peel open a case and find out who is who -- the ones lying to me and the ones telling me things I can use -- until I finally meet the suspect and know I've got him by the nuts. The arrogant bastard who couldn't believe you'd ever take him down until you present the evidence and watch his face, watch his 'fuck you' expression fade as he looks at twenty-five to life without parole. There is nothing like that moment for me."

Andrews smiled and nodded. "I agree."

Mo came in carrying a tray with a carafe, monogrammed Chicago Police Department cups and cream and sugar packets. She set everything down on a side table and poured two cups.

Andrews thanked her and she winked at me while her back was to him and left.

"I could quit detective work and live without the money or the hassle," I said. "I've squirreled away enough to pay off my debts, but I'm too stubborn to stop. Every time a case takes hold of me, I feel that old adrenaline rush and I remember that I love what I do. Even though I'm no longer working homicide for the department, I'm still performing a public service."

"I get that, and I can't say as I blame you." He held up the sugar shaker. "Cream and sugar?"

"No, black's good."

"More than once, I've seriously considered getting out," said Andrews. "Some of this shit is just plain madness. It makes it hard for a man to sleep at night, ya' know?" He paused and gave a long loud sigh. "Just last month, we had a case, some guy from the Chicago Heights blew away his wife and two kids because the wife brought home a bucket of regular instead of extra-crispy chicken from KFC. Then he goes in his bathroom and blows his head off. The scene was so bad our guys working the case had to take umbrellas in the bathroom."

"Need I say more about doing your own thing, Bill?"

"Point well taken." He paused for a beat. "Well, what have you got on this Hubbard deal?"

"I want to see if you can pick up Keith Alcott or Benjamin Walker, my two suspects. I believe the Hubbard death is definitely a homicide, LT. Hubbard was abducted by these two and subsequently murdered. It may look like a drug overdose because that's what they want us to believe, but it's bullshit."

"I don't know, Hawk. I have to believe the Medical Examiner and coroner's reports. Both say there were needle marks in both arms and his left thigh. Lots of them. The consensus is Hubbard was a closet addict and simply went on a bender. He evidently overdosed. The coroner says there was enough coke in his body to kill five men. Heart attack, most likely. You know Stoney. His report has to count for something, right?"

"Yes, I suppose, but remember, to the coroner another human being is just a bucket of guts sewn up in a sack of skin."

The Lieutenant heaved a sigh and looked up at the ceiling as if the real answer might play out there like a movie on a screen.

I sipped my coffee and began to fill him in on how I acquired the original Thad Hubbard abduction pictures obtained from the kid, Jesus Rodriguez, and then went on to tell about the video from the parking garage I'd obtained from Charlie Gretsch.

"It takes huge balls to go through with a kidnapping in broad daylight in the Loop, for Christ's sake. These fuckers must be harebrained. Especially if they've got rap sheets and the cops are already all over them like a bad rash."

He paused to drink some coffee before he said, "My guys got copies of the Sinclair Building tapes on the first day Hubbard went missing. How the hell did you...?" He grinned. "Never mind. Go on."

"The problem is the tape is so damned grainy that if I didn't have those pictures the kid took of the two perps, I would never have been able to identify them. The Gretsch videos show the same two suspects packing Hubbard into the trunk of a Buick. They were looking right at the security camera when they piled into the car."

"That's a plus, eh?"

"Well, yes and no. It was dark as hell in the lower level, and when these guys rounded the corner to go up the exit ramp, we only caught a glimpse of their Illinois plates. The color of the car is impossible to distinguish, too, by the way."

"Yeah, I don't get it," he said. "What's the point of having those damned cameras if they use the tapes so many times we might as well be trying to watch cartoons from Mars."

"They need to go digital."

"Costs money."

"Cheap pricks," I said under my breath.

"Well, we can get our techie geeks to go over the video from the parking garage ASAP. With any luck we'll have an enhanced version to look at shortly. Maybe we'll get lucky."

A guy rapped his knuckles on the door frame and I recognized him.

Andrews acknowledged. "Come on in, Mac." He stood and pointed at the man. "You know Patrick MacAnenney, don't you, Hawk?"

I stood to shake the man's hand. "Yeah," I said. "He and I go back a ways, don't we, Paddy?"

"Yeah, we've got some time logged together, that's for sure."

Patrick MacAnenney was his real name, an old-time cop from the kick-ass-and-take-names school. Everything was black or white for the guy they called The Mad Irishman. There were good guys and there were bad guys. Mac hit the streets armed with the law and about five concealed weapons. A real gladiator for justice.

I always admired the man. He was about fifty-five and heavyset. He had his suit coat off to work in his shirtsleeves and his blue-and-yellow-striped tie pulled down. He was slightly scruffy with salt-and-pepper beard stubble.

Andrews said, "Have a seat, Mac. Hawk was just filling me in on that Hubbard case we've been going over, the cocaine overdose found in Jersey." He glanced at me. "Cleve, the Mick is my number two. He's been following this thing right along."

Mac said, "Yeah, but we all know the first couple of days of any investigation are crucial. Trails cool fast, wits start losing the details of their memories, perps slither away into their holes. Oftentimes three days is as much priority time as we devote to a case before another dead body turns up and we have to move on that one because the first two days are critical. And around and round it goes."

"Anyway you were saying, Hawk?" said Andrews.

"Well, we've nailed down the identity of the two suspects so I need help with a BOLO. I figure an All Points may kick these guys loose and they might try to run, but we could get lucky, too, and have somebody turn them in. It's better than nothing. A running man is easier to spot than a hiding man."

"Well, even if we locate them, it's going to be a rough road getting the noose around their necks. I can tell you this much, Hawk. There were no useable prints on Hubbard's body. At least a half a dozen people touched him before processing, including the derelict homeless guy who called the Newark cops."

"So far, none of those prints came back with a rap sheet," said Mac.

"Both of these two assholes have sheets and neither of them have been keeping dates with probation for months. And, both had at least one count of assault on their record," I said.

"We know assaults are the homicides of tomorrow," said Andrews. "But finding them is the thing. When I was riding a blue and white years ago, I once put the cuffs on a scumbag who was so stupid he couldn't find his dick in a dark room. But he knew every way possible to create a false identity and evade the cops."

"These guys have got nothing to lose now. We nab them and they go down for at least two murders and God knows what else. They'll never see the light of day. That is if the jury don't make them ride the needle."

Andrews got up, poured more coffee and studied me through squinted eyes before he said, "You think these fuckers have any conscience, Hawk? Shit. Look at John Wayne Gacy. He was the killer of dozens of young men and boys whose bodies he stuffed in the walls and crawl spaces of his own house. Supposedly, his last words to one of the guards who escorted him to his execution were 'kiss my ass.'"

"Perps don't always get their just desserts in this life, ya' know," I said. "That's one reason we need to keep believing in God. The hope being he will kick ass in the afterlife."

"We can hope," said Mac. "You know the media is going to be crawling up our asses like cheap underwear."

"I hate the fuckin' media. Their usefulness is far outstripped by their ability to annoy, to misinform, to fuck up, and do outright damage to a case," I said. "Their stock in trade is human tragedy, the more horrific, the better. A woman with no name dying is of no interest to them or their papers. But murder her and they are all over it. Include rape and abuse of any kind and they come running. Label it a serial killing and they piss their pants getting to the scene."

"So, is the BOLO all you want right now, Hawk?"

I gave my crocodile smile. "It doesn't matter what I want, LT. Shit, I want world peace. I want not to have gas and acid reflux after I eat Italian. Truth is, nobody gives a shit what I want. I want the truth. I want to know who killed Thad Hubbard and why." I got up to leave.

Andrews stood with his hand extended. "You got it, Ace. We need to get on this like stink on shit. Further checking for sure, and pronto, eh, Mac?"

He nodded. "Meanwhile you'll keep us posted if you discover anything we can use, right?"

I shot him with my thumb and forefinger. "You've got it," I said as I turned to go.

"Hey, Hawk?" Andrews called after me.

"Yeah?"

"You get tired of doing private, you could go into sales. You're a natural. You could sell dope to the Pope."

A shot of electricity went through me as I walked to the elevator, the way it always does when a piece of the puzzle falls into place or I gain some ground. I wanted to run right out and cuff Alcott and Walker. I knew that the obvious suspects almost always turned out to be the perps in homicides.

Triple Crossed

Chapter Twenty-Five

The numbers 2:33 glowed green on the alarm clock sitting on my nightstand, a.m., not p.m. After I had called Mo, I sprawled out on the bed and tried to sleep, but sleep was like love. It wasn't always available when you needed it.

My mind was wrestling through my next moves in the Hubbard case, and daylight couldn't come soon enough so I could get started. This was my calling, a case with a sense of urgency. I was like a hound on the scent, but as I threw my legs over the edge of the bed, a familiar voice in the back of my head told me "you've got to take time out for sleep, asshole."

I tried to rub the grit out of my eyes with the heels of my hands before I slipped on some old sweats and went to the kitchen to look for something to eat. I sat down in the living room with nuked, leftover pizza and turned on an old *Bonanza* episode. I was still dwelling on the case, but at the same time hoping to see Hoss kick a barroom hick's ass. Then I dozed off and when I woke with pizza sauce on my chest, daylight was just visible.

With about four hours of sleep, I shaved and showered and got dressed in Levi's, a button-down Ball and Buck shirt, my Bear's cap and my leather bomber jacket to cover my Smith and Wesson.

I walked outside the apartment I had called home for the past couple years just as the sun was beginning to break. The horizon was painted in stripes of hot orange, bright pink and banana yellow. I like that time of day before the world wakes. It's silent and still, and I feel like I'm the only person in it.

An October chill was in the air and there was still frost on my windshield when I stopped at the nearby 7 Eleven to grab a cup of coffee, a newspaper and a couple of doughnuts to keep the stereotype alive. Then I sat in my car and scanned the paper to kill some time.

I had decided to start my day by visiting Thad Hubbard's workplace one more time. I took off for the Sinclair Building. It was after nine by the time I finished parking, a couple of blocks away, and I grabbed another cup of coffee at the concession stand and stood off to the side of the lobby to check my notes before getting on the elevator.

I was counting on speaking to the big cheese, Hugh Carrington, of Carrington Enterprises. I couldn't help but wonder what his attitude would be now that his ace chemist was laid out in the city morgue. Since I sort of got the bum's rush the last time we met, I made up my mind he would see me whether I had an appointment or not.

When I opened the gold-lettered door that said Carrington Enterprises, the same two mature female clerks I'd seen last time were still stationed in cubicles off to the left. They glanced up in unison and gave me what I considered to be the stink eye. I sensed there was no indication that anyone was in mourning for Thad Hubbard.

A mall-type wannabe cop stood just inside the door, an overweight guy busy gnawing on a Slim Fast bar. Slouching against the wall, he quickly straightened up and tugged at his jacket in an attempt to disguise the gut that draped over his shiny black belt. He got a bad case of torque jaws when he saw me.

The receptionist's desk still sat next to a mahogany door, evidently to guard Mister Carrington's private office. I remembered the middle-aged woman's name from my notes. It was Edith, Edith Chalmers.

She stood and removed her glasses when I came in and slowly skirted around her desk to greet me. She showed me a slight smile, pleasant. She wore a black-and-white-printed dress that wrapped around her slender frame. Her blonde hair had been slicked back into a simple ponytail, but her mouth appeared small and her lips resembled those of a goldfish.

"May I help you, sir?" she asked. She hugged her arms tight across her chest and looked around the reception area as if looking for permission from some unseen authority to ask me to just leave so she could go back to pretending she was busy.

"Yes, Ms. Chalmers. I am here to see Mister Carrington."

She looked at me with her head cocked to one side like an anxious little bird. "I see. And do you have an appointment, Mister...?"

"Hawkins, Cleve Hawkins. Don't tell me you have forgotten me so soon. I remember you, Edith." I flashed my ID and her eyes widened.

"Oh my, yes. The detective. Well, Is Mister Carrington expecting you, Mister...Hankins?"

I smiled. "See. You did forget. It's Hawkins, and my time is as valuable as his so please go tell him I'm here."

With a hand on her hip, she feigned a smile and said, "Wait right here. I'll see

Triple Crossed

if Mister Carrington will see you." She rubbed a trembling, manicured hand across her forehead and let a slightly shaky sigh escape.

She shoved her way through the cushioned door and I waited as I was told. A few moments later she politely ushered me into Carrington's private lair.

"Good morning, Mister Hawkins," Carrington said as he stood abruptly from behind a huge mahogany desk. Paperwork and manila folders were stacked in neat little piles. The blotter was clean and clear except for a few pens and a legal-sized yellow tablet, two open folders and a monogrammed Carrington Enterprises coffee cup.

He was a tall man with weathered, tan skin that resembled an old catcher's mitt. Clean-shaven, he wore a pin-striped white shirt, neatly pressed. The crease in his gray slacks was sharp. A tasteful gold bracelet clung to his left wrist. He looked tired and sad.

I edged over to his desk and pumped his hand. "Good morning, sir. Sorry for the unexpected visit. I have a bad habit of not calling ahead."

"I noticed. Yes..." Carrington lowered himself into his cushy executive's chair, his hands on the desktop as if physically bracing himself for bad news. "I remember you now. You are the same fellow who stopped by to inquire about our chemist Thad Hubbard. Please, have a seat. May I have Edith bring you something to drink? Coffee, or tea perhaps?"

"No, I'm good, thanks." I paused and sat down in the plush armchair across from him and we began the verbal dance. "But you are correct. We discussed the same Thad Hubbard who is now deceased, as we all know."

"Oh, my God, yes. Isn't that terrible? What a tragedy. I mean, the way they found poor Thad."

"You mean dead."

He frowned. "Yes, but in an alley, in New Jersey. How disgraceful and yet so sad."

"Yes, Newark, to be exact."

"Yes. My, how he must have suffered. One can only imagine. We are still waiting for them to release Thad's body so we can have a proper funeral, Mister Hawkins. Do you have any idea how long before that will occur?"

"I'm not a cop anymore, Mister Carrington, but I would guess there is an investigation underway to determine cause of death. That may take a little longer than usual due to the circumstances."

"Yes, of course." Carrington skirted around his desk and fidgeted around, first putting his hands on his head, then on his hips, then he crossed his arms in front of him. He paused and looked off at the wall as if he were watching a scenario play there like a movie on a screen. "They told us Thad died of a drug overdose. It's difficult to grasp the insinuation that Thad was addicted to cocaine." He squeezed his eyes shut and rubbed his forehead with one hand. "Unfathomable."

"Maybe he wasn't."

"What's that you say?" His mouth was agape. "That is a grim notion, Mister Hawkins."

"True enough, but I'm a suspicious man. I wouldn't believe my own mother without a corroborating witness. Maybe Thad met with foul play and was murdered. Now then, I'm here to ask you -- as I did last time I was here -- what was Thad working on which may have been so valuable that someone might kill for the information?"

Carrington seemed to deflate and shrivel. "Oh, no. I simply cannot divulge that information, Mister Hawkins. I'm sorry, but the police told me they had the coroner's report and it showed Thad died of a drug overdose. Regardless of the reason for his demise, the project Mister Hubbard was working on should have no bearing whatsoever on the case."

"Sorry, sir, but you are mistaken. If the investigation warrants it, you will be compelled to reveal that information by way of a subpoena." I paused a moment to let that sink in before I said, "Tell me, to your knowledge were there ever any rumors about Thad or his wife doing drugs?"

Carrington shoved his hands in his pockets and turned his back to me. "As far as Thad goes, no. We had no reason to believe he was doing drugs. He was a very reliable employee, dependable to a fault."

There was another long pause before he turned to face me. "Now, as for his wife, Bethany..."

"Yes?"

"May I be frank with you, Mister Hawkins?"

"I'm listening."

He began to pace. "Well...how can I put this tastefully? You see, Thad had only been married a short time to Bethany and, well, everyone who made her acquaintance from our office had the same opinion, even though we never let on to Thad."

"That seems unfair, but what was that?"

He cleared his throat then said: "Mrs. Hubbard was a self-centered nag and a gold digger. There, I've said it."

I shrugged. "So what? A lot of women are guilty of that, I'm afraid."

Triple Crossed

"Yes, but, with Bethany, Mrs. Hubbard rather, we always felt she was very inconsiderate and greedy and as a result she treated Thad very badly. She embarrassed him and used him, that's all I'm saying." He paused and rubbed his face with both hands. "I would appreciate it if you didn't repeat that to anyone, Mister Hawkins, but it's the truth as I see it."

I ran my fingertips along my lips from left to right. "My lips are sealed. But, I'm sure his wife is suffering a lot of pain, just as you and his associates are."

"I'm not so sure of that either."

"Oh, really?"

"Well, I'm not sure you understand, but there had been gossip floating around to the effect that Mrs. Hubbard was having an affair." His eyes widened in a what-do-you-think-of-that manner as he dropped back into his leather chair.

"I have to be honest with you, Mister Carrington. While I appreciate your candor, you do appear to have a personal dislike for Mrs. Hubbard."

He frowned. "You are wrong, and I don't like your attitude, Detective."

I stood to leave. "Nobody does. Lucky for me, I don't give a happy rat's ass." I paused. "See, Hugh…may I call you Hugh?"

He frowned again. "I suppose."

"Okay, here's the scoop. I can stoke my anger the moment I open my eyes in the morning and feel it through the entire day, much in the same way a person tosses sticks on a bonfire."

I inched towards his desk. "My anger allows me to create my own menu, with many choices on it. I can become a moralist and reformer and make the lives of my friends a living hell. I can spit in the soup from morning to night and feel as high as a balloon in a windstorm without breaking a sweat."

Putting on my cap, I walked to the door, and turned. "See, I'm going to find out what Thad Hubbard knew that was so important, Hugh, with or without your help. And I'll find out who murdered him. You go ahead and spread that around."

R.C. Hartson

Chapter Twenty-Six

Maxee's was the kind of gym where sweating and grunting were the name of the game. After my usual routine, the front of my gray workout tee was soaked in sweat.

I stretched my leg out straight while I cranked out several reps on the bench. Sliding an extra plate onto the bar, I performed twelve more reps. When I racked the weight and sat upright on the bench, a bald Mister Clean type by the name of Eddie Glinski was standing nearby, unimpressed.

"Next time, slower," he said. "And pause when the bar hits your chest. Don't bounce it. You'll get hurt that way."

"I can get hurt doing a lot of things, Eddie." I thought about his face later on when I pounded the speed bag. It had been a while since I had attacked the heavy bag and exchanged my frustrations.

When I was done, I showered, shaved and changed. Dressing casually for the day in jeans with a black polo shirt, I also wore my bomber jacket and Bears' cap. That's part of the beauty of working for myself, no dress code but my own. I've found that people don't always like talking to the suit and tie. There are times I want people as relaxed as possible when I interview them.

• • •

It wasn't my place to judge Beth Hubbard and in doing so close off my mind to possibilities in the investigation. Instead, it was my responsibility to see her for who she was and to see every path open to me from there. I decided to pay her another visit, this time armed with additional insights into her character. I thought she was not being forthright from the get-go and I needed to get a handle on it.

In the meantime the media would spotlight the possibilities in the investigation and get people talking, get them staying alert for the faces of the two suspects.

Triple Crossed

I took my time driving, playing everything through in my mind, trying to sort in chronological order all I had learned, mending the gaps with educated guesses and trying not to react to any of it in an emotional way. I reminded myself that Beth Hubbard had just lost her husband, after all, and I should try to go easy on her.

The Hubbard property was beautiful. I admired the tall oaks and maples as I turned onto the concrete driveway that led to the tri-level house. Those huge trees that shaded the yards and streets half the year now stood as naked, bony sentinels for the long winter months ahead. A new silver Mercedes CL65 and an older model Dodge Ram pickup faced the three car garage.

As I sauntered up the walkway, I noticed the fading landscape was still well tended, even for the fall, and was an expression of joy, filled with old-fashioned climbing roses, tall blue delphiniums and mums of all colors. Flower boxes under the front windows spilled over with ivy and pink geraniums.

I rang the bell and heard it play the first few chords of "Hello, Dolly" while I waited. Beth Hubbard answered and I tipped my cap when she opened the door.

"Mrs. Hubbard, I'm sorry for not calling ahead. I'm just following up. I have a few quick questions, if you don't mind."

"Questions? What sort of questions would you possibly want to ask me?" she said with a nervous tremor in her voice. "Don't you realize how hard this is for me?"

"I apologize, but I was hoping you could give me a little more insight into the sort of man your late husband was. It will help me close my files on the case. Mind if I come in?"

Her face seemed to turn pale in spite of thick make up. She nodded and I thought I saw tears welling up. "Well, I suppose," she said, as I edged past her.

Dressed to either play polo or go horseback riding, she wore tan jodhpurs, tall boots and a butter-soft suede jacket. A beautifully patterned silk scarf was wound around her throat into an elaborate cravat. Her hair was up in a messy topknot with long curls slipping free all around. A sparkling diamond tennis bracelet was on one wrist, a bejeweled Rolex on the other.

I glanced over her shoulder. "Sorry if I interrupted something," I said as I followed her. "Where's your butler by the way, what's-his-name, Carl?"

"Carl is *not* my butler. He's my personal assistant, and he's presently running errands for me. I was just on my way out to Oakbrook to ride my horse and try to get my mind off of all that's happened.

She abruptly turned and walked away, leaving me to follow. I wandered to the edge of the foyer and looked into a living room with a stone fireplace and overstuffed couches. Blue smoke was heavy in the air and hanging like a ghost over one of the couches. I was sure more than one person had been smoking there.

"Is that his truck by the garage?"

"Probably. He may be back…I'm not sure." She paused briefly. "I still can't believe my husband is dead," she said, as she sank down into a chintz-covered chair in the living room. Her hand trembled as she dabbed a tissue under her eyes.

"I'm sorry about your husband, Mrs. Hubbard." I watched her eyes for reaction. "We never imagine something like this will happen to someone we love. Nobody should die violently. A person dies only once, but the loved ones left behind, suffer every day. That's just the way it is."

She nodded, crying a little into her crumpled tissue. "It's like a nightmare, yet I'm awake. It's, it's terrible. I can't believe he died that way. I never had any idea he was doing drugs. It's all so strange. And what in the world was he doing in New Jersey, anyway?"

She took a pack of Virginia Slims from the pocket of her jacket and shook one out. I thought about how much I used to like smoking, how soothing the ritual of it was, how a cigarette was like an old buddy you called up every time the world screwed you over, and you went out and got drunk together and felt like shit afterwards.

"You had told me you and Thad weren't married long." I paused, waiting to see if that information was correct. "Still, I can imagine you have a lot of fond memories."

She lit her cigarette and squinted at me through a cloud of exhaled smoke. "Well, yes. We were quite happy until recently. He became so distant. That's why I suspected him of being unfaithful." She pointed to an armchair. "Please, have a seat, Mister Hawkins."

"Thank you." I sat and leaned forward from the seat of a large armchair across from her.

"I must tell you, however, Mister Hawkins, I thought our arrangement was over since Thad was found. Frankly, I'd rather not talk about it with you or anyone else for that matter. Do I still owe you something?" She inhaled deeply and blew the smoke out through her nostrils.

"No. We're clear on my fee. However, there are still a few things about the case that trouble me." I took out my notebook and smiled. "Call it cops' curiosity, okay? As you know, the autopsy on your husband showed that he was a cocaine user." I paused. She said nothing so I marched on and flipped through my notes as

Triple Crossed

if I needed them.

"And he died of an apparent overdose according to the coroner."

She fidgeted with her hands and cleared her throat. "Yes, two detectives and an officer came by here with that information." Dabbing her eyes again, she said, "I find it hard to believe, but they said they found drugs on Thad's body, too."

I nodded. "...and needle marks on both arms and one thigh."

I was about to continue when the man named Carl suddenly appeared from the hallway. He had his silver hair combed straight back and he wore a double-breasted black suit and a gray shirt with a bolero string tie knotted up tight. He was about five ten, perhaps 200 pounds, with a large faded tattoo on the right side of his neck. He also had brown shifty eyes that didn't blink.

"Oh, Carl. There you are," said Beth. She failed at feigning surprise.

"I was just out back. Sorry, I didn't know you had company." He sat on the settee without invitation and spread both arms out along the back of it, as he stretched out his legs. I thought this guy's got balls to just plop down as if he owned the place. Interesting.

"Carl Cosgrove, this is Cleve Hawkins. Mister Hawkins has stopped by to ask some questions, Carl." She sniffled and blotted her nose with a tissue.

Cosgrove studied me. "Hawkins, eh?" He snapped his fingers. "Yeah, I remember now. You're the detective she hired. You were out here once before, when Mister Hubbard come up missing."

He shook a cigarette out of a pack of Marlboros and hung it on his lip. After lighting up, he took a long pull on the cigarette and exhaled a jet stream of smoke.

Beth quickly said, "Yes, but he is no longer in my employ, are you, Mister Hawkins?"

"No, that's true, but I must tell you, Mrs. Hubbard, I have gathered new information, evidence that can prove that your husband was in fact kidnapped and subsequently murdered."

Beth sat forward, visibly shaken. A sense of deep, quiet desperation appeared to circle around her. The air hissed out of her lungs. She buried her face in her hands and pressed her fingers against her closed eyes in an effort to stop the flow of impending tears and said, "What in the world do you mean?"

"I mean he was killed, murdered and injected with the cocaine. The drugs were actually planted on his body."

She began to cry. At first, just a few tears in a slow trickle, then a dam burst somewhere inside her and the emotions came in a flash flood of tears, snot and spittle, like something in her head had exploded.

"The police didn't say anything about murder," said Cosgrove. He gave me a cold look. I think he knew he had spoken out of turn. He flinched when my eyes darted in his direction.

"Well, what I mean is," said Carl, "Mrs. Hubbard told me about the visit the police made out here the other day and she never mentioned them calling it a murder case."

She suddenly stopped crying and agreed. "No. No, I didn't, because this is the first I've heard anything at all about it. Oh, my God! Murder?"

"The case has never been closed, ma'am. The police have more information now and are in the process of investigating." I pulled out the pictures of Alcott and Walker, leaned over and handed them to her.

"Have you ever seen either of these two men?"

I watched her body language and her eyes. Her breathing turned quick and shallow and she barely looked at the pictures before handing them back. There were tears on her cheeks and she shook her head.

"No. I've never seen them before. Why? Who are they?" She had that I-want-to-hurt-you look in her eyes.

"Let me have a look," said Cosgrove and he took the pictures.

A long moment passed while he studied the pictures and I was reminded that sociopaths and most mainline deviants share the same characteristics. No matter how ignorant and uneducated they are, they believe they are more intelligent than law-abiding people. They also think they can read the minds of others. They all seem to wear that same corner-of-the-mouth smirk that crawls under my skin. There was a trace of that on Cosgrove's face as he handed them back to me.

"Well?" I said.

"Well, what? I never seen them either. I was just curious."

"Thanks." I stood, put my cap on and shook my head. "The thing to be afraid of with ignoring the possibility or the reality, for that matter, is there's a good chance the perpetrator could get skittish and paranoid. He, or she, might strike out at a perceived threat like a relative or acquaintance who might know or suspect something."

Cosgrove looked sullen as he stood up. He took a long pull on the cigarette and exhaled. "You're not a cop anymore, Hawkins, isn't that right?"

"That's right, I'm not."

"Well, honestly, I think this thing is way above your head and I'd let the cops handle their job if I were you." His face flushed red with anger. "Quite frankly, I am not impressed with you at all. In fact, if you told me the time, I'd want a second opinion."

"Oh, my God," Beth mumbled behind her hands.

I gritted my teeth and said, "Mrs. Hubbard, thank you for your time, and again, my condolences for your loss. I'll see myself out, thank you."

As I drove back to the city, I let possibilities run through my mind unchecked, uncensored. None of them pleasant, but then that was the nature of my job and the bent of my mind because of the case. I couldn't afford to trust, to discount, to filter possibilities through a screen of denial the way most people do.

Innocent people are usually quick to react in outrage to false allegations. Even though I hadn't accused him of anything, I felt that Carl Cosgrove knew too much about the Hubbard case that didn't concern him and probably a lot more than I did.

But I would soon be up to speed.

Chapter Twenty-Seven

They were both lying and I knew it. When I left the Hubbard mansion, my suspicions that I had been played were substantiated. The question was to what extent were Beth and her so-called assistant involved with the disappearance and murder of Thad Hubbard.

The next morning was Wednesday. The weather that had brought rain and fog over the area for the last few days had moved out, leaving the air clean and the sky a robin's-egg blue. A stiff breeze off the lake was having a fit and made leaves scuttle along sidewalks like crabs.

When I walked up the one flight of stairs to my office, Deckle was huddled by my door. He was evidently sleeping in. I often wondered how he survived when I didn't show up at the office, which could often amount to a few times a week…depending.

I shook his shoulder. "Rise and shine, Deck." With that he jumped like a firecracker had exploded under his ass.

"Oh, Lordy, it's morning out." He coughed three or four times and wrapped his arms around himself in an effort to warm up. He reeked of cheap wine and stale cigarettes. Squinting up at me he said, "Cleve?" Unshaven and bleary-eyed, Deckle straightened his cap and rubbed his stomach. "Man, I'm glad you're here, boss." He scrambled to get up and I gave him a hand.

"Yes, sir, I sure could use a donut. How about you, Cleve? Huh? Want me to go to Whalen's and get some donuts for you?"

"Thanks for guarding the door, partner. Hold on. Give me a minute here, okay?" I unlocked the door, flipped on the lights and picked the mail up off the floor. Deckle was right on my heels. He shuffled in and quickly grabbed a chair.

"How about making some coffee for us, Deck?"

"Coffee? Yep. Yes, sir, Cleve. I'm right on that, my man. You know I make good coffee, don't you, Cleve, huh?"

I watched his hands tremble as he filled the carafe with water. I hung up my jacket, tossed my cap on the top of the filing cabinet, skirted around the desk and

Triple Crossed

parked in my swivel chair.

Lacing my fingers behind my neck, I leaned back and pondered the likelihood of Cosgrove and Beth Hubbard having an affair. My mind kept returning to the one thread I had working for me, that of Lieutenant Andrews and his crew actually locating the two thugs responsible for abducting Hubbard. There was an All Points Bulletin out on them, but I couldn't sit still and wait for results. I had to keep grinding away on my own.

Jeebers had called and wanted to meet me at one of his favorite breakfast joints called Fast Bobby's on Diversey Avenue. I was hungry and didn't want to ruin a good breakfast with raspberry-filled donuts, but Deckle was anxious. I figured it best to be sure he ate something before I left.

Jittery and hung over, he shuffled over to the front window, clasped his hands behind his back and stared out at Wells Street, where the morning rush hour traffic was building. Then he jerked around to face me.

"Coffee is makin', Cleve. It won't be too long." Rushing back over to the pot, he leaned down and with an eyeball mere inches away from the carafe, he stared at the dripping process until the coffee was done.

I pulled a sawbuck out of my wallet. "Here, go ahead and get six of those fat makers at Whalen's, but when you get back I want you to sweep and dust. I'll be waiting, so don't get lost okay?"

"Yes, sir. I gotcha, Cleve." He stood and stared at me. The inner workings of his mind always seemed to move at the rate of grass growing. Finally, waggling the ten in the air, he said, "Oh. This here's ten dollars, you know that, right? I'll get the donuts and bring you the change like I'm supposed to, okay, Cleve?"

"Yes, that'll be great, Deck."

He scooted for the door, but slid to a stop and turned. "Oh. What kind you want today, Cleve?" Before I could answer, he snapped his fingers and said, "Oh, I know! I know! Don't tell me." He smiled, showing me his toothless grin. "Jelly inside, right? Jelly donuts."

"Right, Deck. Hurry back now, okay? I've got to be leaving as soon as I check out the mail."

"Yes sir, Cleve." He shot out the door and I grabbed a cup of coffee and started sorting through the bills, trash mail and more bills. No checks.

The landline phone jingled and I picked up. A woman's voice sounded on the verge of tears when I said, "Hello."

"Mister Hawkins?" That was followed by a long pause and sniffles before she spoke again. "Sorry. I mean, is this Cleve?"

I could tell it was Beth Hubbard, but it was difficult to hear her. It was as if she was whispering. I leaned forward and covered my left ear with my free hand.

"Yes. This is Cleve."

"This is Beth Hubbard." There were sniffles and snuffing and then a pause before she continued. "I...I need to see you as soon as possible. I'm terrified and I need your help."

"I don't understand. What's the trouble? You didn't say anything when I was out there. Calm down and tell me what's wrong."

"I need to meet you someplace so we can talk. I couldn't speak freely with Carl here. Please listen to me. I can't talk long."

"You're not alone?"

"For now, yes." There was a hitch in her voice and she started crying again. "But he could come back any time."

"If you're in danger, call the police. I'll come out right now."

"No, no. That won't be necessary. I'll be able to get away for a while later this afternoon. I'm sorry, but it has to be this way, right now. No police. You'll understand after we talk. Just meet me at the Brewpoint Coffee Shop on Park in Elmhurst?"

"Okay. But you're a poor liar, Beth. Your heart's not in it. It doesn't come to you naturally. Who are you trying to protect? Did you make a promise to some bad characters you're now scared to death of? Can I just ask what this is about?"

"Please. It's just...well, I just cannot go on living with myself...I mean...there are things you don't know. It was all a mistake. There was no reason for Thad to die. I've got to hang up now. I just saw him pull in. I knew it. This is far too dangerous."

"Okay. What time?"

"Between three-thirty and four?"

"Okay, I'll be there. You're coming alone, right?"

Her voice suddenly changed pitch and the sounds of fear were gone.

"Yes, of course. Well, I'll need time to check my calendar. I'll call you back if you're going to be around later, okay?" There was a pause before she said, "Okay, good. Bye bye, Carol."

"Damn!" Somebody had obviously walked in on her. I dropped the phone back on its cradle and stared at it for a moment. Somehow I knew that Cosgrove was there.

When Deckle got back I took one donut. "And keep the change, Deck, but promise me you'll get some decent hot food for your stomach, okay?"

Triple Crossed

"Cross my heart, I will do, Cleve. Thanks." With that, he stuffed a donut into his mouth and grabbed the broom from the bathroom. Sweeping was no big deal, but when he finished ten minutes later, Deckle blew out his breath like a man who had just defused a bomb.

He saw me watching and he laughed and snorted. His nose was running. Instead of wiping it, his tongue swept across his upper lip and he used his sleeve to wipe a smear of jelly from his chin.

I always felt a little disappointed in myself when I had to shut down and leave Deckle outside, but I just couldn't risk giving him the key to the office. I knew he could leave to buy booze and forget to lock up. Either that or fall asleep with a cigarette and burn me out. I slipped into my jacket, bid him goodbye and headed for my meet with Jeebers.

On the way my gut churned with a myriad of thoughts about what was up with Beth Hubbard.

• • •

Fast Bobby's Coney Island, on Diversey, had a sign in the window that boasted "Breakfast Served All Day." Finding a place to park was a real grin, but I managed to find a spot a half a block away.

The restaurant was crowded and noisy, the air thick with conversation and the welcome smell of fresh-brewed coffee, fried potatoes and sausage. The walls were time-worn brick, the floors scarred wood, and the ceiling beams exposed.

Jeebers was sitting in a booth in the corner nursing a cup of coffee when I walked in and spotted him. I worked my way past the occupied tables and took a seat across from him.

"Mornin', Jeebs."

He looked up from the sports section of the *Tribune*. "Hey, hotshot. How's it hangin'?"

"About like yours." I glanced around. "So...you say the breakfast is number one here, eh?"

"Yeah, the place isn't The Drake, but looks are bullshit, you know that." He handed me one of the menus. "Try the French toast. It's the bomb."

"Ya' think so, eh?" I never needed a menu to order breakfast and I put it off to the side.

Jeebers wasn't ordinarily very talkative, but this morning he seemed half asleep and there were purple circles under his eyes. Somebody had a hard night, I thought with some amusement. I know the symptoms, having had a few hard ones myself.

A rather heavy, middle-aged woman with dark skin and a mole on her chin came to take our order. She had an empty cup with her. "Good morning, sir. Coffee?"

I nodded and smiled. "Thanks."

Jeebers closed the paper, folded it in half and put it down. "Sherrill, this is my friend, Cleve." He grinned. "Don't give him the stuff left over from yesterday, okay?"

She had her pencil and pad at the ready and smiled at me as she shook her head. "Don't mind funny man here. What'll you have, Cleve?"

I nodded. "You put up with him much?" I asked.

"Not often enough, it seems." She patted Jeebers on the shoulder. "This big lug is alright."

"I guess so. Glad to meet you, Sherrill. I think I'll have three soft scrambled, ham, home fries with plenty of onions, and wheat toast."

Jeebers said, "Scrambled eggs? That reminds me. Did you know there was a Paul McCartney tune called 'Scrambled Eggs'? It eventually became 'Yesterday.' the most widely covered song in music history." He looked at Sherrill. "I'm ready now, babe. Give me a double order of French toast and sausage links, okay?"

"Gotcha." She gathered up the menus and was gone.

I noticed in the corner, next to an ATM machine, a table of overweight tourists with long shirts and cameras, drinking coffee. They were all talking at the same time while glancing at their menus. The apparent leader, a guy with an unbuttoned shirt, a heavy gold chain draped upon his chest hair, thick gray sideburns and a Phillies baseball cap, looked repeatedly toward the grill in search of a waitress.

I sipped my coffee and Jeebers made a sound like a horse blowing air through its lips. "So, what's happening, Hawk? You still chasing after those two perps that heisted what's-his-face?"

"Hubbard?"

"Yeah. The chemist, right?"

"Yeah. Funny you should ask. I think I caught a break this morning. Hubbard's widow called me, crying, I think. She sounded shaky anyway. I was just out at her place yesterday for chrissakes." I leaned in a bit and lowered my voice. "So, check this out. She asked me to meet her this afternoon, away from her house, mind you. Sounds like she wants to tell me everything I don't know, but wish I did."

Triple Crossed

Jeebers arched a brow and settled back. "Careful. It could be a setup, pal. When it sounds too good to be true...well, you know."

"So, we got cut off. Somebody walked in on her conversation and she switched gears real fast and had to hang up."

"What do you mean?"

"Ah, you know. It was like somebody walked in that wasn't supposed to know she was talking to me."

"Makes you wonder," he said. "Just be sure to take your piece with you, my friend."

Sherrill brought our food. Jeebers cut up his French toast like a surgeon and poured half a bottle of syrup on it. We worked on our food for a moment, but the silence stayed palpable until he chuckled. "So, before I forget...what do you call a lesbian dinosaur?"

I shook my head. "What?"

"A Lickalottapuss."

We both laughed. He took another bite of toast and thoughtfully chewed. "Seriously, maybe you've got the goose with the golden egg there with Hubbard's widow, eh? I still say, don't trust her, though. Know what I mean?"

"Yeah." I forked up a mouthful of potatoes and felt the phone vibrate in my pocket. I pulled it out and checked the screen and told Jeebers "Andrews" before I answered.

"Hawkins."

"Cleve? This is Andrews. We've caught a break."

"Really? What's up?"

"Our all points paid off. Crime Stoppers got a tip from an informant telling them where to find Alcott."

"No shit?"

"Yeah, they called ROPE, the Repeat Offenders Program, part of a federal fugitive task force with Chicago cops on it. ROPE had Alcott's file and flight warrant to pick him up wherever he might be. The cops thought he had gone to the New York area, but according to the informant he's staying in a house out in Des Plaines."

"Dumb shit stayed right here in Illinois?"

"Looks that way, or he left and came back. One of our guys, Detective Jim Ashbaugh, and his partner were staking out the house until they saw a guy fitting Alcott's description. He came out on the balcony. That "made" the house and it gave us probable cause to execute the flight warrant. He was living there and they cuffed him and stuffed him. He's ours."

"Great."

"Yeah, they call him Toad. Remember, you guys said he looked like a frog in his mug shot? Yeah, it's him alright. So we've got one of them, Hawk. I'm sure he'll give up his buddy, but be sure to get your ass in here if you want to be in the room when we work him over. It won't be much before tomorrow in the a.m., though."

"I'll be there." My heart was beating faster. The anticipation was like a coffee buzz, like speed. I brought Jeebers up to date and left.

This was the big break I had waited for. I knew one partner was always dominant, the other a follower. And when the chips were down in the cop's interview room, invariably one would turn on the other in a heartbeat in order to secure some sort of break, like a shorter prison sentence. They possessed no loyalty to anybody but themselves. I was counting on it.

Chapter Twenty-Eight

Attorney James Folgelstein was a persistent prick. A smart prick, but a prick, nonetheless. Some called it terminal assholeitis. As Keith (Toad) Alcott's attorney, he insisted on speaking to Alcott as soon as possible after his client's arrest early Wednesday. He would not wait until Thursday morning.

Lieutenant Andrews wanted a go at Alcott before he had the chance to consult with Folgelstein, and I headed for the jail as soon as he'd informed me of the change in plan.

"I'm letting you in on this one, Hawk, but Detective Jim Ashbaugh and I will be asking the questions. You remember Ashbaugh. He worked vice before we got him in homicide."

"Yeah, I remember Jim. Good man."

"Yes. So all you can do is observe. I don't want Alcott or his rat-fuck mouthpiece to find any fault with our procedures, when and if it comes to trial."

"I understand, Phil, and thanks. I'll be a good boy. Promise."

I knew how these interrogations went and figured with my commitment to meet with Beth Hubbard in the afternoon, things could be tight. Our meet was for between three-thirty and four o'clock. Now that the Thursday morning interrogation of Toad Alcott had been moved up, I didn't want to miss anything one way or the other. I suddenly found myself moving faster, talking faster, thinking faster.

The high that was building in me was almost better than sex.

It was actually for the best because Andrews knew as I did that the element of surprise was always best. Forewarning only gave people time to get their lies straight. The sudden interview with homicide cops armed with a lot of questions had a tendency to rattle a suspect into talking.

I turned through a wide chain-link gate and drove around the back side of the building past the garage and about three dozen parked blue and whites.

I was led into the building by two uniformed cops who brought me inside by the evidence lockers and went through my pockets. They took my wallet, watch and personal belongings. An overweight property sergeant noted every item on a large manila envelope while they pulled off the hip holster for my .357 and the ankle holster for my .22.

The two uniforms brought me through a heavy metal door and into a long sterile hall that had all the charm of a urinal stall in the men's room. There were little rooms on either side of the hall with pea-green walls and water-stained acoustical tile ceilings. I knew the rooms had the latest in interrogation room technology and there was heavy duty soundproofing so passing liberals couldn't hear anything from the outside. Cameras were mounted on the walls to ensure that phony complaints related to police coercion and brutality could be proven unfounded.

I entered one room on the right. A hardwood table sat in the center of the room with some straight backed metal chairs on either side of it.

Toad Alcott came into the interrogation room with a swagger in his step as if he had something to be proud of. He immediately reached for the pack of Marlboros on the table. His hands were fat and stubby like the paws of a bear. He had a big nose and no neck. One big vein stood out in a zigzag on his forehead, like a lightning bolt. He had some prison ink on his wrist, a green dragon with a snake hanging from its jaws.

Alcott wore a three-piece suit, navy in color, made of at least ninety percent polyester. The tie was cheap imitation silk. The man wasn't much of a dresser, but there was a certain neatness about him. His smile widened enough to show he was missing a molar. He smelled like an ashtray and his lungs made sounds like he had just run a mile in four flat. His eyes were cold and as flat as buttons.

The common threads among professional killers, in my experience, were greed, sometimes desperation, and total indifference to the fate of their victims and their families. They have neither anger nor curiosity and have no conscience whatsoever. I figured Toad would fit into all of these categories.

Detective Ashbaugh was at least six feet tall and built like a weightlifter. A grin lit up his face, an interesting, lived in face, that was a bit rough, a little lined, not exactly handsome, but utterly compelling. He sported an inch-long scar diagonally across his chin. His nose was substantial and looked like it may have been broken a couple of times. His eyes were dark and deep set, and though they shone with traceable humor, they looked tired.

He took the cuffs off Alcott and shoved him down onto a chair.

"Park it right there, asshole." He put the cuffs away in a black pouch on his belt and gave Alcott a light. "Anything to make you comfy, as long as you cooperate here."

Andrews settled across from Alcott and folded his hands together on the table. Ashbaugh took a seat to the left of Alcott. Andrews tipped forward to rest his forearms on the table as Ashbaugh leaned back with his arms folded.

"I shouldn't be talking to you without my lawyer," he said and blew smoke out his nostrils. His nose was bulbous, with a couple of bumps along the bridge.

"This conversation is being recorded," said Andrews. "I'm going to ask you some questions, Keith Alcott, and your answers will be used in court unless you elect to consult an attorney. You have that right, you know. If you haven't got a lawyer, we can get a public defender for you."

"You know damned well I've got a lawyer and he should be here by now." Alcott's face was flushed. His voice sounded thick.

"And who is that?"

He sighed and rubbed a hand across his forehead. "Folgelstein."

"Ah, yes. The friend of the felon. Okay, well, while we wait for Jimmy, let's go over a few things."

Andrews opened the manila folder he'd brought with him.

"Let's see, Keith Parker Alcott." He flipped through a few of the pages and stopped to read. "Your rap sheet is a gamut from soliciting, to drugs, dealing toot, burglary and robbery. Damn. Then, you've got armed robbery, three counts of breaking and entering, assault and of course your last little infraction, assault with intent to kill."

Andrews looked up, tilted back in his chair and folded his arms.

He paused and said, "Want to know what I think?"

Alcott stared at the wall, pretending he hadn't heard any of it. He had kicked back in his chair, his arms crossed over his chest, his legs stretched out and spread a little, a practiced pose to suggest arrogance.

Andrews continued, "I think you graduated recently when you and your buddy, Benny Walker, abducted Thaddeus Hubbard and killed him. I don't understand why they let you out. It was up to me, your ass would belong to the state for life.

Ashbaugh leaned in. "They do call you Toad, right?" He was right down in the man's face when he said, "I can see why they'd call you Toad, asshole. You are one ugly, froggy-looking motherfucker."

Alcott glared at him. "I didn't kill nobody, and I don't know nobody named Walker."

A moment of silence smothered the room. The only sound was the rustling of paper as Andrews continued to thumb through sheets in Alcott's file.

My phone vibrated in my pocket. I pulled it out and checked the screen. Jeebers. I'd ignore the call for now, but I couldn't help thinking about the disappearance of protocol if Jeebers was on hand. Asking him to go one-on-one with Toad would be like putting a guppy in a piranha pool.

I couldn't make myself sit still. The adrenaline was beginning to flow. I stood off to the side and found myself slowly shifting weight from one leg to the other. It was my pressure valve, spending a little steam to keep me from blowing up.

I finally said, "Well, at least we know he's not lying right now."

"How's that?" said Ashbaugh.

"His lips aren't moving."

Toad glared at me.

"Anybody actually faint when you were giving them that stare? You know, sort of gasp with terror," I said, "and slide down in the chair and let their head fall sideways with their tongue hanging out? Like this?"

"Fuck you, Hawkins. If I want bullshit, I'd go to one of those AA meetings. What're you doing here anyway? You ain't even a cop no more."

Andrews said, "Not that it's your business, Alcott, but I invited Detective Hawkins. Now, this is all nice and chatty, and I'm sure you'd be an interesting person to spend the day with if I didn't think you were such an asshole, but let's cut to the chase. Suppose you tell us about the abduction and subsequent murder of Thad Hubbard."

Ashbaugh said, "We've got you guys on camera leading Hubbard away from his job and down to your vehicle in the parking garage. You're also on tape cramming his body into the trunk. We'll be showing that to you later on."

Andrews leaned across the table. "You're holding out for nothing, Toad. Your buddy has already come clean. So you see, you have to get in line for any kind of deal. Tell me, do you want to change your story a bit? Maybe we can still spare you the twenty-five to life.

The look on Toad's face was priceless. A little information and a lot of attitude goes a long way toward rattling people with something to hide. All the years of wading hip-deep in the garbage of the criminal mind had taught me more about human nature than any degree in psychology ever could. Andrews had opened both barrels of bullshit and hit some nerves.

Alcott licked the corner of his mouth. "I told you. I don't know nobody named Walker."

"Listen, Alcott, I'm not in the mood to have a scumbag like you fucking with my morning," Andrews said and Alcott looked up. "You can tell me some big shot paid you to do it or you can say you killed Hubbard for fun. I really don't give a shit. The way I got it figured, if you'd stayed on the street much longer, you would've disappeared too."

"I don't give a shit what you think, Andrews." Alcott's eyes shifted up and to the left, an involuntary movement. I had seen it in a great many interrogation rooms over the years. It meant he was either going to duck the question or just plain lie.

"Yeah, I can see you don't give a rat's ass about anything. So you'll try to feed me what you think I'm waiting to hear because you're looking for a deal."

Toad glanced at Andrews like he was an annoying mosquito buzzing around his head. He fiddled with an unlit cigarette, twiddling it like a pencil between his nicotine-stained fingers. There was no denying the scent of fear had touched him.

Ashbaugh reached over and snatched the cigarette from Alcott's hand and squeezed it in a fist. "No more smoking, asshole."

A landline phone jingled on the wall. Ashbaugh got up and answered it.

"Yeah. Okay. Send him in."

He turned to Andrews. "Jimmy Folglestein is here."

"Good. Maybe he can convince his client that he's screwed."

Toad's lawyer walked in, pulled out a chair, sat down and immediately picked at his nails, brow furrowed. He didn't open the briefcase, but slowly and deliberately surveyed the room.

Folglestein was like a character out of an old movie where the men wore hats and fancy suits and everybody smoked cigarettes and talked fast. In his late forties, he was a short, trim, bald man with a few strands of black hair slicked back just above his ears. His eyes were also black and partially concealed behind a pair of tiny reading glasses perched halfway down his narrow nose.

We had crossed paths before when I worked in homicide. He hadn't changed much and looked right at home in his dark blue Armani suit, starched white collar, bow tie and suspenders. He was lugging a tan, expensive-looking, Henk briefcase.

"Good morning, gentlemen. I am here to represent Mister Alcott and I am assuming you have enlightened him as to his rights?"

"Of course," said Andrews.

Folglestein slumped down in his chair and steepled his fingers. He glanced at Alcott with brows raised and Alcott nodded ever so slightly.

"I take it that means yes. They did comply, Keith?"

"Yeah, they gave me the usual bullshit. Just get me some bail so I can get the fuck outta here."

The lawyer's half-moon eyebrows gave him a happy look, even when he wasn't smiling. "In that case, this little premature interview without counsel is terminated." He hugged his briefcase to his chest as he stood up. "We are done here, boys."

"Whoa, counselor. This guy's not going far. Right around the corner, as a matter of fact," said Andrews. "He's violated his parole. He hasn't been near his probation officer since August. That's over three months ago. I think the judge will frown on that. He'll side with us on this one. So Mister Alcott will be spending quite some time with us. Have a good one, Jimmy."

Cops know how it works when two people have exactly the right mix of bad chemistry. First of all, there are no partnerships with two dominant partners. The egos won't allow it. There is always the dominant partner and the one who will claim he just came along for the ride or that he was coerced. If there were ever guys that smart, one wouldn't give the other one up on a minor point. If one cracks, they both go down. If Alcott and Walker were partners, Alcott would be the killer. The interrogation hadn't produced much, but perhaps we got the ball rolling by shaking up Toad. We needed to find Ben Walker, pronto.

Chapter Twenty-Nine

The adrenaline from the interrogation of Alcott had burned off and I was headed for the lowest of lows as I shrugged into my coat. If we'd had Walker's ass there at the same time, it would have been a different story, or so I told myself. I checked the time and thought about my meeting with Beth Hubbard.

When calling on the scared shitless, it's important to make a good appearance, so before driving out to keep my appointment with her at the coffee shop in Elmhurst, I had a couple of hours to spare and decided to run by the apartment for a shower and a change of clothes.

There wasn't a whole lot of other preparation necessary for my departure. I wore jeans, a white dress shirt, tie and a corduroy sport coat. Slipping my .38 into a clip-on holster, I attached it to the inside of my waistband and left my jacket hanging over it.

Feathery clouds had stolen into the sky and the wind had picked up. Red and yellow leaves of the maple and elms fluttered chaotically and a flurry of them rattled across the street from my place and whipped against the parked cars.

I hadn't seen Mo in a few days and guilt plagued my mind as if it had been a month. I knew everything, including Alcott's arrest, was knotting me up, and I felt I had been unfair with her. She was still at work and I brought her up on speed dial.

"Homicide, Lieutenant Andrews' office."

"Hi, Mo."

"Well, hello, stranger."

"Sorry, I've been so scarce. This Hubbard case is coming to a head. How about doing dinner tonight?"

"Really? Are you asking me out on a date, Detective Hawkins?"

"I'll even pop for dessert."

"Oooooh. How could any girl in her right mind resist such an offer? What time?"

"Ah...I'm on my way out to Elmhurst, but should wrap up that business and still be outside your door by seven-ish. Is that okay?"

"Sounds good. I can't wait, big guy."

"Good, see you then."

"Okay. Hey,..."

"Yeah?"

"Please try not to get lost on the way over, okay?"

"No way, beautiful. Bye."

Closing the phone, I tossed it on the passenger seat and drove in silence as I left the city. Traffic always got heavy at the end of the day with people getting off work and it took almost forty-five minutes to drive from the Loop to Elmhurst. I worried I would get there too late. With the condition Beth was in, she might panic and leave.

The Brewmeister on Park Street was predictably crowded, but I sensed this was one of the reasons for her choosing it as a meeting place. She was bound to feel safe with other people around, even though she had no reason to fear me, but she had been truly upset about something when she called. That was for sure. Cosgrove's name came to mind.

I arrived ten minutes early, ordered a coffee and seated myself at a table with a clear view of the door. I wanted Beth to have an unobstructed view of me when she walked in. I wanted her to feel at ease. I kicked back, expecting she might be late on purpose in order to let me know the power in this meeting was hers and hers alone. I didn't care one way or the other as long as she told me what I wanted to hear. I knew that all of my questions wouldn't be answered, though, and the most I could hope for was enough answers to build a case.

She had said between three-thirty and four o'clock. I was positive of that, yet I waited and watched the clock until nearly four-thirty. I figured maybe she simply changed her mind about telling me anything. It could have been an anxiety attack and she blew it off. Maybe she was crying on a girlfriend's shoulder instead. Perhaps she was visiting relatives who were, even now, giving her comfort with a cup of coffee or something stronger. But I doubted it. It didn't figure that Beth Hubbard would not show up to the meeting she had requested so urgently.

It was only about ten miles to Oak Park and I decided to jump on 290 and head for her house.

Beth's Mercedes sat in the driveway. Cosgrove's pickup was gone. I parked behind her car and got out. The wind gusted and sprayed leaves against my ankles as I walked up the sidewalk.

Opening the storm door and using my knuckles, I knocked on the inside door several times. Getting no response, I tried again, this time pounding with my fist. I waited for what seemed like a very long time and then looked behind me before making the decision to try entry. I slowly turned the knob and shoved the door. It was unlocked and swung open.

I shut the door behind me, carefully, so the click was no louder than the second hand ticking on my grandmother's clock. The house had a stark stillness that I didn't like and a sense of being empty and I moved with caution through the foyer and into the living room. The big screen TV was on, but the sound was muted. I drew my gun and called out.

"Beth?"

With no response, I tried again. "Beth...it's me, Cleve Hawkins." I paused before going any further.

"Hello! Anybody home?"

I continued to move around in the living room and saw the message light flashing on a phone. I eased over, pushed the button and listened to five messages on the answering machine. Three were from somebody named Nick, one from a lawn service, and another from a woman named Carol. I jotted down the names and phone numbers that had been left. They could lead to something if I needed them for some reason.

I slowly continued through the house, checking the den, dining room, downstairs bathroom, a pantry and the kitchen. I tried turning the knob on the back door and found it was locked from the inside. I spotted nothing out of order, but paused, stopped and listened for what seemed like a full moment before calling out again.

"Beth? Hello! Cosgrove? It's me, Hawkins."

Dread fell like an anvil on my chest and my heart beat like my fist rapping on that door. I held my gun down at my side and slowly edged straight ahead toward a spiral staircase leading upstairs.

I began to worry. Though I would not admit it to anyone, I thought I could sometimes feel the echo of raw emotions at the scene of a violent crime. Terror, anger and panic were all part of it.

"Beth? It's me, Cleve Hawkins. Where are you?"

The smell hit me first. It wasn't overpowering until I reached the landing halfway up the stairs.

"What the fuck?" I swore to myself as I edged closer to the top of the stairs and a bedroom door that was ajar on my left. I aimed the gun and nudged the door with the toe of my shoe. "Beth?"

Swinging my gun from left to right and back again, I scanned the room but it appeared empty. It could have been a spare room. The king-sized bed appeared unused and the furniture was bare except for doily coverings and lamps. I froze for a second when I caught a fleeting glimpse of myself in a mirror on a dresser. The hair on the back of my neck bristled.

I backed out of the room and walked carefully along the upstairs hallway to what I figured would be another bedroom on the left. A sick feeling churned in my gut as I moved. That putrid smell was becoming stronger.

Using my foot, I opened the door, went in, but found nothing. Nobody, just an empty queen-sized bed with a white chenille spread and the usual bedroom furniture. An oil portrait of Jesus hung in an expensive frame on the wall by the dresser.

Again I backed out and moved toward a third room located on the right. I figured it had to be Beth's bedroom. The door was barely ajar. The images of what I would find on the other side poured through my head. I stood to the side as I turned the knob and took a deep breath and shoved the door open with my free hand.

The bed was unmade and looked as though more than one person had slept in it. Women's clothes were tossed helter-skelter on the carpet by the foot of the bed. A brandy tumbler sat on the nightstand with a splash of what looked like whiskey still in it. More clothes were scattered on two big armchairs.

The walk-in closet door was open and a light was on in there.

The smell now hit me like a rolling wave. I stared at the bed as I anticipated my next move and tried to erase the images I'd already formed in my head. Blood and excrement and urine and the unmistakable smell of gunpowder hung in the air. The bathroom door was directly across from me. It was closed.

I stood to the side with my gun at the ready and knocked. I spoke again, only this time barely loud enough to hear myself. "Beth, it's me, Cleve Hawkins. Are you alright?"

Getting no response, I turned the knob and pushed the door open.

The first glimpse was of the shower curtain. It looked as though someone had butchered a cow. Bloody chunks of brain tissue and hair clung to it. I gagged.

Beth Hubbard sat on the toilet wearing nothing but her panties and bra, her head and shoulders flung backward, arms hanging to her sides. Her legs were canted over to the left. Her mouth hung open and her eyes were wide open as if she knew in that final second that the reality of death was different than she imagined it would be.

Triple Crossed

"Beth," I heard myself whisper aloud.

I moved into the room carefully, absorbing the details automatically, even as my brain tried to comprehend the gross tragedy in front of me.

The back of her skull was gone, blown wide open with a chunk of scalp clinging to the crown of her head by a mass of bloody blonde hair. Brain matter that resembled oatmeal and tiny bone fragments had all splattered the ceiling and wall as well as the floor. A .45 pistol lay on the floor to Beth's right side, flung there with the force of the body's reaction in that final instant.

I touched two fingers to her throat, a mere formality. She was cool to the touch. Rigor mortis had set in, so that put the time of death within the last eight to ten hours, maybe longer, but not much.

I wondered if she slept the night before or lay awake, sorting out the harsh realities of living, and had concluded she would take her own life. I got no further with that assessment. Beth Hubbard didn't have the guts to kill herself. I may have been wrong, but that was my conclusion until proven otherwise.

In all of my twenty-plus years in law enforcement, I'd never gotten used to the smell of death. There is nothing else like it. It hangs in the air at the scene so thick and heavy, it's an unavoidable presence. I knew that logically the smell would disappear after the body was removed, but the memory of it never dies. More than once I had to throw my clothes away after working a scene. It seemed as though the smell clung to clothing and never went away.

I left the room and sat on the stairs, bent over with my forearms resting on my thighs, my head down. As many of these as I had witnessed, I was still shocked and I felt like puking.

After a while, I walked downstairs and out the front door. I stood on the front steps and wished for that cigarette I had done without for so long. I wanted a stiff double shot of scotch, too, but instead reached for my cell phone and punched in nine-one-one.

R.C. Hartson

Chapter Thirty

I spoke to the dispatcher, Sergeant Tereasa Granger, a veteran cop I knew from my days on the road in a blue and white. I told her who I was, but I was actually surprised she remembered me.

"Hey, Hawkins. What the hell is going on? I thought you were retired."

"Yeah, over two years ago. I'm private now. So, I'm in Oak Park. Long story short, you'd better send the coroner along with the bag and tag 'em boys. There's a female DB out here, at 2016 Lone Pine Road. Looks like a suicide."

"Got it. Is she anybody you know?"

"Just from a case I'm working."

"Okay, Hawkins. I'll notify the duty officer and Lieutenant Andrews. What in the name of hell are you doing there?"

"Ah, it's a long story, Sergeant, but go ahead and do what you have to do. I'm calling Andrews, too, just so you know."

"That'll work. You'd better stand by out there, though."

"I planned to, Granger."

"Okay, catch ya' later. Hey, stop by sometime. Fill me in on what's been happening, you handsome devil."

I punched in Andrews' home phone number. His wife, Helen, answered and she handed it off to him.

"Hawkins here, Phil. Beth Hubbard is dead. I called dispatch, but figured I'd touch base with you, too. Apparent suicide at her home in Oak Park. Could be homicide, though. You know how it goes."

"Hold on. What was her address again?"

"Two-oh-one-six Lone Pine Road."

"Okay. Question is, what the hell are you doing out there?"

"Oh. I thought I mentioned to you at Alcott's grilling. Beth Hubbard had called and asked me to meet her this afternoon. She was upset, claimed she had some reliable information for me on her husband's disappearance. Remember, she hired me before all this shit hit the fan? Anyway, I was supposed to meet her at

Triple Crossed

The Brewmeister in Elmhurst. She didn't show. Now we know why."

"Hmmm, something sounds strange there. But okay, pardner, I'm on my way. I take it you're gonna' hang tight 'till I get there?"

"You've got it, LT."

I flipped my phone closed. The side of my face was tingling and I let out a deep breath and tried to decompress. The visuals and the odors were usually the most difficult things to get used to in homicide work. I hoped to confiscate a mask from the first responders.

Every moron who has ever watched an episode of *CSI* thinks they are experts in forensic sciences and criminal investigation, but I knew in my gut there would be evidence of foul play found here. A forensic pathologist will collect evidence such as hairs and fabric fibers. A rape kit will be performed looking for foreign pubic hairs, semen, signs of sexual assault.

Few of those so-called experts realize a violent death scene is a putrid mixture of blood, bladder and bowel content. It's thick, choking and underscored by the sharp, acidic smell of puke.

Beth's decomposition had filled my nose. It would be a while before I would smell anything but death.

It was six-fifteen and the sun had turned into a red ember inside a bank of maroon-colored clouds above the city. Mo and I had a date at seven. I had to call her, but figured I'd wait until the homicide squad showed.

I couldn't get Carl Cosgrove out of my mind. I suspected he was involved and would never return, even after the cops were gone.

It wasn't long before I heard sirens. An EMT and an ambulance pulled in a few minutes later. They were eventually followed by three blue and whites. Andrews and Ashbaugh were not far behind.

Andrews was driving his black Explorer. Ashbaugh stepped out of a Crown Vic like he was stepping in soup. He must have come right from the office because he still wore a gray suit with a gray and red tie. The wind blew the tie over his shoulder as he crossed the front lawn. Andrews hadn't bothered with the dress code. He wore slacks and a polo shirt under his top coat and his hands were buried deep in the pockets of the coat as he approached me.

They ducked under police tape, and the sedans in the driveway had become radio cars. It was a crime scene.

"Hey, Hawk," said Andrews.

"Yeah, Loot. Hell of a way to spend a quiet evening at home, eh?"

"Yeah. Come on, let's go inside. You can bring me up to speed." We walked the rest of the way in silence. The smell was overpowering and Andrews pulled out a handkerchief to cover his nose and mouth. To save time I took the lead and Andrews followed me. Ashbaugh was right behind him. I saw him fishing around in his coat pocket for his own handkerchief, but finding none, he held his arm up over his nose, the same as I did.

Two Oak Park Police Department uniforms stood just outside the bathroom door, securing the actual scene with their presence. I stood to the side and let Andrews edge past the two cops.

"Fuckin' A," he muttered when he saw Beth Hubbard. "Why do they always pick the bathroom?" I saw him look at the gun on the floor. "Christ, a forty-five? She might as well have used a cannon."

I shook my head. "Never seem to get used to it, do we?" I murmured as Detective Ashbaugh looked over our shoulders.

"You were supposed to meet her at the coffee shop, eh?" said Andrews.

I nodded. "Between three-thirty and four o'clock. She didn't show, so I drove over here. I guess it was about twenty to five."

"Doesn't add up, does it?" said Ashbaugh.

"Hell, no," I said. "Why bother to ask for a meeting with somebody and then decide to kill yourself instead? It's bullshit. Speaking of bullshit, I think you'd best put out an APB on Carl Cosgrove ASAP, Phil. Remember? He's the asshole I told you about that lived here posing as the butler or personal assistant. I know damned well his prints are all over this scene."

Andrews pulled out his iPhone, punched in something and spoke. "Yeah, Gorman? Andrews here. Listen, I want you to get an APB started on one Carl Cosgrove." He paused. "No. I don't have a middle name yet. What? Hold on." He looked at me. "Hawk, what did you say the address was here?"

"Two-oh-one-six Lone Pine, Oak Park."

Andrews continued on the phone. "It's two-oh-one-six Lone Pine, Oak Park. What? No, but get somebody moving on a mug shot, too. Cosgrove might be an alias, but I've got a hunch we've got this clown somewhere in the books." He paused again then said, "Yeah...yeah. Okay. Well, get it done pronto and get back to me tonight if possible."

The crime scene crew came through then, lugging their cases and cameras, just as I was headed for the front door to make my call to Mo.

The place would be photographed then video-taped. The death scene would be dusted for prints. I tried to remember what, if anything, besides the door knob, I had touched. Not that it mattered, but it's just not done by a professional.

Triple Crossed

If there was any evidence to gather, it too would be photographed, its exact position measured, noted, logged, marked and packaged with extreme care taken to establish the chain of custody so that its every moment could be accounted for. All that time, Beth Hubbard's body would remain just as I'd found it, until the Medical Examiner arrived.

Outside I saw that the first responder uniforms had immediately made sure yellow crime-scene tape had been wound around a couple of small saplings. They fluttered in the strong breeze like banners around a used car lot.

A small group of reporters had followed the blue and whites and were being held back by deputies.

A radio was playing country music while portable cop radios crackled with static and mumbled messages. Red and blue lights flashed and swirled everywhere and the voices of the cops on hand to investigate ran together in an indecipherable mish-mash.

A crowd of neighbors gawked from across the street, and the line of cars edging past made it seem like a traffic fatality had occurred.

It wasn't long before news vans and more police cars were parked in front of Hubbard's house. Transmission dishes swayed over the vans like spindly fronds, and uniformed cops and news people chatted together on the sidewalk. A news helicopter fluttered overhead. An ambulance was parked in the drive, its back doors yawning open.

The Oak Park Police Department had three cars on hand, too. The case would be in their jurisdiction, but homicide cases automatically attracted the Chicago homicide people, too.

I edged over to a spot under the bay windows in the front of the house, pulled out my cell phone and called Mo.

"Hi, Mo. I just wanted to let you know. I got tied up in a miserable scene out here in Oak Park, but I'm on my way."

The sound on the other end had the quality of a held breath. Or maybe the held breath was mine.

"What happened?" she asked. There was an obvious fright reflected in her voice.

"Suicide or homicide. It's Beth Hubbard...she's dead."

"Whoa! What in the name of God hap...?"

"I know, I know. I was supposed to meet with her. Listen, I'll be late, but I wanted to let you know, I'm on my way. I'll tell you about it when I get there."

"Okay. Please be careful, Cleve. See you soon."

"Yeah, the traffic is gonna' be a bear this time of day, but I'll squeeze through. Don't worry. Bye."

I went back inside, hung around for a few minutes watching the crime scene guys do their thing before I told Andrews I had to leave.

"If you need anything, feel free to call. Otherwise I'll be stopping in HQ tomorrow morning. Maybe I can help you ID Cosgrove."

"Okay. Later, Hawk. Thanks."

I clamped a battery-powered emergency light on my roof and took off. I still had to squeeze in a stop at my place for a shower and change of clothes.

On the way home, my mind began to wander every which way. Cosgrove was out there someplace thinking he got away with murder. I'd bet my life on that pistol being his gun. When the traffic slowed, I completely switched gears and thought about my beautiful Mo and her red hair, big blue eyes and sexy voice. I knew I was one lucky sonofabitch to have her in my life. *Maybe I should give some serious thought to spending more time with her and less on worrying about scumbags like Toad, Walker and Cosgrove.*

I was squeezed in bumper-to-bumper traffic before I reached the North Side. I caught myself looking in the rearview, checking myself with a critical eye. I still looked like hell in the aftermath of the scene in Oak Park.

. . .

When I got to her place, Mo slipped her arms around me and hugged me tight for a moment. I held her and kissed the top of her head. She looked up at me and said, "I'll bet you're not hungry now, are you?"

"Honestly? No, but I asked you to do dinner and we will do dinner, Mo. I'm keeping my word."

She was wearing a black turtleneck sweater and a string of white pearls with designer jeans and black leather boots. Her leather jacket hung on the back of a dinette chair. She was wearing very little makeup, but I could tell she had spent time on her face, the way women do. She laid her head on my chest and the scent of her hair was wonderfully potent.

She wet her lips. "How about a scotch and soda?" She pointed a finger in the air. "Just one. You look like you need it."

With my fingers under her chin, I tilted her head up. Looking in her eyes, I said. "I appreciate it, Mo. Believe me, it sounds good, but some people can't handle alcohol. It doesn't mean they're weak willed or bad. With me, we both know, it's like gasoline and matches. I'll have a Diet Coke if you've got one."

"Of course," she murmured, almost as if she were talking to herself. Her hand settled briefly at the base of her throat and then moved away.

"I'm proud of you, Columbo." She smiled as she peeled off my coat, took my cap and said, "Have a seat."

She pulled a bottle of Coke from the fridge and kissed me lightly on the lips. "I've decided we're ordering carry-out. It's Chinese tonight and we're eating it right here."

"Oh, dammit. Are you sure you don't mind?"

She shook her head and sat on my lap. "Just tell me what went down in Oak Park? Bottom line, detective, okay?" She slid a cigarette out of the pack of Mistys lying on the table and lit up.

"Well, you knew I was going out to meet Beth Hubbard, right?"

"Yeah."

"She didn't show. So I went over to her house and found her dead in her bathroom. Gunshot. Looked like it was self-inflicted. Your boss and Ashbaugh and the rest of Cook County, I think, are out there sorting things out."

Mo stood and pressed an elegantly manicured hand to her lips, as she always seemed to do when a moment became too difficult for her.

"Oh, no, that can't be right," she said with a half an inch of ash glowing red on the end of her cigarette. "From what you've told me before, she doesn't seem like the type to pull something like that." She paused. "Whatever that type is...but you said she was needy and greedy, and due for a lot of money after her husband was gone."

"Exactly. That's how I feel sure it wasn't suicide."

Mo laid the cigarette in the ashtray and paced the living room. She looked out the window at the city below. Crossing her arms over her breasts, she cupped her elbows, a self-comforting gesture, I thought. I followed her movements as she watched the traffic still clogging the streets of downtown Chicago with headlights and taillights glowing in the night. She turned and came back over.

"What's the story with her and this guy Carl Cosgrove?" she asked as I sipped my Coke.

"Good question, babe. They're looking for him as we speak. I think the whole thing was staged. Once a homicide cop, always a homicide cop, I guess. I think everyone's murdered. It's my natural mind-set."

She stubbed her cigarette out in an ashtray and kissed me on the lips. Not a long passionate kiss, just soft, wet and sweet.

"The Chinese should be here anytime," she said. "I told Chen's eight-thirty. I ordered your favorite, Mongolian Beef with white rice. Try to eat something, will you?"

I looked at my watch. It was eight-twenty. "Wow, you did good on the time." I grinned. "Yeah, I'll try to eat something, you went to all that trouble."

"Good. I got a half dozen Crabmeat Rangoons, too."

"Perfect."

Much later, after we'd eaten, Mo hooked her arm in mine and we went to the bedroom. She sat on the edge of the king-sized bed and I helped her pull her boots off. She wrapped her arms around my hips and looked up into my eyes.

"You're an honorable and brave guy, Hawkins. That's why you'll always be both feared and respected by the world."

"You think that's it, huh?"

"Yes," she murmured as she pulled back the covers. "I love you," she said. "Get in here, just as you are."

I slid under the sheets and held her in my arms.

"I love you, Cleve."

I kissed her and said, "I love you, too, beautiful."

That night we made a different kind of love. We just lay in each other's arms, fully dressed, and slept until dawn.

Chapter Thirty-One

Mo was still sleeping soundly when I got up before dawn. Just before I left, she stirred and I bent down to kiss her on the cheek. I left a note telling her I would call later in the day.

After I went to the gym, I stopped by my apartment for a shower and change of clothes and then headed for the office. It seemed odd that Deckle was nowhere in sight, but the temperature had dropped. A severe cold front had quickly chased away autumn and a freezing mist settled over the city. It always seemed to happen overnight. I felt sure that my raggedy friend was sheltered at the mission on Canal Street.

I had no sooner turned the heat up and made a pot of coffee when my phone vibrated. It was Jeebers.

"Hey, Jeebs. What's shakin'?"

"Cleve, I'm glad I caught you. I've got some good news and some bad news."

"Really? Well, go ahead and give me the good stuff first. It's too damned early for the bad. What's up, partner?"

"We've got a bead on your man Walker."

"Great. How'd that happen?"

"Lieutenant Andrews put me in charge of overseeing the BOLO for this asshole. Actually I sort of volunteered, but anyway, we checked for your perp, Benjamin Culver Walker, in all the databases available for guys with that name in the Chicago area in case he stood out in some way. We got nothing but hundreds of random hits, as was to be expected, I suppose, given ethnic names and historic patterns of movement."

"Of course."

"Anyway, as you know, he's got one hell of a rap sheet, but that didn't help in tying anything together. Some of these guys should be required to wear full body condoms. This scumbag was hidden like a grain of sand on a beach until I got a tip from one of my snitches. We think we know where he's staying…with some broad out in Wheeling."

"Great, Jeebs. I'm surprised Andrews didn't let me know. Christ, he knows how much I'm involved with this case. What's the bad news?"

"Take it easy, Ace. Remember, I said he put me in charge of this. He'll probably fill you in, but meanwhile, I'm going out there. I don't think we'll need SWAT, but I'm taking two other men with me for back up and going there to check it out. They're stretched pretty thin on detectives right now, so a couple of lucky uniforms get to wear plainclothes for a while. Bad news is you can't do anything but tag along. I'm not supposed to do this, but I know you've been in this up to your eyebrows. I figured you'd like to be in on it, so that's why I'm giving you the heads up. Maybe we'll be able to put the cuffs on Walker."

"You need a warrant?"

"No. Warrants are about what you can prove. Not what you know."

"And we can prove he's our guy, right?"

"Right. We've got him with the other asshole on your film, snatching Hubbard, so we should be good to go. You in?"

"Is the Pope Catholic? Hell, yes! When are you going?"

"According to my informant, Walker has been living in Wheeling in a rundown apartment. He rents in a two story on a dead end street where most front lawns have a vehicle sitting on cement blocks. You get the picture, right?"

"Yeah, where do you want to meet?"

"Are you at your office?"

"Yeah."

"Stay there, Hawk. We'll swing by in a few and you can ride with us out to Wheeling."

"Roger that. I'll be here. Semper Fi, Jeebs."

I felt the spark ignite in my bloodstream and I ruminated while I drank my coffee and waited. Rounding up Walker was not the bottom line. He wouldn't have all the answers, but the charge of adrenaline came nonetheless. After we questioned him, I knew something had to give.

I could put the pieces of the puzzle together and there was always a definitive high when even the smallest of pieces had a new fit. With this case, I realized how free I was to follow my own instincts and cast my net in any direction I wanted.

When I was with the homicide division, I certainly had followed my instincts, but there was always a captain or lieutenant holding me up with approval. There were so many rules and procedures to follow. Everyone had to be briefed before action could be taken. There were rules of procedure and rules concerning evidence. A partner was a must, and budgets tied my hands in many cases. I always felt that every move I made, every word I typed, was subject to review and could possibly be held against me in the long run.

We had proof positive that Walker and Alcott had abducted Thad Hubbard, and I believed they had killed him with injections of cocaine that stopped his heart. But they didn't act on their own. Someone much higher up on the food chain was calling the shots.

Somebody had murdered Beth Hubbard, too. It was no suicide and I was sure the Medical Examiner would have the same opinion when he was finished with his business.

. . .

I rode in the back seat of Jeebers' SUV with a sergeant named Steve Kyer. Detective Dick Martin was in the front with Jeebers. We parked down the street from where Walker was living in a little two story house on a thirty-foot lot, no driveway, green and white metal awnings over the windows.

There was a statue of the Virgin Mary holding a dish as a bird bath in the front yard. Nice touch for the digs of a killer, I thought.

Jeebers took a dead cigar out of his mouth and threw it out the window. He took another thin cheap one from the breast pocket of his jacket. Stripping the cellophane from it, he stuck it in his mouth and said, "We're gonna' go real careful here, guys. This prick is probably armed and definitely dangerous." He looked at the cop in the passenger seat. "Martin, I want you and Kyer to circle around back. Take up positions on each side of the door and keep an eye on any other possible exits. Clear?"

They both answered, "Yeah, we're good to go."

"Good." Jeebers stared at me with serious eyes. "Hawk, you're coming with me to the front door. I'll do the talking. I assume you're carrying?"

I patted my chest. "My .38 and the .22 on my ankle."

"Okay. I don't want you using them unless it's absolutely necessary, but you've got my back if things go sideways for some reason, okay?"

I nodded. "You've got it."

He looked at Martin and Kyer again. "We know Walker has no qualms about using a gun to settle scores. His priorities are cocaine, women and whiskey, and not necessarily in that order. In other words, he's a crazy fucker, so stay on your toes, men."

I said, "Yeah, but I'm betting he's a punk. Probably has to squat to piss."

"Just be cool, Hawk. I know you want to help, but let us take him. You get to watch this time."

Martin and Kyer left and I saw them skirt down the block to eventually cover the rear of the house while Jeebers and I moved slowly down the block and up to the front door. Jeebers pushed the doorbell and we waited.

A tired looking, overweight woman answered the door. She was short, built like a corner mailbox and her makeup was overdone, but she had smooth skin for a fifty-something female. Her eyes were big and blue, and her hair was bleached blonde. I could see the dark roots. I figured her to be Italian or Gypsy. She wore huge triangular gold earrings, which, if connected to a shortwave radio, could have picked up Naples. A cigarette dangled from a corner of her mouth.

"Yeah, what is it?" she said without opening the inside storm door. She looked around as if the trees had ears. Loud television voices were coming from somewhere inside.

Jeebers badged her. "Good morning, ma'am. I'm Detective Mulvaney, Chicago Police Department, and this is Detective Hawkins. We need to speak to Benjamin Walker."

With hand on her hip, she hesitated. "He ain't here right now. What's this about?" Her breath came in short, shallow, unsatisfying gasps.

"Police business, ma'am."

"Jesus Christ," she said, as she took a long drag on the cigarette. "What in the world did he do? He got in another fight, didn't he?" The cords stood out in her neck and her face turned red. Her blue eyes narrowed and filled with both venom and tears as she opened the door and flicked her cigarette out on the ground.

"Can we come in?" Jeebers asked.

She shied away a bit and tried to smile, the way people do when their problems are so intolerable and without answers that you want to leave the room. "I don't usually let strangers in my house, you know. You got a warrant or something?" She waved a hand in dismissal. "I suppose I can make an exception for a badge," she said in a two-pack-a-day voice.

"I'm telling you, it's a waste of time, though. The man you want isn't here, and I still think you need a warrant or something."

A big screen TV had the Steve Wilkos show blaring in the background.

"That's good," said Jeebers as he pushed the door, forcing the woman to step back. He pulled his Glock from the holster inside his coat and continued edging forward. While he talked, his eyes constantly scanned the room.

"What's your name, ma'am?"

Triple Crossed

"Killigan. Jessica Killigan. Why do ya' need my name? What is this, anyway?"

"Procedure, ma'am."

"Procedure? Jesus Christ!" Killigan shouted.

"Thank you. Please stay back out of the way," Jeebers said and kept passing through the living room, past Steve Wilkos saying, "Does that make you feel good? Talking to your brother that way?"

We moved down through a narrow hall to the kitchen and toward the back of the house when a man suddenly rushed down a set of stairs to our left and bolted for the back door. I knew it had to be Walker. Instinct made me draw my .38.

"Stop!" Jeebers yelled. He leveled his gun and aimed at the man's head. "Hold it, Walker!" He froze in place. "Down on the floor," Jeebers yelled. "Now! Do it!"

Walker raised his hands and dropped to his knees.

Jeebers was on him. He shoved Walker down on the floor and pinned him like an insect to a board. Kneeling in the middle of Walker's back, he yanked his arms back and clamped the cuffs on his wrists.

"Oh, my God! Oh, my God!" Scream after scream tore from Jessica Killigan's throat and she fell to a couch, sobbing. "I told them you weren't here, Benny."

"Shut up!" Walker growled.

He was a body builder type with a head the size of a moonshine jug, his hands as big as baseball mitts. He was wearing an undershirt, jeans and cowboy boots. He had dressed in a panic evidently. His belt wasn't through all the loops and dangled like a black snake from his hips.

I saw the shadows of the other two cops through the curtain covering the top half of the back door and I unlocked it to let Kyer and Martin inside. They rushed in as far as the stairway with guns raised. They lowered them when they saw the situation.

"All clear in the back. This is Walker, eh?" said Martin.

"Yeah, it's him, alright," said Jeebers. He grabbed Walker by the hair of his head and yanked him up onto his feet. "That's you, isn't it, asshole?"

"Benjamin Walker, you are under arrest. You have the right to remain silent. Anything you say can and will be used against you in a court of law. You have the right to speak to an attorney and to have an attorney present during any questioning. If you cannot afford a lawyer, one will be provided for you at government expense. Understand? Good."

He nodded at the two other cops. "Check upstairs. See if this asshole has any friends hiding out." He lit his cigar and said, "Hawk, you'll probably want to sit in when we question this piece of shit. It will take time to book him and so on. Check with me tomorrow."

"I wouldn't miss it, Jeebs. Thanks."

So, we had Walker. I was hoping he'd try to make a deal and give us everything we wanted. I suspected he could have given Carl Cosgrove the heads up to get out of Dodge, and Carl might be in the wind already.

Loose ends and unexplained details always bother me, like odd pieces in a jigsaw puzzle box. Sometimes they were big questions, sometimes not, but they were always a sliver in the ass.

For instance, what was Cosgrove's role in Beth Hubbard's life and death? Was he her lover or her stooge? Surely, he was more than a handyman or bullshit butler.

When you hear hoof beats, you don't think kangaroos.

Chapter Thirty-Two

The on-again-off-again rain spackled my windshield with diamonds. The windows steamed up and I cranked the defroster on full blast. The clouds broke open one final time, hammering me with a downpour so hard the wipers were useless. I squinted into the oncoming threat but didn't slow down.

I was still thinking about Cosgrove when I drifted through a yellow light at State and Roosevelt and heard a horn behind me. Glancing in the rearview, I saw a maroon SUV that was right on my ass. The clown driving it stayed on his horn and as he passed, gave me an Italian hand signal that didn't mean left turn. My collar felt a bit tight, but I continued on my way to the police department on Michigan Avenue where they were holding Walker.

Finding a parking place was impossible, but I managed one, even though I knew my black Charger parked among the blue and whites would stand out like a rhino among cattle.

During the day, the Chicago Police Department is always swarming with urgency of one kind or another. Uniformed cops rush around bantering crudely with those working behind desks. Detectives in cheap suits strut through the halls, scowling as if they are pissed off at the world. Frightened people sit on wooden benches waiting for anticipated bad news. Often there's a uniformed cop huddled up with a lawyer involved in an intense negotiation about an ongoing trial.

After checking in with security, I was escorted to The Major Crimes squad room, which was typically crowded and busy. A half dozen detectives who looked like they would rather be home in bed were engaged in conversations with uniformed officers who floated around listlessly with Styrofoam coffee cups.

A cop I didn't recognize was sitting alone in one cubicle with his legs stretched out, his arms folded. He was watching me like I was about to make his long day longer.

I went to Jeeber's office, one he shared with another detective named Paul Blondell. It was a small gray cubby full of books, binders and file folders. Yellow post-it notes were stuck to every surface, reminders to do anything from calling for lab results, to checking with witnesses, to court dates. Cop cartoons gleaned from the internet were taped to the filing cabinets and walls. Detective Jeebers Mulvaney was not there.

A uniformed cop led me to the interrogation rooms where Jeebers stood with Lieutenant Andrews and Detective Jim Ashbaugh. They were looking into a one-way mirror, eyeballing the arrested Ben Walker, alone in the interrogation room.

Sidling up to the glass, I said, "Hey, LT, thanks for letting me in on this one." I nodded at Ashbaugh and Jeebers. "Guys, how's it going? Has he said anything?"

"Nothing except his full name," said Ashbaugh.

"And he wants to lawyer up," said Jeebers.

I nodded and smiled. "Wow! You couldn't see that coming. So, who's steering the interview?"

"Jeebers," said Andrews. "He'll continue to be the lead. He brought Walker in, so I figure I'll let him play this one out, see where it leads."

He glanced at Ashbaugh. "Jim, you take second chair. Be there for good cop, bad cop crap if need be. I may pile on too if things get sticky. Right now, I've got a meeting upstairs. Keep me posted, okay?" The lieutenant turned to me. "Sorry, Hawk. I know this one was yours, but you'll have to keep a low profile in there, right?"

I nodded. "Check."

We watched Walker's body language for a few minutes while we talked. He sat kicked back in a folding chair with his arms crossed and his cowboy boots propped up on the table. He scowled and fidgeted and looked as if his skin didn't fit him right. His dark, thinning hair was unruly and he had the obligatory prison tats on both of his arms and his neck. Under his thin lips, he had the tiniest tuft of hair, which he stroked several times. There was a small scar above his right eyebrow, a silver earring in his left earlobe and a diamond ring on his right pinky.

"It shouldn't be a problem with this guy, LT," said Jeebers. "He's dead meat. Just doesn't know it yet. Let's get in there, guys."

Inside, we grabbed folding chairs and sat at the table. Jeebers placed his chair directly across from Walker and used a meaty hand to sweep Walker's feet off of the table. "Get your fuckin' feet off our table."

Walker sneered as his boots hit the floor with a thud. He scooted his chair around a bit and leaned back, tipping his chair so the front legs were suspended in the air. "I don't know what I'm here for, but I want my lawyer."

"He's been notified, you cocky asshole. You need to adjust your thinking and your attitude." Jeebers opened a manila folder and laid it on the table in front of

Triple Crossed

him. He flipped through a few of the pages and looked at the smirking Walker.

Walker twiddled his thumbs and stared at the folder. He didn't respond and Jeebers pressed on.

"First of all, you don't believe in following the rules of your parole, tiger. You haven't checked in with your probation officer in over four months."

I tried to read through Walker's scowl, but found nothing. I found myself staring at the man who I'd tracked down from video camera pictures weeks before and comparing his features to those of the man on the video. Behind his eyes, I could see him pulling a rake through his thoughts, as though he was trying to figure out the source of all his trouble. He picked at his nails and didn't return my stare.

"I can't be sayin' shit to you about anythin' without my lawyer." The man had yet to look my way, but now he turned and glared at me.

Jeebers thumbed through a few more of the pages and looked up at the smirking Walker. "Quite a rap sheet you've got here, Ben. Is there any bad shit you haven't tried to pull in your illustrious career?"

Walker continued to mess with his fingernails and said nothing. The air was strained and tense.

"Let's get right to it, Walker. We can save some time before your mouthpiece gets here. You're being charged with kidnapping and murder, and we can prove it, so wipe that silly-assed grin off your fuckin' face before I decide to punch your ticket myself."

Jeebers paused and cleared his throat then continued. He slid an eight by ten picture of Thad Hubbard across the table. "You know this man?"

Walker leaned in and studied the picture very briefly. He shook his head. "No. I can't help you. Never saw him before."

"Let me refresh your memory. His name is Thad Hubbard." Jeebers paused, pulled the picture back and laid a different one in front of Walker. It was a mug shot of Keith Alcott. "How about this guy?"

Again Walker shook his head. "Never seen him before either."

"You make a piss poor liar, Ben. Mister Hubbard was abducted as he was leaving work in the Loop. His car was found untouched on the bottom floor of the parking garage on Jackson. The footage from the garage surveillance cameras were analyzed for that time period, as well as the twelve hours prior, and they clearly show you and your partner, Keith Alcott, stuffing Mister Hubbard in the trunk of a car. The cameras also captured the license plate of the car you used."

"Bullshit. You've got the wrong guy," said Walker. "I don't know who those two jokers are. I never heard of nobody named Hubbard, or Wolcott neither." He crossed his arms. Smug. He also had that lop-sided grin you see on stupid people who think they are smarter than you.

"That's Alcott, not Wolcott, asshole, and you know it," said Ashbaugh.

His lying churned my insides and I felt the blood rush to my head. I hadn't wanted to smack anybody in the head that badly in a long, long time.

Walker crossed his arms over his chest and cupped his elbows, a self-comforting gesture, I thought. "I said I want to wait for my lawyer."

Jeebers glanced at his watch. "Yeah, we get that, but we're not gonna wait all day. I don't have time for this bullshit. By the time he gets here, I'll be long gone and you'll be stuck with the bill. Don't worry, though. I'm sure your guy will drop everything for a scumbag like you and will be here in a flash to save your ass." He paused and flipped through a few more pages in the folder. He stopped and steepled his fingers under his chin. "Problem is, he can't save you, Ben. You're screwed."

"Ha! You got nothing on me except not showing for my probation meets."

I was so pissed I couldn't help myself. I jumped in and said, "Really? The kidnapping wasn't your fault, right? Nah, it was Mister Hubbard's fault for walking to his car by himself. He was clearly an idiot. You must think you should be commended for taking him out of the gene pool, eh?"

Walker's face was covered in sweat when he gave me the bad eye. He glanced at Jeebers and Ashbaugh. "This is all bullshit. I'm not giving you nothin', detective." He paused and tapped his fingers on the table in a staccato rhythm. "Certain people think I'm talking to you, next thing my ass is horizontal. So, fuck that."

I shouldn't have said anything, I guess. Usually I've learned to bite my tongue. In fact, my tongue has scars.

My phone vibrated and I checked the number. I didn't recognize it, but decided to take it. "Excuse me, Detective Mulvany, I've got to take this one," I said as I stepped outside and closed the door.

"Hawkins."

On the other end a woman spoke in a low, whisper-like voice. "Mister Hawkins, you probably won't remember me. I'm Edith Chalmers."

"Sorry, no, I don't recall the name. What can I do for you, ma'am?"

"I'm Hugh Carrington's personal secretary. I met you when you visited him a couple of times a few months ago."

In that instant, I got it. Of course. She was the one with her nose in the air who was downright rude. She was such a tight ass, I suspected it would have taken a tractor to pull a toothpick out of her ass.

"Oh, yes, sorry. I do remember you now. What's up?"

Her words became almost melodic. "Does the name Carl Cosgrove mean anything to you, Mister Hawkins?"

I hesitated and swallowed hard before I said, "I have a feeling you know it does, Ms. Chalmers, or is it Mrs.?"

"It's Ms., and I didn't want to talk to the police. I have some information regarding Mister Cosgrove, but I don't want to discuss it over the phone. Can we meet somewhere and talk?"

"Yes, of course. When and where?"

"I thought perhaps at the Starbucks on State near Division, say tomorrow morning around ten-thirty?"

"Yeah, I can do that." My heart was hammering in my chest, but I didn't want to sound too excited. I knew it was better to pretend there was no fire at all than to poke around in the ashes and stir up the dust. I took a single breath. "Do you happen to know where Mister Cosgrove is, Ms. Chalmers?"

There was a heavy sigh on her end. "Let's wait until I see you, shall we? I'll be sitting in the back."

"See you in the morning then," I said, but I had a feeling she was already gone. I clicked off and went back into the interview room.

Jeebers and Ashbaugh continued to press Walker, but he had totally clammed up, so we all stepped outside to take a break and left Walker to dwell on his fate.

About fifteen minutes later his attorney, Sid Maret, showed up. Ashbaugh saw him coming down the hall and whispered, "It's Sid Maret. If he had been a light bulb instead of a lawyer, he would have been about a twenty watt."

He approached and said, "Good day, gentlemen."

We shuffled back into the room and Maret followed us.

Walker jumped up, and hooking his thumbs in his back pockets, said, "It's about time, Sid. Jesus Christ, These cops are busting my balls over shit I had nothing to do with."

"Shhhh. Don't say another word without my permission," said Maret.

Maret had a reputation as an ambulance chaser and a sleaze ball who had been busted at least three times for soliciting prostitutes. He looked to be over fifty. Trim body. Tennis on Tuesdays and Fridays, no doubt. He had a prominent cleft in his chin and a head that was slightly too large for his body, all the more emphasized by a wild thatch of curly black hair shot through with silver. He was dark eyed and olive complexioned with a chipped front tooth. When he set his briefcase down, I noticed his hands were covered with liver spots. Although the man wore thousand dollar suits, he was still very much an asshole with a law degree.

He pulled up a chair and gazed into space, a spec of light in his eye, a slight smile on his mouth. He zeroed in on Jeebers since Jeebs had the folder in front of him and appeared to be in charge.

He hadn't bothered to open his briefcase while he gazed at Jeebers, "What is my client accused of, detective?"

"Your client has been arrested for kidnapping and first degree murder, counselor. And by the way, it's a lock. We have him on tape while he's dumping the body of the victim into the trunk of a car."

"Bullshit!" said Walker.

Maret quickly gripped Walker's forearm and glared. "I said not a word, Ben. Shut up." He paused briefly. "Gentlemen, this interview is over until I've had an opportunity to confer with my client."

"Yeah, your client should have come in a couple of weeks ago. We could have made a deal. Maybe. Now it's too late. His partner, Keith Alcott, was also arrested." Jeebers focused on Walker. "He spilled his guts, Benny, told us the whole story."

Jeebers grinned as he continued to look at Walker's surprised eyes.

"That's right, mister innocent. We've got your buddy in the cage. He gets the plea deal, if there is one. You get the shaft, hotshot. Sometimes, life is a misery carnival with shit for prizes, ya know?"

I was glad to finally get out of there. Mo was visiting her mother in Aurora, so with nothing else to do, I headed for home. I wondered what Edith Chalmers had for me. Somehow, I knew I would have trouble sleeping that night as I pondered the possibilities.

Chapter Thirty-Three

It seemed like such a distant memory, that first day I'd met Beth Hubbard and had agreed to tail her husband in order to uncover the suspected infidelity. Now, almost three months later, there I was meeting a co-worker of her husband's and I hadn't even met the man, not while he was still breathing anyway.

Crazy conspiracies are fodder for novels and movies, but after meeting Edith Chalmers a couple of times at Carrington Enterprises, I was convinced she was either extremely rude or wasn't to be trusted. I didn't attend our meeting at Starbucks with my eyes closed. I had my 9mm Glock in a pancake holster against the small of my back beneath my sport coat.

Thursday morning was crisp, with a slight chance of snow in the air, and I entered the coffee house at ten-thirty per her request.

Ms. Chalmers said she would be sitting in the back, but when she saw me come in, she stood and moved quickly toward me as though we were lovers meeting for a tryst.

I had forgotten that she was a somewhat tall woman who moved with a lot of confidence as if maybe she'd been an athlete in college. She wore a dark car coat and was dressed impeccably in a gray pleated skirt that fell several inches below the knee. Her top was white silk and her boots were knee-high black leather.

I noticed there wasn't one hair out of place. She had it scraped back against her skull and pulled into a flawless, tight chignon at the base of her neck. She wore a beautifully patterned silk scarf draped artfully around her neck. It was pinned in place with a gold encrusted brooch. She offered her hand and I took it.

"Hello, Ms. Chalmers. Good to see you again."

"Mister Hawkins?" Her lips barely moved when she spoke, yet there was an attempted smile.

"Yes, and it's Cleve, by the way." I pointed to some small tables in the rear. "Have you got a place already?"

"Yes. Actually I have been waiting for some time back there. I'm having a vanilla cappuccino. Won't you join me?"

I glanced at my watch as we moved to the table. "I understood ten-thirty. Am I late?"

"Not really. Well, I believe in being prompt, Mister Hawkins."

"Cleve, call me Cleve. If you don't mind, I'll go up and get a cup of coffee and we can talk."

"That will be fine." A brunette, her makeup understated and careful, she had classic good looks with big brown eyes, nice nose and facial lines that gave her a somewhat drawn look but showed wisdom and experience.

"Okay, be right back," I said with a smile.

I went to the counter and ordered a Starbucks' Grande and returned to where she was sitting. She had removed her coat and I had forgotten she had a shapely body. I removed my topcoat and took a seat across from her.

I sipped my coffee and waited. She said nothing and I decided to get things rolling. "Please forgive me, but my curiosity is similar to that of watching a train wreck. It's irresistible. Why are we here?"

She shook her head and appeared to be holding back tears, fighting some emotional battle I couldn't read. I looked at the moist eyes and asked, "Okay. So what's the problem, Edith?"

"It's a long story, and please believe me, it was difficult to convince myself to relate what I'm about to tell you. I've not been sleeping well at all. I even thought about calling the police, but changed my mind."

"The police? Why? Is this something they should be made aware of?"

"No. No. Not the police." She wet her lips and began again, but her voice had the quiet, tense quality of a woman who had bought seriously into a private piece of discontent.

"I couldn't stand the embarrassment. I'm counting on your discretion, Mister Hawkins."

"Why me?"

She looked into my eyes and said, "I'm...I'm not sure. I know you've been working on the Hubbard case and I've been assured you're a good man who can be trusted."

"Well, I thank you for your faith in me. Although you may not want to disclose whatever it is, it must be one hell of a burden. And, don't look now, but you're shaking under the weight of it, Ms. Chalmers."

She nodded. "I know. Living with this on my conscience has been . . ." She sat back a little and stared at me over her coffee mug, one knee crossed over the other. She tossed her foot back and forth for a moment while she decided whether to finish or not. "I am just so frightened."

"Look, Edith. Somewhere in their careers, most cops come to a bad tasting conclusion about themselves. They realize they are in danger of becoming like the people they have investigated and put behind bars. But when people lie to you every single day, and lawyers work to free killers and drug pushers or you investigate cases involving child abuse and murdering so horrendous your beliefs are called into question, you have to re-evaluate your own life and outlook. At that time you check your belief in justice and protection of innocent people or you don't. I still feel comfortable in my skin. So, let's have it. What's going on?"

She smiled, but it was a phony smile, a smile you can see on the faces of visitors to the animal shelter, a smile for the doomed mutts who weren't quite cute and cuddly enough to make the cut.

She wrapped her fingers around her cup and looked at me with pleading eyes. "I hate when people ask questions like that."

I shrugged. "Well?"

There was a long pause before she said, "I do trust you, Mister Hawkins, or I wouldn't have called." She cleared her throat and said, "Everybody suspected Thad cheated on his wife. He was a brilliant chemist, but he would never have been smart enough to pull off total discretion." She paused to sip her drink.

"So we're talking about Thad Hubbard?"

She nodded. "Yes."

"You and Thad were having an affair?"

She shook her head and pressed an elegantly manicured hand to her lips as she rocked her head back. "No, no. Of course not. I wasn't attracted to Thad Hubbard in the slightest. My goodness. Beth became suspicious because Thad worked such late hours. That's when she hired you, I guess."

"Why didn't you call me when you found out Thad was kidnapped and murdered? It may have helped the police in apprehending the perpetrator."

"Yes. I know. I feel terrible that I didn't, absolutely terrible. I'm so sorry, but there's so much more, I just couldn't at the time."

"Quite honestly, that doesn't make any sense. By the way, you probably aren't aware but the police now have Thad's killers behind bars."

Her eyes widened. "Really?" She paused. "That's good."

"But it's not a done deal. Lots of loose ends. For instance, I still need to know why Thad Hubbard was targeted in the first place. And who else is involved in the killing?"

Edith sighed. "Yes, I know. I feel so damned responsible."

"What? Hold on, Edith. I think you'd better start at the beginning."

She leaned across the table and lowered her already dim voice. "It's all about oil. The oil industry is controlled by some very greedy and vicious men, Mister Hawkins."

"What do the oil barons have to do with Thad's murder?"

Once again she hesitated before she spoke: "Carrington Enterprises has a so-called 'top secret project.' They call it Operation Solid. The rumor is their people have formulated a method to harness the sun's power in such a manner as to enable mechanized vehicles to operate on solar power rather than gasoline. Imagine how that would affect the oil industry. Think about the stock market alone, when and if it were ever to be made public."

I sighed and rubbed a hand across my jaw. I needed a shave. "So, oil people are behind this whole thing and they figured Thad Hubbard could give them vital information about this Operation Solid?"

"Yes. As our number one chemist, he knew practically everything there was to know about the project. Poor Thad. I feel so terrible knowing that he was killed over such a thing."

I processed that information for a moment. "So big oil hired the two thugs we've got in custody to kidnap Hubbard and things probably went sideways, so they killed him? Hmmm. Somebody else must be involved, though. The two men we have in custody have neither the smarts nor inclination to kill for something they know nothing about."

Edith Chalmers nodded. "Much more important people are involved."

I shrugged. "I don't get it, Edith. Why are you telling me all this? If you weren't seeing Thad, how did you get so wound up in this whole deal?"

She took a drink of her cappuccino while staring sullenly at the bookcase on the other side of the room. She hesitated, reached in her purse and retrieved some Kleenex. The tears came and she dabbed at her eyes. "It's Carl."

"What do you mean, Carl? Carl who...Carl Cosgrove?" I found myself staring at the top of her head as she gazed into her lap.

"Edith? What about Cosgrove?"

"Carl and I...we were lovers."

I suddenly felt as though I had been zapped. There was a flood of adrenaline like nothing I'd ever felt before. My heart hammered in my chest. I stared at Edith, unable to speak for just a beat.

Obviously, grief had surrounded her like a force field. She didn't seem to be hearing anything but the voice of regret in her head and in the deepest part of her soul.

"Oh, I tried to break it off when I found out he was staying with Beth Hubbard," she said, "but he assured me that their affair was over. Of course, I found out he was lying."

She knotted the Kleenex in her hands as she talked. "I foolishly believed him."

I leaned in. "Listen, don't blame yourself, Edith. I know guys like him. Around fifty years old, nasty and thinks he's untouchable. He's very independent, one of those guys whose life is invested with imposing control and power over others, especially women. Don't blame yourself. You are doing the right thing by exposing him."

I felt she had gone this far, so I'd go for the jackpot:

"Did Carl tell you that Beth Hubbard is dead?"

She nodded. "That poor woman. I really had nothing against her. It was Carl who ruined my life."

I felt like I was hovering outside of my own body as I went for it.

"Did Carl kill Beth Hubbard?"

She nodded. "I think so."

Big tears filled her eyes and her face tightened into an unattractive expression. She turned one way and then the other, not knowing what to do or say next. She looked away again, wrestling with her thoughts. A tear rolled over her lashes onto her cheek. Then a flood of tears started coming and I looked around to see if we were attracting an audience, not that I cared. My eyes back on her, I squeezed one of her trembling hands.

"Edith, listen to me. No matter what has happened, no matter who is involved, nobody is blaming you." I paused for a fleeting moment before I asked, "Do you know where Carl is?"

She dabbed at her eyes and after clearing her throat, groaned and said, "I don't want to get involved with the police, Mister Hawkins. Please understand. I am trusting you to do the right thing, but I have said enough."

"I understand, but now is the time to start fixing this."

"Yes, that's right, of course." she murmured, almost as if she were talking to herself. Her hand settled briefly at the base of her throat and then moved away. "I've made up my mind. Carl needs to be caught and punished. As far as I'm concerned, they can castrate the son of a bitch."

Chapter Thirty-Four

I still wasn't sure how much of what Edith Chalmers said was fact or was part and parcel of a scorned woman's story. Before I went at Carl Cosgrove, I needed the autopsy report on Beth Hubbard. I had to be sure she had not, in fact, committed suicide.

Monday morning, after I worked out at the gym, I grabbed two jelly donuts and a large coffee from Dunkin and went back to the apartment to shower. I called Mo and told her I'd come by later that day. She was a bit put off, but true to form, very understanding.

Watching the pathologist, Stoney, conduct an autopsy was like watching ballet. Classical music played softly in the background while the bone saws and the clank of surgical instruments against stainless steel overrode the music. The stark whiteness of the room was like a blank canvas, clean and austere.

Stoney and his assistant skirted around the table like a pair of ballroom dancers in blue surgical gowns, elegant and smooth and synchronized with each other.

I had hospital booties covering my shoes as I watched them work on Beth Hubbard, snipping free the woman's rib cage with a long handled pruner. I still will never understand how Stoney could perform his job without puking. The mask covering my face was as useless as tits on a wall locker. The stench was overpowering, to say the least. However, I felt privileged that he was a friend and allowed me to observe like a dog waiting for scraps.

He removed and weighed the organs, took tissue samples and then returned the organs to her body in a plastic bag. About an hour later, Beth's body was being stitched back together, a section of skull refitted and her brown hair smoothed into place again.

"So, obviously, this one's pretty important to you, Hawk," he said. "Well, I don't have all of the tox reports yet, but I can tell you this much. There's no fucking way this woman fired a gun and killed herself. Somebody helped her out literally. I'd follow your intuition on this one being a homicide."

Triple Crossed

"Thought so, Stone. Between your consensus and that partial thumb print they found on the gun, I think we can bag the sonofabitch who did the deed. Thanks a bunch. I owe you big time."

He pulled off his gloves and we stepped out in back of the building so Stoney could have a smoke. He plucked a pack of Pall Malls from his pocket, tapped it against his forefinger twice, gripped the now exposed cigarette with his lips and lit up.

"Cleve, I've got to give you credit. You should have given up on this case a long time ago. In fact, as soon as they found the deceased's husband over in New Jersey or wherever. Know what I think? You should never have resigned your post, my friend."

"Thanks, Stoney. I just can't quit in the middle of shit like this."

He smiled and tapped me on the arm. "I know."

I had a lot of faith in Stone's conclusions. He was a brilliant individual who among other things had written pages about selenium poisoning that mimicked the symptoms of a heart attack and wouldn't show up in a regular basic toxicology screen. He was good at his profession. And reliable, as well as skilled.

Armed with my information, I got on the horn and called Jeebers. He wasn't in at first, but when I tried back later in the morning, I got lucky.

"Hey, Jeebs, how's it hangin?"

"Hey, Hawk. Glad you called. I had your boy Keith Alcott back in the interview room again this morning. We had him convinced his partner had given it up and he spilled his guts regarding the Hubbard deal."

"Hey, that's great, Jeebers."

"Yeah, he was very cooperative after we showed him the videos. Now he thinks Walker ratted him out so he's looking for a plea bargain because he says it was Walker who actually pumped the cocaine into Hubbard's veins. Duh! Boy that makes a big difference, huh?"

"Well, I just got the inside dope on Carl Cosgrove yesterday. Carrington's private secretary, Edith Chalmers, may be a classy tight ass, but evidently she likes her men bold and slimy. The two of them were having an affair until Cosgrove pulled his zipper open for Beth Hubbard."

"Yeah, I can see where that could piss her off."

"The lady says she is certain Cosgrove killed Mrs. Hubbard. Not only that, but she gave me a lead on where he's staying. I figured you'd like to take a ride with me and put the cuffs on him. I think we have enough for a warrant, don't you?"

"You sure you can trust her info?"

"Let's just say her body language doesn't lie. Can I count on you?"

"For sure. How much time have I got to get a warrant?"

"I'd like to go out there tonight, if possible, Jeebs. You know, catch his ass off guard."

"Ah, I don't know about that, but I'll get right on it. I'll bring the lieutenant up to speed and call you back."

"Yeah, sounds good, buddy. Cosgrove is a con, Jeebs. He will sell you a bowl of rat shit and call it chocolate chips, but I think we can nail him. Right now he's standing up to his bottom lip in a lake of shit and the motorboat is just about to pass."

. . .

Edith Chalmers had told me that Carl Cosgrove admitted he murdered Beth Hubbard when the two of them had met about six days earlier. He tried to convince Edith that he did it so the two of them could renew their relationship. "Besides," he'd said, "she knew too much about her husband's business that could get my ass involved, even though it wasn't me that killed her old man."

According to her, she didn't believe or trust Cosgrove and wanted nothing further to do with him. He had called her a few more times from where he was staying at a rented house in Half Day, Illinois. He'd asked her to drive out to the suburb, roughly thirty miles north of Chicago, to have dinner and talk things over. He claimed he left the Hubbard house not because he was worried about the law, but because he just needed to get away for a while.

Jeebers called back. He had everything lined up, but unfortunately he couldn't get the warrant before the next morning. I wasn't happy, but at least we'd be able to make our move the next night. In a way, it was perfect because I could spend some time with Mo.

She looked absolutely stunning when she answered the door. "Come on in, McGruff." She wrapped her arms around my neck and we kissed long and deep. We didn't speak for a moment and I just held her in my arms and buried my nose in her hair, soaking up the essence of the woman I knew I was in love with.

"God, you're beautiful, Mo. I missed you."

She giggled. "Well, you would never know it. I haven't been honored with your presence in nearly a week, mister." She looked up at me and smiled as she ran her fingers through my hair.

"I *have* been calling, though." I traced my fingers along her cheek. "There's a glow on your skin, baby. You smell like flowers in the morning and I have sexy dreams about you every night."

"That's true. You called, but I prefer you in the flesh, know what I mean?" She took my hand and guided me into the living room. I thought we'd order a deluxe pizza from Malnati's, if you're hungry."

I tossed my topcoat on the back of the couch and encircled my arms around her again. "Maybe later," I whispered.

"Fine." She rested her arms on my shoulders and said, "How's that Hubbard case going anyway?"

I brought her up to date and finished by saying, "We know where Cosgrove is and we're hoping to pick him up with a warrant tomorrow."

She studied my eyes. "Are you worried?"

"Not really. Jeebers is the arresting officer. I'm just along for the ride tomorrow."

She suddenly took my hand and began to steer me to the bedroom. "Hey, gumshoe, don't you know you shouldn't live in tomorrow's problems? Tomorrow has no more existence than yesterday, but you can always control now."

My heart was racing and my legs felt weak. I suspected there would be no pizza for quite a while. I pulled Mo close against my body and she felt electric and incredibly warm.

"I'd only be a half a person without you, Mo," I whispered. "You're more than my lover. You're my confidante, my best friend and all the good things that women are. No one could ever take your place."

We both felt the urgency. After we undressed each other, I drew her down onto the bed and rolled over her, holding my weight on the palms of my hands. I dipped and kissed her beautiful face and each of her breasts. I pulled at her nipples with my lips and licked them with my tongue. I kissed all around her slender ankles, up her legs and then between her legs.

Arching herself up toward me, she gasped. She moved her body against me and we found a wonderful rhythm. We were both breathing faster and harder.

"Please, just do it," she whispered. She bit into my shoulder. "I want you inside, Cleve."

I felt a fire ignite inside and take over my entire body. I slid inside slowly, but I went as deep as I could and we made love slow and easy at first. After a while the need took over and we climaxed together.

While the first hint of daylight crept in through the bedroom window, I felt guilty as I tip-toed out, like a man leaving church early.

Chapter Thirty-Five

Two plainclothes cops staked out Cosgrove's place during the day in order to get an idea of the area, the actual property layout and any obstacles for our approach. We needed to know what we were getting into ahead of time. The advance team gave us the all clear and we were set to go.

Jeebers had obtained the warrant from Cook County's Judge Kilbourn, and although we hoped Cosgrove would be caught off guard, we knew he might not be so easy to cuff and stuff.

In a planning session with Lieutenant Andrews, it was decided we wouldn't request a SWAT team unless it was absolutely necessary. We were on our own.

Each of the Special Forces Department's vehicles is equipped with what is called the police package, flashing lights in the grille, sirens, tinted windows and other bells and whistles, but we drove Jeebers' personal car, a 2014 Explorer, in order to ensure that we wouldn't be spotted as cops.

We stopped to eat at Ann Sathers breakfast joint on Belmont and took two extra coffees with us on the way out. It was a little after nine in the morning when we left the city and headed toward the town of Half Day some thirty miles north of Chicago.

Edith Chalmers had given me the name of Polk Street, but claimed she didn't know the exact address. She did give me enough of a description of the house, though, that we could locate Cosgrove's cave.

We had ridden about five miles when I cracked the window to escape some of Jeebers's cigar smoke and said, "I know we're all set, but is anything else underway to help in apprehending this guy?"

"Yeah, we've got a BOLO out on his car. It says he's wanted for questioning relative to a homicide in Oak Park. I agree with you, though. We can't be sitting on our asses waiting for that possibility to give us anything. Your guy will be in the wind. In fact I'm surprised he hasn't skipped yet."

"When I was out at the Hubbard house a couple of times, I spotted his truck. It's a red 2012 Dodge Ram."

Triple Crossed

"That's what the report says."

The monotonous hum of the SUV engine was all I heard for a moment or two before I said, "So what're you packing for this picnic?"

He glanced over at me and grinned. "My .45. Hell, I've got a nine millimeter with fifteen rounds in the clip, but it's too heavy to carry. I only bring it with me if I think I'll need it. I've got a three fifty-seven too, and a twelve-gauge shotgun. But for deals like this, the .45 is all I figure I'll need. How about you?"

I patted my side. "I'm partial to my .357. It's never failed me. I've got that and a .25 in my ankle holster, but I don't figure we'll need anything to bring this guy in."

"Yeah, I agree." Jeebers took a beat then said, "When I approach one of these scumbags, I always watch their hands. Hands kill. In God we trust, but everyone else keep your hands where I can see them."

I laughed. "Right. Be polite. Be professional. But be prepared to kill everyone you meet."

"No shit. And with me, I don't want anybody messing with my piece. I just tell everybody in the section straight out, keep your shit hooks off."

Jeebers puffed on his cigar, squinted and cracked his own window.

"So this Edith broad said Cosgrove isn't really the mastermind behind the kidnapping? What does that mean? Who in the hell is calling the shots then?"

"An east coast thug named Nick Zagaretti."

"Zorgarotti? Who in the hell is Zorgarotti?"

I laughed. "Zagaretti. All I know is he's from New Jersey. I did manage to do some homework, though. This clown operates out of Newark and all things indicate he's mobbed up. It all figures, if you want to consider Thad Hubbard's body was found near Camden. If this all leads back to Zagaretti, nailing him and the mob for it would be as useless as trying to give a traffic ticket to the guys who brought down the Towers."

"Well, from what you've told me, Cosgrove has got a big mouth and will do anything to impress the women, so who knows? Maybe it's all a bunch of bullshit to cover his ass somehow. Know what I mean?"

"Yeah. I'll tell you what, buddy. This case has gotten real muddled up. Who in the hell would have believed the complications? I was just thinking the other day, all this shit started out as a simple tail on a husband who supposedly couldn't keep his dick in his pants."

Jeebers smirked. "Shit happens. There's no angels walking around out there, my friend."

"Yeah, well, anyway, if I'd wanted to see assholes all day, I would have become a proctologist. Instead I follow them for a living."

Jeebers snickered. "It didn't have to be like this. See, how it is, Hawk? You could be letting some uniforms or suits with Kojak lights on their roof worry about Cosgrove. You should have left this shit to them a long time ago."

"Yeah, my job was to follow Hubbard and report to his wife. Then the case just mushroomed like an epidemic of the clap."

"You're not a bloodhound, Hawk." He laughed. "You've just become the second dog in the team, but everything is basically the same. It's still follow that asshole."

We both laughed.

After a while I said, "What I don't get is why the elegant Mrs. Hubbard wanted to let Cosgrove get in her pants. Maybe he is connected, but I'm thinking it was likely just the sex. She did bitch because Hubbard was never home, you know, always working. I'm thinking she and Cosgrove were both in on getting rid of her husband, but in the end she must have gotten cold feet and he figured he simply had to get rid of her to cover his own ass."

"Either that or she got worried about his mobster connections. Hell, if Cosgrove really is connected, those guys get around a lot and among other things, they pass around STDs like a family heirloom, so she's dead but maybe only his dick will fall off."

I glanced at my notes and looked up ahead. "Okay, we should be pretty close now, Jeebs. Turn left at the next light. There's supposed to be a Sunoco station on the corner. It should be about a quarter mile out of town after we turn. Edith Chalmers claimed she'd only been out here a couple of times and that was at night. She remembered that it's back off the road a ways, though."

In general the homes were old and stately with lots of brick and ivy. It wasn't long before we eased past Cosgrove's place, situated on my side of the car.

It looked benign. The house was about a hundred yards off the road with a gravel drive and dense hedges just below the front windows. It was two stories, with conservative trim colors and a two car detached garage. The place almost seemed abandoned and sat hauntingly behind a dense growth of trees and wild shrubbery. A red Dodge Ram was parked alongside the garage.

"Looks like that's it," I said.

"Yeah, and it's got all the warmth of a cyanide factory."

We circled the block and parked one house down. There was a large field of brambles and dead grass between our position and Cosgrove's house. Jeebers stubbed out his cigar in the ashtray and tossed it out the window. Handing me the warrant, he said, "Okay, you know the drill. Let's bust him or smoke him, Hawk."

"Right. Want me to take the front or do you want to lead?"

Jeebers leaned over the steering wheel and stared at the house. "Well, I've got the badge, but this is your caper, Cleve, so yeah, I think you should take the front door." He pointed. "I'll cut across that field and circle around back." He stared me down. "No need to tell you to watch your ass, buddy."

"Thanks, partner. Let's go."

My heart was thudding hard as I got out, walked up the road, cut in and headed up the cobblestone walkway to the front door. Meanwhile I saw Jeebers hustling across the field until he disappeared around the corner of the house.

The doorbell was dangling by loose wires so I used the knocker. No response, so I knocked again, this time harder, until suddenly Cosgrove came out of the garage to my right by way of a small side door.

"Yeah. I'm out here!" He squinted at me for a beat. "What do you want?" he yelled as he wiped his hands on a blue shop rag.

Cosgrove wasn't over five-foot-six inches tall, but his neck was thick and corded with veins. His shoulders were wide and sloped like a weightlifter's, but his muscles seemed so tightly strung together that one motion would activate a half dozen more. His eyebrows flowed across his forehead in one dark, uninterrupted line and he wore a black wife beater that read "Harleys Rule."

I carefully made my way toward him and saw random smears of black grease on his face and arms. He acted as though he still didn't recognize me.

"Carl Cosgrove?"

"Yeah. What do you want?" He searched my eyes, uncertain, I suppose, of what I wanted.

He looked different, somehow. I remembered him having a short brush cut, but the thing on his head looked a lot like fresh road kill and even though he appeared sturdy in other ways, his stomach made a thick roll at the bottom of his shirt.

I waved the warrant, and as I pulled out my cuffs, I said, 'You are under arrest. You have the right to remain silent. You have the right to have a lawyer present during any questioning. If you..."

"Arrest for what?" He placed his hands on his hips.

"For suspicion of the murder of Bethany Hubbard. Let's take a ride."

"You can go to hell, too." A red scald started at Cosgrove's neck and rose up to his face. He turned and went inside the garage and then wheeled back around to face me. "I thought I remembered your ugly kisser. I don't appreciate the intrusion, Hawkins. Get the fuck off my property."

I continued forward. "You arrogant fuckin' prick. Give it up, Carl. We both know you killed Beth Hubbard. We've got you dead in the water. DNA and fingerprints don't lie."

Jeebers came around the far corner of the garage as I spoke. He had his gun pointing at Cosgrove, but said nothing. He was waiting for me to cuff Cosgrove.

Cosgrove wet his lips to speak again and suddenly one side of his face tightened. He lunged and swung at my head and I ducked but felt his ring graze across my scalp.

Then I hooked him, hard, dead-center in his face. His head snapped back and his nose spurted blood. He came at me again, swinging wildly with both fists, the way an enraged child would. Before I could pound him again, he locked both arms around me, grunting and wheezing in my ear. Then he let go of one of my arms and aimed for my crotch.

His aim was bad and he caught my thigh. I brought my elbow up and into his nose and clobbered him again, this time in the mouth. He bounced off the wall and I hit him hard in the face again. He slid across the cement on his stomach, wiggling like a crab and breathing like a sprinter.

He got up and shook his head once as if there were a horsefly on it.

He started to swing again and then Jeebers was between us, gun in hand, one arm held out stiffly toward me, his eyes wide and glaring. "Back off, Cleve! You're gonna' kill this asshole!"

I was breathing hard and glaring at Cosgrove. "You know, Carl, somebody who kills for a living usually strikes a little more fear into people than what you're showing. You're good with women because you are one...as far as I can see."

His eyes were dilated black and glittered in his feverish face. His breathing was heavy.

"Get out of this, Hawkins," he growled. "You're in over your head." He edged over and leaned on the work bench. Snot and blood poured from his nose as he glanced sidelong at Jeebers. "You're both messing with people who will waste you like popsicles on a warm day."

I had no time to digest the revelation. I caught the motion of Cosgrove's arm in my peripheral vision and dove forward. He had grabbed a small axe from the bench and swung, but it just grazed the back of my head and shoulder. The pain was a hard, hot ball biting into me.

I rolled onto my back as he swung wildly for my head again, but he missed and

Triple Crossed

buried the head of the axe into the bench.

Jeebers stood, stiff-armed, with his gun pointed at Cosgrove's head. "Freeze, asshole! You're under arrest!"

"Gun!" I yelled as Cosgrove dropped down and pulled a blue-back .25 from an ankle holster. I kicked his leg and knocked off his aim. His shot went wild and broke out a small window behind me.

I rolled to the side, but Cosgrove's purpose was now to escape and he was already running, heading for the side of the garage and his truck. He swung his arm back and let a shot go. I heard the zing as the round hit the cement floor.

Jeebers charged past as I pushed to my feet and pulled out my .357. Cosgrove ducked around the corner of the garage and fired two more shots. Jeebers ducked right and the second of the shots punctured the garage door. Then Cosgrove was nowhere in sight.

I stumbled through the opened side door and crouched behind several fifty-five gallon drums, straining to hear, to get some bearing on which way he had gone. I couldn't hear anything but the wind and my own ragged breathing.

I felt the back of my head and came away with bloody fingers.

Jeebers yelled, "Damn! Which way did he go? He gets away, we're in a heap of shit," he groaned. "I'll be doing school crossing duty until I retire."

Then I spotted Cosgrove. He had passed his truck and was behind the garage, trapped between me on one side and Jeebers on the other.

"Give it up, Cosgrove!" I shouted. "There's nowhere to go."

"Fuck you!"

Jeebers yelled, "Alcott and Walker have both spilled their guts. You're finished, Carl." He paused. "We know there's somebody else in this, so drop the gun and come out. Maybe we can cut a deal for you."

"You're right, detective. And that somebody else will fuck you up. You won't be seeing him, but he'll find you. You think you're up to dancing with him and the boys? Ha! I saw a time when they had another grease ball hold a motherfucker down on the floor while my man cut off most of the guy's ear with a pair of tin snips."

"Enough of the bullshit. Come on out. Now!" I yelled.

I started moving towards the back of the garage. Only TV cops and movie gangsters stick a gun out in front of them like a hard dick before turning corners or tilt their weapon on its side. I held my .357 in front of me with both hands and pulled back the hammer to full cock.

I spotted Cosgrove with his gun raised at the same time he saw me and we both fired.

The air echoed with my shot and the round cored through Cosgrove's left shoulder. That should have taken him down, but it didn't. He was still standing up against the garage wall, shooting wildly.

My ears were ringing, my heart was pounding with fear and my wrists had bucked upward with the recoil of my weapon.

At the same time, two things happened in what seemed like one single action. I felt the stinging pain of a round drill me in my left side just below my ribs, and Jeebers appeared from the other side of the garage.

He fired three shots from his .45 and Carl Cosgrove crashed across the back of the garage before I went down. I saw him smash into the wall and hang there like a broken doll before he slumped to the ground.

I barely remembered the drone of Jeeber's voice as he used his iPhone to call for help.

Chapter Thirty-Six
Epilogue

When I woke up in the hospital, Mo was standing by the bed.

"Hey, Columbo. How you feeling?"

I tried like hell to smile as she squeezed my hand and kissed me on the lips. "You seem to be breathing okay."

I looked down at the tape wrapped around my side and stomach. "It hurts like hell."

"I imagine it does. You took one in the side. That's bound to cause a big oweee."

My brain was still fuzzy, but I searched her eyes.

"How much damage is there? Did the doc tell you?"

"Oh, just a few little things to slow you down for a bit. A ruptured spleen, a slightly nicked liver, one shattered rib and a lot of blood loss. You'll have a scar you can brag about for the rest of your days. Other than that, you're fine, Doctor Plemphy says."

My throat and mouth felt parched. "I guess I'll live then," I groaned. I pointed to the Styrofoam cup on the nightstand. "Would you hand me that cup of water, Babe?"

"Sure."

She held it for me while I sucked on the straw.

"You know you have this little gizzy," she said, "which should help with your pain." She handed me the pain pump. "Just push this little red button and the morphine will kick in. It helps. Trouble is, it may put you out again, and it's timed so you can only get so much every so often."

"Yeah, I've heard that somewhere before."

She set the cup down, adjusted my pillow, pulled up the covers then leaned over and caressed my face with both hands. I saw tears welling up in the corners of her eyes. She kissed my forehead and whispered, "Good thing Jeebers was with you. I can't bear to think what might have happened if he hadn't been."

She cleared her throat. "Quite a few visitors have stopped by to look in on you, big guy, but they weren't allowed in. A few will be back, they said."

I grimaced from a throbbing pain in my side. "Anybody I know?"

"Of course, silly. Lieutenant Andrews, Jim Ashbaugh and Harve Bidden, for instance. I was surprised to see Doctor Stone, the pathologist here too. Jeebers is just outside. He said he wasn't leaving until you were awake. Andrews and Ashbaugh said they'd be back in a couple of hours."

Tears filled Mo's blue eyes and spilled down her cheeks.

I reached up and rubbed them away with my thumb. "Hey, don't you start with the tears, baby. I'll be okay."

"I was afraid of this. Once I start crying, I won't be able to stop. It doesn't matter that I'll be crying because I'm happy. You know I'm not an attractive crier, Cleve." She giggled. "My nose runs and my face gets blotchy and people stare."

"I'll be up and as good as new before you know it."

"Good attitude, flatfoot." She paused. "Well, they told me not to stay too long this first time, so I should be going, but I'll be back later this afternoon." She gathered her things and stood to leave.

I felt a jolt of pain again. "What? You're leaving me already?"

"Yes. I can't stand to see you hurting. I want you to use that pump right now. Get some sleep, okay? Don't be afraid to use it, either. Like I said, it won't let you OD." She feigned a smile and kissed me on the lips. "Be back later." She squeezed my arm and said, "No flirting with the nurses, either."

"Yeah, that'll happen. Send Jeebers in, will you?"

She sighed. "I love you, Cleve. I'll send him in, but please don't let him stay too long. Promise?"

"Okay. Promise." She turned to leave and I croaked, "I love you, too, Mo."

I heard what seemed like muffled voices for a moment, and then Jeebers stood at the foot of my bed. Lieutenant Andrews was with him.

"Hey, Hawk, how ya' feeling?" asked Andrews.

"Ahh, you know. I've got some stitches and a shitload of pain, but I'll be fine." I looked at Jeebers. "How about you, buddy? You okay?"

"Sure, I'm good. You're the one lying on your ass, not me."

We all laughed.

"And Cosgrove?" I asked.

"Gone. Two slugs caught him where it counts."

Triple Crossed

I looked at Andrews. "Hey, LT. Thanks for letting me in on the takedown. I appreciate it. Sorry it didn't go as we planned."

"No sweat. You're a good man, Hawkins. As a matter of fact, you may want to consider coming back on the force someday. We'll get together on everything when you're up and around. Now, my understanding is Detective Mulvaney here took down Cosgrove, but you had his back all the way. We all appreciate that, Hawk."

I knew then exactly what story Jeebers had used on the report. It was a good deal because we both knew he should have been the lead in performing the arrest of Cosgrove. Good old Jeebs.

"By the way, we're done on this end as far as Chicago is concerned. This now falls into the laps of the FBI and various New Jersey police agencies. We've got enough to handle right here in Chicago without handling another department's problems."

"Amen to that," said Jeebers.

I asked, "What about Alcott and Walker, lieutenant?"

He hiked his shoulders in a half-hearted shrug and raised an eyebrow. "They're both going to go down for the murder of the chemist, Thad Hubbard. We have plenty of DNA and their confessions. They'll be going away for life, no doubt."

Jeebers walked up to the head of the bed. He squeezed my shoulder. "If it wasn't for your hard-headedness and tenacity of a Pit bull with a steak, we wouldn't have got any of these clowns. Good job, buddy."

"We'll stop back," said Andrews. "You just rest up and get well."

I still had questions, but I was tired of tolerating the pain. When Jeebers and the lieutenant walked out the door, I pushed the red button that would make me do something I rarely did well. I relaxed.

I still smelled Mo's perfume as I drifted off.

Purchase other Black Rose Writing titles at www.blackrosewriting.com/books
and use promo code PRINT to receive a 20% discount.

CPSIA information can be obtained
at www.ICGtesting.com
Printed in the USA
FFOW03n1240030616
24558FF